RENTING SILENCE

Mary Miley

This first world edition published 2016
in Great Britain and the USA by
SEVERN HOUSE PUBLISHERS LTD of
19 Cedar Road, Sutton, Surrey, England, SM2 5DA.
Trade paperback edition first published
in Great Britain and the USA 2017 by
SEVERN HOUSE PUBLISHERS LTD

British Library Cataloguing in Publication Data
A CIP catalogue record for this title is available from the British Library.

ISBN-13: 978-0-7278-8653-8 (cased)
ISBN-13: 978-1-84751-754-8 (trade paper)
ISBN-13: 978-1-78010-820-9 (e-book)

Typeset by Palimpsest Book Production Ltd.,
Falkirk, Stirlingshire, Scotland.

RENTING SILENCE

ACKNOWLEDGMENTS

My special thanks to Dr Mark Pugh, a pharmacist who helps me figure out historically appropriate ways to poison people; Donna Sheppard, who more than any teacher taught me how to write; Mike Shoop, the world's best librarian and book sleuth who can lay his hands on any obscure tome I request; Linda Crowson and Ursula Jones at the Hattiesburg Area Historical Society who saved me from several mistakes; Hays T. Watkins, retired CEO of CSX who explained the intricacies of railroad operations in the 1920s; Mike Condren, who helped with historical information about Mississippi trains in the 1920s; Brooks Wachtel, Hollywood writer, producer, director and film historian for his advice on filming techniques of the era; to everyone at Severn House for their work on the book; and everyone in my very excellent writing critique groups: Vivian Lawry, Marilyn Mattys, Linda Thornburg, Susan Campbell, Kathy Mix, Sandie Warwick, Heather Weidner, Susan Edwards, Josh Cane, Tom Fuhrman, and Libby Hall.

ONE

Filming silent movies is noisy work – directors shouting instructions through megaphones, cameras grinding away like machine guns, studio musicians playing the mood from the corner – which is why I was perplexed when I walked on to the set of *Little Annie Rooney* that morning and found it frozen in silence. Actors, electricians, make-up artists, grips, carpenters, script girls, and cameramen stood motionless, as if drawing a deep breath would shatter the spell. Only one person gave life to the scene, and all eyes were on her. Mary Pickford, 'America's Sweetheart' and the star of the film, was slowly pacing the edge of the set, her head down in fearsome concentration.

I looked to Director William Beaudine who motioned for me to stay where I was. He waited until Miss Pickford faced away from him before gliding to my side, so his movement wouldn't distract her.

'A note said Miss Pickford wanted to see me on the set,' I whispered. 'Maybe I'd better come back later?'

Tall and stick thin, Beaudine had to bend to get close to my ear. 'Hang on a minute, Jessie. This is the last take before we break.'

One glance at the chalkboard in a young assistant's hand raised my eyebrows. Sixteen takes? That was a lot, even for a perfectionist like 'Retake Mary Pickford.'

'I could strangle Rudolph Valentino,' the director whispered, almost to himself. 'He barged in here, broke her concentration. She hasn't—'

Miss Pickford stopped and lifted her chin. 'I'm ready.'

The scene lurched to life. 'Hit 'em once!' shouted Beaudine and the set was instantly flooded with silvery light from an array of Kliegs, baby spots, and barrel lights. 'Camera!' Cameramen cranked up their Mitchells, and the four studio musicians in the corner began playing a gloomy number to set the mood. They were shooting the tearjerker part, where Little Annie learns her policeman father has been killed in the line of duty.

As I watched, thirty-three-year-old Mary Pickford, playing a twelve-year-old girl, scampered out from her hiding place under the table, ready to surprise her beloved father with his birthday cake, only to find herself face to face with a policeman sent to deliver the tragic news. Her expression started at mischievous and slid rapidly through puzzlement, confusion, disbelief, denial, futile hope and horror, only to end with heart-rending tears. It was an astonishing display of acting skills. In all my years in vaudeville, I had never seen the equal. No wonder she was the most famous actress in the world! I hoped everyone in the audience would have hankies in hand – I was misty-eyed myself. The scene reminded me all too forcefully of having been orphaned myself at the same age.

'Cut! Good work, good work, everyone,' called Beaudine. 'No more shooting for now, boys and girls. We'll break for lunch, and well deserved it is. Take a whole hour.'

A solemn Mary Pickford came over to exchange a few words with Beaudine. Catching sight of me, she gestured to one of the simple wooden chairs on the set, indicating that she would be with me shortly.

I sat down and swung my legs. The seat of the chair was high, maybe three inches higher than normal. I'm small – just over five feet, the same height as Miss Pickford – but I can't usually swing my legs in a chair. I studied the wooden kitchen table. It was made to the same scale, a little higher than typical.

Mary Pickford walked over and sank into the chair beside me. 'What are you smiling at, Jessie?'

'I just realized what you are doing,' I said, in awe of her mastery of the craft. 'With the furniture, I mean. The whole set is overlarge, isn't it? And that policeman who delivered the bad news, he was very big and tall.'

Suddenly she was Little Annie Rooney again, grinning like a youngster caught up in mischief. She swung her feet too. 'When I'm doing a young role, I always hire tall actors. They make me seem smaller by comparison. A couple of extra inches on the furniture don't hurt either.'

'I saw the final take. You were wonderful.'

You'd have thought I'd insulted her. Her shoulders slumped, her grin fell away, and her honey-colored ringlets bounced as she shook her head. 'Thank you, but I wasn't. And I had it! I really had it!' She slapped the table for emphasis. 'Before Rudy walked in, I was twelve years old. When he left, I couldn't get it back. No matter how hard I tried, I just couldn't get it back.'

There was nothing I could say. The scene had looked great to me, but what did I know? I was just a lowly assistant script girl new to Hollywood, having been hired by Mary's husband, Douglas Fairbanks, a few months earlier.

'I'm not blaming Rudy,' she went on, more to herself than to me. 'I invited him to stop by the set any time and say hello, bless his heart, and that's all he did. But it distracted me. It was my fault entirely. My fault.' She swung her legs a little longer, sighed, then looked toward the twin cameras. 'Oh, Rob!' she called. 'Rob Handler!'

One of the cameramen turned at the sound of his name and nodded that he had heard. Pulling a reel of film off the Mitchell, he methodically packed it in a soft case before joining us in the middle of the set.

'Have you met Jessie Beckett?' asked Miss Pickford.

The cameraman nodded. 'I've seen her around,' he said, then turned to me. 'You're the girl who used to play vaudeville. I heard how you helped solve those gangster murders last month. Pleased to know you.'

He was referring to the murder of a prominent film director and a waitress who served drinks at his party one night. The waitress was an old vaudeville friend of my mother's, someone I'd known as a child. Everyone was focused on the director's murder, which they wanted to hush up because of his scandalous links to drugs, sex, and bootleg alcohol. No one cared about the waitress except me. I'd become involved at the request of my boss, Douglas Fairbanks, whose famous face prevented him from doing any anonymous investigating. After two more murders and a gangster shootout in the desert, Douglas and I figured out the murderer's identity – something that nearly killed us both.

'Rob Handler is one of the finest cameramen at our studio,' Miss Pickford said by way of introduction. 'One of the finest in all of Hollywood, actually.'

A wiry, middle-aged man who would have passed unnoticed in a crowd, Handler looked like he'd done a week's worth of work in the past few hours. His forehead was creased with worry, his eyes heavy with dark circles. The compliment from Mary Pickford brought the merest twist to his lips. He sank on to the hard chair like a marionette with slackened strings.

'You used to play kiddie roles, didn't you?' he asked, more to be polite than from any real interest.

'Most recently, yes. I was with the Little Darlings for a few years. But I've also worked for the Kid Circus, a couple of magicians, a Shakespeare troupe, and a variety of song and dance acts.'

'And now you're an assistant Script Girl.'

'She'll be working with Douglas on his new pirate picture. But I was hoping she could stand in for me this afternoon. That hospital scene we're shooting only uses my back. If you would, Jessie, that would free me up for a meeting.'

Miss Pickford had mentioned once before that she might want to use me as a double. We were the same size and build, and while my auburn hair was bobbed and her ringlets were long and golden, there were wigs in Costume that would solve that in a jiffy. From the back, we would be indistinguishable. Imagine, me, Jessie Beckett, a stand-in for the incomparable Mary Pickford! Last year's vaudeville wash-up, when I was turned down at every try-out, had squelched any ambition I might have had about acting in the pictures – I simply didn't have that sort of talent – but the prospect of this small connection to the woman I idolized thrilled me. My heart beat faster.

'Sure!' I said, too quickly. My excitement crashed as fast as it had soared. I held up my right hand, the one that had been injured during a struggle with the murderer last month. Two fingers were still in a splint. 'Is this a problem? I'm sure I can get Wardrobe to remove it for the scene.'

'That would be wonderful. I'll let Beaudine know. Thank you, Jessie.'

I thought I heard dismissal in her voice, so I stood. 'I guess I should go see about costumes . . .'

'No, no, sit. That wasn't the only reason I called for you. What I really want is for you to hear Rob's story. If you don't mind, Rob, dear, please tell her what you told me yesterday,' she said.

Handler glanced back and forth between us, and I thought for a moment he was going to say he was too tired to speak. Instead he sighed and leaned forward, rested his elbows on his knees, and started to talk in a monotone that brooked no interruption.

'Well, it's like this. I was called to jury duty for the Ruby Glynn trial,' he began, staring down at his clasped hands. Of course I knew about the Ruby Glynn case. Everyone did. It had been in all the papers. In fact, I was even grateful to Ruby Glynn for making me old news when her own sensational trial had pushed me and the Hollywood gangster murders off the front page. But I hadn't realized that someone in our own Pickford–Fairbanks Studios had been on the Glynn jury.

'Well, I need to tell you how it was, because the newspapers, well, they got a lot of things wrong.'

That didn't surprise me, not after my experiences with the yellow press during those murders last month. Pulitzer and Hearst had fought their customary inky battle for readers, printing speculation as fact, inventing outrageous stories, and slandering innocent people with no concern for the consequences. Any lie was printable as long as it boosted sales. I'd never again believe a word I read in the newspapers.

'At the trial, the lawyers kept saying it was a cut-and-dried case. They had so much proof, we didn't even need to deliberate. Well, they did have good evidence – the murder weapon with fingerprints, her scream, the fights, Ruby's ticket, the rented car . . . The defense, well, they didn't have much to say about these things other than to say they were just coincidence. So you'd think it would be an easy call, wouldn't you? But through it all, I just had this feeling that wouldn't go away. I believed her when she said she didn't do it.'

Miss Pickford started to say something, but Rob didn't notice; his eyes were glued to the floor as if he could only keep going if he didn't raise them. Running his fingers through his thinning hair, he continued.

'When we went in the back room to deliberate, the foreman took a preliminary vote to check the lay of the land. Three of us voted for acquittal, the two women and me. The others were patient at first, reviewing all the evidence, showing us where we were wrong. But we wouldn't budge. Hours went by. Finally the foreman had to tell Judge Peters he had a hung jury. The judge wouldn't accept that. He ordered us to go back and keep trying. Said we weren't going home until we had a verdict. That's when things turned nasty. The others, they shouted at us and said they wanted to go home to their families and their jobs. They accused us of . . . well, I don't need to go into all that. It's no excuse anyway.'

He paused to wipe his eyes and rub his nose with the back of his hand. Miss Pickford waited, respectfully silent, until he could gather himself.

'Pretty soon they bullied the older lady into changing her mind, and that convinced the other woman to give in too. That left me alone. They all said how impossible it was that I could believe Ruby Glynn was innocent with evidence like that. I couldn't give any hard reason except that I had this feeling that she was telling the truth, that she didn't kill that girl. She didn't look like a killer. I didn't know Ruby Glynn, never worked with her, never met her, but she just didn't seem like the kind of girl who would kill someone.'

Miss Pickford reached over and gave his arm a pat. 'Well, I know Ruby Glynn,' she said, 'and I don't think she could kill anyone either.'

'Still, feelings don't hold up against facts, and finally I gave in too. The logic was all on their side. I thought, how can I be right and all these people be wrong? I'm not so much smarter than they are. So I voted guilty. We all went home. But that night, I knew I'd made a horrible mistake. Never mind how I voted, I still don't believe Ruby Glynn killed that girl. I can't tell you who did, but I don't think it was Miss Glynn. Now she's going to hang. If I had held my ground, the judge would have had to declare a mistrial, and another group of jurors would have heard the case. Maybe they'd have come to the same conclusion, who knows? But one thing's certain – I put the noose around that girl's neck, and I don't know how I'm going to live with that for the rest of my life.'

Finally he looked up and his sorrowful brown eyes found mine. 'I haven't been able to sleep since. Or if I do fall off for a minute, the nightmares start.' He leaned back, a lost soul facing a pain-filled eternity.

For a long while no one spoke. At last Miss Pickford broke the silence.

'I wonder if you would look into this for us, Jessie. Investigate this murder. I've already talked with Douglas, and he thinks it's a fine idea. The pirate picture doesn't need to take up your whole day, not at this stage anyway. And you have a knack for this sort of thing.'

I looked at the cameraman. Not a flicker of hope crossed his face. Or maybe he had sunk too far into his own private hell to hear. I looked at Mary Pickford. For the past ten years, she had been my idol. Studying her in moving pictures had taught me how to play young roles, my bread and butter for most of my adult life. She was 'our Mary', 'the girl with the curls', the most popular person in America, the founder of one of the most important film studios in Hollywood, and, some said, the most recognized face in the whole world. We had much in common – a childhood sacrificed to the stage, growing up in rundown boarding houses, sleeping on trains to save the dollar for the hotel, living on cheese sandwiches and pickles or whatever a friendly grown-up would buy you without asking for a return on his investment. I had loved Mary Pickford long before I had the amazing fortune of meeting her. I hesitated not a second.

'Of course I'll try, if you want me to. But I'm no detective . . . what can I do to investigate that the police haven't already done?'

'That's just it,' she said. 'The police never investigated the case. Tell her, Rob.'

The cameraman pulled himself out of his reverie. 'That's so, Jessie. The police got called right when the landlady heard the scream. This was back in February, remember. The victim – Lila Walker, her name was – screamed when she was stabbed.

The landlady ran upstairs and a couple girls from down the hall rushed in. They all saw Lila lying on the bedroom floor. She was still alive then, just barely. Ruby Glynn was lying there too, the bloody knife in her hand. She had fainted. First, everyone thought they were both dead, then one of 'em brought Ruby around and helped her sit up. Lila kept pointing at her, trying to speak but she couldn't get the words out. The doctor and the police arrived fast. The doc said Lila wouldn't make it to the hospital, and he was right. But before she died, the cop asked her again, "Who did this to you?" and she pointed one more time, real weak-like, to Ruby, then she went limp.'

'How awful,' I managed to say.

'Ruby said she didn't do it. Said Lila was already stabbed when she got there. Maybe a good while before she got there. Who knows? She said she was the one who screamed, not Lila, then she fainted. Said she'd never do anything like killing somebody, even if they had quarreled. She said they'd made up weeks before. She said Lila asked her to come over that day. Her lawyer said it was just coincidence that Ruby was planning to leave the country the next day.'

'And you believe Ruby?'

He swallowed hard. 'Don't think I don't know how daft it sounds, but I do. She was so confused looking, so innocent and scared. Reminded me of my daughter when she got lost one time. She just couldn't have done it. I know, I know. Then, who did? Lila didn't stab herself, and there was no one else there.'

TWO

Beaudine's frown telegraphed disapproval. He didn't want me standing in for Miss Pickford. He wanted Miss Pickford. But we all knew who was boss, and I was ready, having been dressed by Women's Wardrobe in Annie's old plaid dress and a head full of bouncing blonde ringlets. 'Annie, you're over here,' he said gruffly, calling me by the name of my character. It worked that way in vaudeville too; performers assumed the names of whatever role they were playing. Sometimes, like in my case, the moniker stuck. Jessie was a girl I'd impersonated last summer. I kept the name, in part to honor her, in part because it fit better than any name I'd ever had.

I stood where Beaudine pointed. The hospital scene would be shot on a bare set that had a door on one side and a gurney near the back wall. Pickford–Fairbanks Studios used the more expensive panchromatic film for its truer gray range, so it wasn't necessary to fiddle with the prop colors to get the right shade of gray. A doctor stood beside the gurney. 'You walk to the gurney and climb up on it,' Beaudine ordered tersely. 'Lie down with your head to the right.' He moved away to criticize the Klieg lights.

Determined to live up to Miss Pickford's faith in me, I worked through the scene in my head. I would climb on to the gurney knee first, like a kid would, keeping my back to the camera. A voice broke into my thoughts.

'You know what this scene's about?' A good-looking young grip standing at the edge of the set spoke up.

'Annie is going to give blood,' I answered.

He shook his head. 'It's more than that. Look, this is just my opinion, but seems to me this scene is one of the most important parts of the story. See, Annie is in love with Joe Kelly, even though she's just twelve. Joe is the one accused of killing her father. Annie's sure he couldn't have done it, but her brother is out for revenge. Joe gets shot, and the doctors say he'll die unless he gets some blood.'

'And Annie volunteers.'

'But the kicker is she's too young to understand what giving blood means. She thinks she's giving him *all* her blood. She's willing to die so he can live.'

I nodded my thanks to the grip. With only a few seconds to plan, I concentrated fiercely on Annie's selfless bravery, putting myself as much as possible into her head. What must it have taken for a young girl to sacrifice herself like that for the man she loved? I had to show that strength and emotion with my body.

Beaudine called for action. The cameras started grinding. Above the set, the 110v lamps shone like small suns. I began walking slowly toward the gurney – toward my death. I hesitated once for a fraction of a second, as if gathering my courage, took a deep breath and continued more resolutely than before. Beside the gurney, I straightened my shoulders and lifted my chin before putting one knee up and scrambling awkwardly on to the stretcher. Angling my face away from the camera, I lay back, folded my hands on my chest, and heaved a deep sigh.

'Cut!'

I sat up and met Beaudine's eye.

'Not bad,' he said.

My heart soared. 'Thank you,' was all I said.

THREE

A few hours later, I was standing on the sidewalk, looking up at the four-story boarding house where the late Lila Walker had lived. And died.

As soon as the excitement of doubling for Mary Pickford had ended, I changed out of costume back into my cotton day frock, hopped an eastbound Red Car on Hollywood Boulevard, and walked north through a busy commercial area until I found the address Rob Handler had told me.

The streetcar ride had given me time to mull over my unusual assignment. Rob's conscience was eating him alive, poor man, and I fully understood. Sending someone to the gallows would require a degree of certainty that left no room for even a smidgen of doubt. The facts of the crime as he described them should have overwhelmed any of his qualms: Ruby Glynn had been caught red-handed – blood-red-handed – and Lila Walker had identified her as the killer with her last breath. No wonder there had been no further police investigation!

Still, Miss Pickford had made a personal request, and I would gladly face a jeering audience throwing rotten fruit to please her. By copying her mannerisms, I'd kept myself in work six or eight years longer than should have been possible. And I was forever in debt to her and Douglas Fairbanks for giving me this job when I was at the lowest point of my life. While most studio bosses and directors were tyrants, Pickford and Fairbanks, the acknowledged queen and king of Hollywood, were famous for their kind treatment of their employees. I knew this was their way of helping a valued cameraman get through his guilt after compromising his convictions. So I would examine the circumstances around Lila Walker's death and reassure Handler that Ruby Glynn was indeed guilty, despite her youth and pretty face. I hoped that would allow the poor man to put this sad episode behind him. My plan was to start by visiting Lila Walker's residence to satisfy myself that there could not have been another killer. Could someone else have sneaked in and killed Lila before Ruby Glynn arrived?

Lila's boarding house was purpose-built and a fair cut above the old farmhouse on Fernwood I shared with four other girls. Its creamy stucco walls were topped by a red tile roof and rimmed with a tangle of geraniums and fragrant roses. An iron fire escape clung to the side of the building, but as is usual, its lower ladder did not extend to the ground in order to prevent anyone from climbing up. A small hotel, a drug store, and a few houses shared the block. A white church hugged the corner. Lila could afford a nice part of town. Not ritzy, but nice. According to Rob Handler, she had lived here for about two years.

My rap on the front door triggered furious barking. After a moment, I heard footsteps and the sound of two thick bolts being released. No one would be wandering through the front door of this house unnoticed. But had that been the case back in February? A thin woman with the beginnings of a widow's hump opened the door, clutching the collar of a small, yappy mongrel desperate to defend hearth and home. The woman greeted me with a stony stare.

'Good afternoon,' I said. 'I'm new to Hollywood and looking to rent a room. A friend recommended this place. My name's Dolly Baker.'

Now that she knew I wasn't selling vacuum cleaners, her

face relaxed and her lips turned up a little. Picking up the
mutt, she said, 'Won't you come in, Miss Baker? As it so
happens, I have a fine suite for rent that just came available.
Only twenty-five dollars a week, breakfast and dinner included.
I am Mrs DeWitt, the landlady.'

When I didn't blanch at the price, Mrs DeWitt bolted the
door behind me and showed me into a pleasant parlor. 'Excuse
me a moment while I close Fluffy in the kitchen,' she said,
disappearing around the corner. I seized the moment to take
note of my surroundings. It would be my only chance to learn
anything about the scene of the murder – if, indeed, there was
anything to be learned.

'Now, then,' began Mrs DeWitt, settling herself on a
chocolate-brown sofa. Under normal circumstances, a landlady would dig into my family background, my father's
occupation, my new job, my salary, and my morals in order
to judge my suitability as a boarder. But these were not
normal circumstances. Mrs DeWitt had an empty room
tainted by its association with scandal and murder, a room
that no one who'd been in Hollywood since last February
would touch. Her good fortune in landing an out-of-town
patsy led her to purr a few pleasantries and glide past the
usual questions. Heck, I could have been Siamese twins and
she'd have signed me up.

I fed her the fictional background I had prepared. The truth
wouldn't have worked – she'd boot me out the door if she
thought I was reopening the murder scandal. In a matter of
minutes, she was showing me the dining room where I would
take my breakfast and dinner with seven other female residents
and encouraging me to peek into the kitchen where Darla, the
stout cook, was frying onions. As we prepared to go upstairs,
a heavy footfall on the front porch preceded a pile of letters
and magazines tumbling through the mail slot on to the floor.
With some effort, Mrs DeWitt stooped to pick them up. 'I'll
sort these later,' she said, dropping them on a table beneath a
dozen pigeonholes mounted on the wall. All but one was
labeled with a resident's name.

She unlatched the small gate at the foot of the stairs, a
barrier that effectively kept Fluffy on the ground floor where

he would not bother the boarders. She motioned for me to precede her.

'Fluffy looks like a good guard dog,' I said. 'Have you had him long?'

'Five years. And he's a she. No men allowed in my house. Now, as you can see, there are four units on each floor,' she said as we climbed to the third floor, 'each with two rooms: a parlor and a bedroom. But first, let me show you the bathing room.' We turned down the hall and walked to the door at the end. 'Here is the bathtub that you would share with only three other young ladies. This square tub is for your laundry. And you see there are plenty of hooks for your clothing and towels. A colored girl comes every Friday to clean the public rooms, but residents are expected to wash the bathtub themselves after each use.' A washboard hung on a nail beside the laundry tub, and there were several boxes of soap flakes on the shelf above it. Two shelves on the opposite wall contained a jumble of bottles and boxes of geranium bath salts, rose toilet water, lemon shampoo, and dusting powder with a pale blue puff tucked into the top.

'At the other end of the hall,' she continued, 'is the water closet. It has a large window too, like this one, for the fire escape, and so these rooms are always fresh.' A door across the hall opened. A bottle-blonde head stuck out, took one look at Mrs DeWitt and the stranger and ducked back into her room. Ignoring the interruption, Mrs DeWitt opened the door to Lila Walker's rooms.

Furnished with boarding house basics, the room contained a braided rug, two upholstered chairs, a small table with a pair of wooden chairs, and some old-timey fashion prints from *Godey's Lady's Book* on the walls. Daisy-patterned curtains decorated the window. Although tenants took breakfast and dinner downstairs, there was a counter fixed to the interior wall with a breadbox on it and a cupboard above. In my mind's eye, I could see Lila standing there, slicing bread and cheese for her lunch.

'Now, the bedroom is very cheerful,' she said, drawing aside the ruffled curtain, 'with this window facing north and that one facing east, so you don't get the hot sun.' I took a good look outside to the ground below. There were no trees near the building, no rose trellises, no way for anyone to climb up to the third floor.

Mrs DeWitt gestured toward the narrow bed. 'We launder bed linens for our boarders once every two weeks. You have your own sink, with hot and cold taps, and this large, built-in clothes closet,' she said, pulling open double doors to reveal a modest space with a dozen dangling hangers that made me wonder where Lila's clothes had gone. Who had cleaned out her apartment? Did she have family in the area? In this sterile place, it was hard to get a sense of who she had been.

'I'm sorry to interrupt you, Mrs DeWitt,' said a voice from the hall. We turned to see the cook, who had waddled upstairs to say that the plumber had arrived.

'Make yourself at home, dear,' said Mrs DeWitt, 'while I run down to show him the problem. I'll be back in a moment.'

A moment was more than I needed to search the bureau drawers and the dressing table, because they were as empty as the closet. I expected as much. Back in the front room, I pulled open a drawer and found it contained utensils, scissors, and a couple of paring knives – Rob Handler said a knife had killed Lila, but it could not have been one of these, which were surely too small to have done the deed. No doubt the police had kept the murder weapon. I wondered if it had come from this drawer or been carried in by Ruby Glynn.

A lifetime on the stage had equipped me with a keen sense of when I was being watched. The familiar prick on the back of my neck made me spin around. The blonde girl, the one who had stuck her head out of the door earlier, had come up behind me.

'Hello.' She gave me a happy grin full of crooked teeth. 'I'm Emma Lansing. I live across the hall. Are you thinking about boarding here?'

'Yes. I'm Dolly Baker. I—'

'Did you know this was the place where Lila Walker lived?'

'Who's Lila Walker? I'm new in town.'

'You must be new if you don't know about Lila Walker. She was murdered a couple of months ago. Right here. You'll sure hear about it if you rent her place. I'm not trying to scare you; I just want to make sure you know what you're getting into because Mrs DeWitt won't tell you, that's for sure. And I can tell you all about it, because I was there that day.'

'You were?' I could hardly believe my luck. Emma Lansing needed little encouragement to take center stage. Glancing over her shoulder in case the landlady should reappear, she began her tale in a rush of words.

'Like I told 'em at the trial, I heard a scream and came across to see what was what. There she was, Ruby Gynn, right here on the floor—' she pointed to a spot in the middle of the bedroom between the bed and closet – 'with the bloody knife in her hand. I could see only her legs from the door and at first I thought she was dead, but she'd just fainted. I took another step and saw Lila on the floor too, all bloody. It was an awful sight! The worst of my life. I screamed, and Suzie who lives beside me came running.'

Emma Lansing walked past me and gestured at the clean rag rug beside the bed. 'Lila was here, like she'd fallen and just missed the bed. She couldn't talk, but she was still alive, blood was everywhere, and there she was, gasping for breath, holding her stomach like she wanted to hold the blood in. I froze, but Suzie, she's used to nursing her little brother whose always into some scrape, she ran to the sink and got a towel and tried to stop the bleeding and told me to call downstairs to Mrs DeWitt to get the police. The officer was here in a jiffy, and he and Mrs DeWitt ran up the stairs. So did a couple of other girls who live on second. Everyone was screaming and shouting and fainting and crying and the policeman, he figured out that Ruby wasn't dead, just fainted, so he took the knife out of her hand and set it on the dressing table, there. About then Ruby came to and threw up. The policeman tried to help Lila. He asked her what happened. She tried to talk, her mouth moved but no sound came out and she kept trying to move her arms and point at Ruby. You could see she really wanted to talk but she couldn't. Her mouth was full of blood. Finally, the policeman asked her, "Who did this?" and she lifted her arm again, like this, and pointed to Ruby.'

The young woman crouched on the floor with her back against the bed and reenacted the grisly scene with ghoulish glee. 'It was right then the doctor and the ambulance arrived and two men with a stretcher ran up the stairs, and when they came in the policeman asked Lila again, while everyone could see, "Who stabbed you?" and Lila pointed at Ruby Glynn. By that time, I'd moved and was standing right here, behind Ruby, leaning like this against the double door of the closet, because my knees were shaking so bad, and it almost looked like she was pointing at me, and I was scared for a second that someone would think she meant me! Luckily no one thought that. They took her away and she died on the way to the hospital. That's what I wanted to tell you, that if you're spooked by ghosts, you needn't worry because Lila didn't die here.'

'That must have been shocking! Were you good friends?'

'Well, friends, sure, but not so good. I'd only lived here four months, and she was kind of stand-offish. Nice, but stand-offish, you know what I mean? She stayed home when the rest of us went to work every day. I'm a teacher, by the way. She was going to be a famous actress, she said, but far as I could see she only had extra parts and not even many of those.'

I wondered briefly how Lila afforded her twenty-five-dollar-a-week suite when extras earned about five dollars a day. Rob Handler had told us that Lila was a secretary for Warner Brothers Studios, and I almost blurted that out. 'I thought she – um, do you think maybe she had another job?'

Emma Lansing shook her head. 'Nope, just extra parts now and then. Maybe her family had money.'

That put me in mind to the next question. 'Did she have any relations? Someone must have come in and taken up her clothes and things.'

'A sister. She lived right here in LA and came several times, taking away what she could carry each time. She didn't have a car.'

Didn't sound like a family with a lot of money to me. 'Do you remember her name?'

'The sister? Yeah, it was German . . . Baum-something.

Baumgarden. Or maybe Baumgartner. No, it was Baumgarten. Lived in Culver City and took the streetcar. At first, I thought she was Lila's mother. She didn't like it when I said that, I can tell you!'

A noise from the stairwell set her in motion. 'She's coming!' And with a flutter of her fingers, Emma Lansing ducked out of Lila's rooms and into the hall just as Mrs DeWitt rounded the corner. The landlady gave her blonde boarder a scowl, but Emma only smiled and slipped casually into the water closet. When I made no mention of having spoken to the girl, the suspicious lines on her face relaxed. 'Well, now, what do you think of our lovely rooms? Do you have any questions?'

'Could I come and go as I please, or do you have curfew or rules about guests?'

'You may have female guests above stairs. I show male callers into the parlor to wait for you. Of course you will have your own key, but most girls don't carry it with them. I never leave the house unless Darla is here, or the colored girl, so there is always someone minding the door. Curfew is eleven o'clock on weeknights, midnight on Fridays and Saturdays. I don't allow my girls to stay out after that, or they'll be turned out. I run a respectable place, and I expect my girls to behave accordingly.'

Promising to let Mrs DeWitt know of my decision soon, I took my leave. As soon as I heard her throw the bolt, I circled around to the back of Fortress DeWitt and tried the kitchen door. It was locked tight as well. Between the landlady, the cook, and the cleaning girl, someone was on the first floor all day to answer the door and tend to business. Lila had been killed on a Saturday afternoon when the building was half full of residents. The landlady had testified that she let Ruby Glynn into the house that day at four. Ruby had been unaccompanied. Unless she had an accomplice hidden in her handbag, she had to have been the lone killer.

Or had Lila been killed by someone already in the house?

FOUR

Finding the only Baumgarten in Culver City was easy. Persuading her to help me prove the innocence of her sister's convicted murderer would not be. The next morning, I took the streetcar to Culver City armed only with a story that was . . . well, at least it started out true.

Mrs Baumgarten invited me to take a seat on the front porch swing which overlooked a street of modest houses. A breeze brought the scent of freshly-cut grass from next door, and across the street children romped with a puppy.

'I work for Mary Pickford,' I began. 'She is concerned about the lack of a police investigation into the murder of your sister and hired me to look into the matter. Not—' I raised my hand to forestall comment, 'that she thinks Ruby Glynn is innocent. No, not that. Rather, she wonders if she acted alone. If you don't mind, I'd like to ask you some questions about your sister.' What I really wanted was to look over her things, if I could wangle an invitation inside.

Mrs Baumgarten picked at a hangnail for a moment. She was a pudgy woman in her forties with plain features unadorned by rouge or lipstick. Finally she nodded. 'I reckon there's nothing wrong with that. I read about the trial, and I know no one else was seen at Lila's boarding house, but I guess there might have been someone waiting outside, is that what you mean?'

I dodged the question. 'When you last saw your sister, did she say anything about a feud with Ruby Glynn?'

Mrs Baumgarten went back to her hangnail. I let the silence pass without interruption until at last, she heaved a sigh and replied, 'The last time I saw Lila was at our father's funeral three years ago. We're only half sisters, see, and she was just five when I left home to be married. Her mother died of Spanish flu back in 1919 and our brother was killed in France the year before that, so I was her only living relative. But, I tell you, Miss Beckett, I know more about my neighbors than I know about Lila.'

'Do you know where she worked?'

'Last I heard, she was working for Jack Warner at Warner Brothers Studio. Dad paid for her to go to secretarial school. He used to say a good stenog would always be able to support herself.' I didn't tell her that Lila had left that job months ago. 'And she got some acting jobs. Little ones. Dad didn't approve of acting, but he never said anything about it to her, only to me. I suppose she wanted to be a screen star, like all the girls do these days. I never saw her in the pictures, but I don't go to the pictures much. I do know she got some acting work. She was working on some picture with Steve Quinn. There was a check from him for a hundred dollars in her mailbox. It arrived the day after she died.'

Steve Quinn was Hollywood's biggest cowboy star. Rough, tough and handsome, he, along with his white horse Bullet, regularly bested Indians, rustlers and bandits without missing an opportunity to romance the rancher's pretty daughter. I didn't tell her that extras weren't paid with personal checks from stars. I wondered if Lila had been sleeping with him. It was a tried-and-true way to get parts.

'You were her only heir?'

'That's right. Like I said, there wasn't anybody but me.'

'I hope she didn't leave you any debts?'

Mrs Baumgarten shook her head. 'Not Lila. That girl was good with money. We got that from our father. After I paid the boarding house, there was four hundred and some dollars left in the bank. Five hundred after I cashed Steve Quinn's check.'

'It was good of you to clear out all her things. That must have been sad work.'

She nodded. 'I had to make four trips on the streetcar to get everything here.' There was an awkward pause as I waited for her to offer to show me the stuff, but she didn't.

'I don't mean to pry, but I wonder . . . might I see some of her things?'

Her eyebrows shot up in surprise. 'There isn't much left. I sold most of her clothes to the second hand shop – I don't share Lila's face or figure, as you can see for yourself. I held back a few things that might fit my daughter who lives in San Diego. I'll give 'em to her when she comes to visit next month.' She eased herself out of the chair. 'Come along. I suppose it doesn't do any harm to have a look.' She led the way through the tiny house to a spare bedroom where six or eight of Lila's garments hung in a closet.

Anyone in vaudeville could give lessons in fabric quality and workmanship in clothing. We were all so dependent upon our costumes and their durability that we quickly learned to pay close attention to cut, stitching, seam allowance, lining, and other features that enhance value by extending the garment's life. Lila's clothing was professionally made of fine fabrics. Of course, everything may not have been as chic as these few items in the Baumgarten closet, but the conclusion was clear: Lila liked nice things and knew the difference.

'Did she have anything like papers or notebooks? Scrapbooks, letters, things like that?'

'You mean stuff from her desk?'

I nodded.

'I put all that in a box. I was going to go through it more closely, but my Frank took it down in the basement last week.' She motioned me toward a door that led to a flight of wooden steps into a cool cellar.

By the light of a single bulb dangling from the ceiling, Mrs Baumgarten dragged a couple of cardboard boxes from the corner. 'This one here's got her kitchen things. This one's got the things from her desk. The bath things I've already used up myself.' Dashing my hopes of being left alone with the contents, she pulled a stool out from under a laundry sink and settled down to watch me sort through the sad remains of Lila's life.

The kitchen box held nothing but utensils and trinkets. The desk box interested me far more. I emptied it completely and began returning the items, one by one, to the box after I'd examined each. Lila had everything most people keep in desks – a letter opener, a paperweight, fountain pens, pencils, a few two-cent postage stamps ('Gimme those,' said Mrs Baumgarten, holding her hand out for the stamps), envelopes, blotting paper, jars of both blue and black ink, a penknife, small tablets, monogrammed notes and so forth. There were also notebooks, laundry lists, sales receipts, stationery, grocery lists and several pages of dialogue that must have been left over from a screen test. I skimmed each item, looking for anything out of the ordinary.

An address book isn't usually out of the ordinary and this one didn't start out that way. Turning each page of the alphabet, I examined the entries. I had lived in Hollywood only a short while, but a few of the names sounded familiar. At the last page, the XYZ page, there were no regular entries, only a list of five letters and numbers:

PT 50
ET 100
AL 75
SQ 100
VM 100

The fourth combination nearly leapt off the page. SQ 100. If the letters were initials and the numbers were dollars, it could stand for Steve Quinn, one hundred dollars. That much coincidence did not exist in the entire state of California. Lila was supporting herself all right, but not as an extra or a stenog. She had found a more lucrative line of work, one that was all too common among Hollywood's ambitious young actresses.

Tucked into the XYZ page was a piece of paper folded in half. I opened it and found, to my astonishment, a vaudeville program. I had seen thousands in my lifetime – cheap throwaways that lasted until the performance was over – and this one was nothing special, although the date at the bottom showed it was fifteen years old. I scanned the nine acts without recognition. No surprise there, this was a Gus Sun program and my mother and I had never played his circuit. Still, everybody in vaudeville knew of Gus Sun, a former circus juggler who developed a Small Time booking agency with a Midwest circuit of a couple hundred theaters. I knew many performers who had started in Small Time circuits such as Sun Time and moved to Big Time, but I knew no one on this list.

Why did Lila save this old scrap of paper? Why was it tucked into the XYZ page with the letters and numbers?

I handed it to Mrs Baumgarten. 'Have you seen this before?'

UNIQUE THEATRE
Strictly Moral Family Theatre at a Popular Price

Overture
Selections from *Babes In Toyland* . . . . Herbert

FIVE STAGPOOLES
Australia's funniest acrobatic act
EMILIA FRASSINESE
Violinist
JESSUP AND SHADNEY & Co.
Entertainers in Ebony
GRACE HAZARD
Costume novelty, 'Five Feet of Comic Opera'
RALPH CUMMINGS & Co.
Presenting 'The Typewriter Girl,' a one-act play
Staged by Cecil Beck

INTERMISSION

LESTA AND FERN
Novelty Sister Act
THE LANDRIEUS
'Two minds with but a single thought'
HOWARD'S PONIES AND DOGS
Most attractive animal act in the Varieties
THE FOUR MAGNANIS
Musical Barbers
CRYSTALGRAPH
Animated pictures

Exit March:
The Stars and Stripes Forever . . . . Sousa

She frowned and shook her head. 'Vaudeville, eh?'
'Do you recognize any of the acts or the names?'

She gave it due consideration before shaking her head again and passing it back to me. 'I don't go much to vaudeville. And this here's from 1910. Lila was just a kid then. Maybe it was a keepsake from a show she'd seen.'

'Not unless she lived in Canton, Ohio in 1910.'

'We never been within miles of Ohio. Gimme here, I'll throw it away.'

'My mother and I were vaudeville players for most of our lives,' I said, thinking fast. 'Would you mind if I kept it as a souvenir?'

Her expression told me she thought I'd lost my mind. 'Please yourself.'

FIVE

I hate jails. They bring back memories I'd rather keep locked up. Cops give me the willies too, for the same reason. I don't steal any more, and I try to abide by all the laws I know about, so I don't expect to spend any more nights in jail like I did when I was young. But still, going inside a jail, even to visit a prisoner, takes a lot of moxie. The clang of the steel gates and bolts reminded me how close I'd come to a long sentence myself. Last year, when I was unable to find work in vaudeville, I'd joined in on a scam to impersonate a missing heiress for her fortune. It didn't turn out the way we'd planned, and I'd just missed prison by a whisker.

I hadn't intended to talk to Ruby Glynn, but something funny was going on with this investigation. Seems there was more to Lila Walker than came out in court or the newspapers. She wasn't a secretary – at least, not any longer – she was a high-dollar prostitute with five regulars. That wouldn't have raised an eyebrow in Hollywood. With a glut of pretty actresses scrambling for parts, selling sex was a temporary sideline for many hopefuls, 'just until that good part came along'. No one thought of it as prostitution. It was sex with a present after-wards. But it got me wondering. What other facts went missing because the police never investigated the crime? Maybe the list of clients had nothing to do with Lila's murder. But maybe it did.

It was said that Ruby and Lila had some sort of feud over a man. I wanted to know more and newspapers were not the place to find accurate information. Better to hear it from the source.

'I'm here to visit a prisoner,' I said to a bald cop behind the main desk. He looked me over like I was smuggling a Tommy gun under my skirt, then he pointed to a door marked 'Jail'. I walked through the door straight into an argument.

'Sorry,' a young cop was speaking to a young woman. 'Rules are rules. You can go in. He can't.'

'But I'm his best friend,' protested the man.

'Wife, yes. Friend, no.' He opened another door and let the wife pass. The friend slumped on to a bench and ran his fingers through his greasy, too-long hair. The young cop turned to me with a belligerent thrust of his chin, spoiling for another fight. The nametag on his uniform pocket read O'Brien. Hugging a clipboard to his chest, Officer O'Brien challenged, 'And who are you here to see?'

'Ruby Glynn.'

'Your name?'

'Colleen O'Malley,' I said boldly, figuring an Irish name could only help my case. 'I'm her sister.' I looked him straight in the eye while I said it. Self-confidence done right can pass for honesty.

He gave me the once-over, like a stage manager before a show. 'You don't have a ring, she's not married, and you don't have the same last name.' Officer O'Brien was nobody's fool and would not be easy to bluff. But neither am I. If being nervous had ever rattled me, I'd not have lasted an hour on the stage.

'Of course not,' I said. 'She's an actress. She took a stage name, like every actress does. Like my own boss, Mary Pickford, whose real name is Gladys Smith. Ruby's real name is O'Malley. Ask her.'

Our eyes battled silently for several long seconds before he looked down at his paperwork. 'Sign here,' he ordered, handing

me the clipboard. At the top it read: Visiting Hours 12:00 to
2:00. I had arrived, unknowing, at the right time. 'Wait there,'
he ordered, nodding at the bench where the forlorn friend sat.
Thirty unpleasant minutes later, Officer O'Brien called my
name, and I walked through the door into the cellblock.

Down a flight of stairs, around a corner, down a hall, and
into a windowless basement room I went, following a female
guard who looked as if she could lift me above her head with
one arm. Ruby Glynn was waiting for me, sitting in a wooden
chair behind a wooden table. The place smelled like coffee,
sweat, and cigarettes, although I saw no evidence of any of
those.

I'd not have recognized her. Ruby Glynn wasn't exactly a
household name, but she had played several small roles with
big-name actors and had a promising career ahead of her. Or
used to. God himself could pardon her now and she wouldn't
land another part ever again. After two months in jail, her
stylish brown bob had outgrown its shape. Held back from
her face by a couple of bobby pins, it hung behind her ears
like limp string. She wore a gray shift, men's shoes with no
socks, and no make-up. Her nails were bitten to the quick.
This was a woman who had given up.

'Hi, Sis,' I said as I took the wooden chair opposite her.
The tabletop was sticky, so I clasped my hands in my lap.
With every breath of the stale, rank air, I wanted to gag. 'You
can leave us now,' I said to the guard in my most imperial
voice. It worked.

'Who are you?' Ruby Glynn said when the guard had left.
She did not smile.

'My name's Jessie Beckett. I work for Mary Pickford. She
asked me to investigate Lila's death, and I need to ask you
some questions. They won't let anyone in here unless they're
relatives, so I said I was your sister. What else could I do?'

The ghost of a smile pulled the corner of her mouth.

'I barely know Mary Pickford. What does she care
about me?'

'She thought there should have been a police investigation
into Lila's death. There wasn't, so she asked me to take care
of it.'

'You're a private investigator?' she asked, her disbelief plain.

'Not really. I'm an assistant script girl for Pickford–Fairbanks Studios. But . . . well, I can figure things out. Better than some, it seems.'

She stared at the blank wall behind me a moment, then looked straight into my eyes. 'What does a script girl do?'

'Well, she's the— Wait a minute, you've worked with dozens of script girls. You know what we do.'

'Yes, but do you?'

Ah, she wanted to make sure I wasn't a reporter in disguise. 'A script girl is the director's right hand,' I began, 'a liaison between him and the film editor. She monitors the script during shooting to avoid errors in continuity so that clothing, props, make-up and weather stay the same from scene to scene. She tracks wardrobe and make-up, keeps notes on each scene, and takes each day's film and notes to the editor.'

'All right, you're a script girl. So what do you want?'

'To help you.'

'Nobody can help me.'

'Maybe not. But Mary Pickford wants me to try.'

'Do you think I'm innocent?'

A shrewd thrust. I folded my hands on the table and leaned forward. 'Totally innocent? I don't know. But there are things going on that need explaining. Was someone else there that day?'

'No.'

'Was she injured when you arrived?'

'Yes.'

'Tell me about that day.'

'I've told a hundred people. It doesn't matter.'

'Please, one more time. There was a feud between you two?'

Ruby folded her hands in her lap and continued staring at them the entire time she was talking. 'The famous feud . . . yes. I don't deny there were hard feelings. I wouldn't call it a feud, though. Lila had been seeing Ricardo Delacruz. He was never very serious about her, but then he met me on the set of *Inca Warrior*. He broke off with her and began seeing me. Our romance was in all the papers.'

'I only moved to Hollywood a few months ago,' I offered

by way of explaining my lack of familiarity with the publicity. But I knew who Ricardo Delacruz was. Who didn't? He had started to nip at the heels of Rudolph Valentino, taking the tall-dark-and-handsome roles Valentino didn't want. Both men had an abundance of that exotic, Latin charisma so popular in leading men – the dark wavy hair, smoldering ebony eyes, terrific physique, and swarthy complexion – but Delacruz was Cuban while Valentino hailed from Italy. Both men played sheikhs, pirates, bandoleros, sea captains, and conquistadors for an adoring, largely female audience. I wasn't aware that Delacruz and Ruby Glynn had been a couple.

'It wasn't one of those romances the studios manufacture for publicity. It was real. Ricardo is the love of my life, and I am his. Lila didn't like being cast off, of course, no one does, and she set off a couple of ugly public scenes. But her bitterness wore away, and she and I were back on speaking terms. There was no feud. Then, two days before her murder, she telephoned and said she had some important news, could I come over for coffee? I was getting ready to leave on a trip to Acapulco—'

'Excuse me, where?'

'It's in Mexico. A tiny village on the coast. It's become all the rage since Prince Edward of England discovered it, and I wanted to see it for myself.'

'You were going alone?'

She nodded. 'I needed a break. Some time to think.' She paused, as if recalling her reason. I pulled her back to the present with a cough. 'So I asked Lila if I could come by after I returned, but she insisted it was urgent, so I made time for her. I drove to her boarding house, which I had never visited before. The hunchback landlady let me in. I went up to the third floor and knocked. No one answered. The door was unlocked, so I stepped into the front room. I saw a knife on the floor just inside the bedroom door. I picked it up. If I hadn't picked up that knife, I wouldn't be here. I don't know why I did it. Then I heard a noise like a gasp for air. Lila was on the bedroom floor, bleeding horribly. I screamed. That's all I remember until I woke up with a policeman beside me, in Lila's bedroom.' She drew a deep breath and leaned back in the hard chair, drained by the effort. I hated to push her, but I needed to know.

'You didn't see anyone else there.'

'There was no one else there, trust me. I told them someone must have come in before me and stabbed Lila and left, and they might have believed me if Lila hadn't said I did it. Twice she pointed at me when they asked her. Twice! I don't know why she did that. I suppose it was for revenge, but who would lie on their deathbed?'

'And the trip to Mexico?'

'Oh, the trip. The prosecution said that proved I was planning to flee the country, so her death was premeditated. They said the rental car I drove was proof that I was trying to visit Lila without being noticed . . . as if anyone could get past that busybody guarding the front door without being noticed!'

Those two circumstances had let them ask for the death penalty. The judge was considering the sentence now.

'Why did you rent the car?'

'I'd lent mine to a friend, because I wouldn't need it for several weeks. She testified to that, but they said she was lying to protect me.'

'What happens next?'

'To me?' She shrugged as if it mattered not one bit. 'I'm only here until the judge pronounces a sentence. Life in prison, my lawyer says, if I'm lucky.' Left unsaid was the unlucky option: death by hanging. 'Then I go to prison, possibly San Quentin.'

'I thought San Quentin was just men.'

'Used to be. Now it's for women too. Those scheduled for execution.'

'Oh.'

'You know what? The honest truth is I'm past caring. I did care. I did want to be proven innocent during the trial, but that's over. No one has any doubt about me having committed this murder; even my own lawyer thinks I did it. Sometimes, even *I* think I did it. Thank Mary Pickford for her interest, but it's over. Don't trouble yourself anymore.'

*   *   *

Hugely depressed, I escaped from the creepy cellar room into the blinding rays of the noonday sun. Squinting against the light, I would have stumbled down the white stone steps had it not been for the handrail. Pausing to let my eyes adjust, I filled my lungs with the orange-blossom-scented air, inexpressibly grateful to be free. My thoughts raced. I'd gone into the jail convinced of Ruby Glynn's guilt; I left full of doubts. Everyone was convinced of her guilt, lawyers, jury, press and public, and Ruby herself had given up.

Suddenly, unexpectedly, I was with Rob Handler. I'd seen some great performances in my time, but the one I'd just seen in that dismal room wasn't one of them. Her sincerity was unmistakable. That's what Rob Handler had sensed and he was right. Someone else had done it, I felt sure. But who? And more to the point, how?

Somebody was calling my name. The last person I wanted to see was coming up the walk toward the police station, dressed in his crisply pressed uniform, reporting for duty: Officer Carl Delaney, my persistent suitor.

'Jessie!' he beamed. 'This is a surprise. Are you looking for me?' The hopeful note in his voice was unmistakable, and I considered, only for an instant, telling him what he wanted to hear. But he'd catch me in the lie soon enough. He always did. I launched into the role of guileless girl without a thing in the world to hide.

'I was just visiting a friend,' I said brightly, and in an attempt to change the subject I asked, 'Are you just coming on duty or getting off?'

He wasn't that easy to deflect. 'Who?'

I sighed. He'd find out anyway. 'Ruby Glynn.'

His eyes narrowed with suspicion. 'She's a friend of yours?'

'Well, she's a friend of Mary Pickford's. Miss Pickford asked me to visit, because she can't. You know as well as I do what happens when she appears in public.' It had surprised me to learn what restricted lives stars like Mary Pickford and Douglas Fairbanks led. Any venture outside their home or studio attracted noisy throngs of reporters shouting outrageous questions and fans pushing for autographs, grabbing bits of their clothing. Everyone said the big stars were virtual prisoners, although, after having just visited Ruby Glynn, this was not a comparison I was ever likely to make.

Carl's soft brown eyes bored into mine. I swear, that man could see my brain through my eyeballs. 'Don't do it,' he said.

'Do what?'

'You know what I mean.'

'I have no earthly idea—'

'You're poking around in that murder case. Don't do it. It's over.'

'But, Carl,' I said, dropping all pretense. 'I really think she could be innocent. There are a number of things that don't add up, things that didn't come out in the trial—'

He took my right hand in his, the one with two fingers still in the splint, and stroked them lightly. 'How's the hand?'

'Almost good as new.'

He lifted my hand and brushed his lips softly against my knuckles. 'Next time, you might not be so lucky.'

SIX

I arrived back at the studio as the cast was breaking for a late lunch. Director Beaudine had ordered plates of sandwiches and bottles of root beer from the commissary and given everyone fifteen minutes to bolt their food. Miss Pickford motioned Rob Handler and me into her dressing room where she kicked off her shoes and propped her feet on a stool. She crunched on carrots and celery as Rob and I tucked into ham and cheese on rye. I gave them a summary of what I'd learned about Lila.

'Looks like Lila was the sort of girl who knew her way around,' said Rob, his eyes still red from lack of sleep. I pitied the man. 'None of that came out at the trial, but if it had, would it have mattered?'

'It might have made the jury think that something else could have been going on,' I said. 'That one of her paramours might have killed her.'

'If so, how?'

'The boarding house doors are kept locked, there's the cook at the kitchen door and the eagle-eyed landlady with a dog at the front. The only unguarded way in is the fire escape, which leads to the hall water closets. You'd need a ladder to reach the lowest part. Or some shoulders to stand on.'

'But that would mean two people trying to kill Lila,' Rob protested.

I took a swig of root beer. 'I didn't say it made sense. The likelier possibility is that one of the girls living at the boarding house killed her and then just slipped back to her room. Did anyone consider that at the trial?'

Rob shook his head. 'The police talked to everyone who was in the house at the time, which was about half the residents. They testified at the trial. None of 'em heard anything before Lila's scream, and none of 'em saw anyone suspicious lurking around the premises.'

'But the police never investigated those girls? To make sure they didn't have some grudge against Lila or some reason to kill her?'

'With Lila saying plain as day that Ruby did it, they didn't see any reason to investigate further.'

Mary Pickford reached for another carrot and made her first comment. 'Let's think about the initials.'

I repeated the letters PT, ET, AL, and VM. 'I've tried to match them with actors or directors without much luck.'

She closed her eyes and considered the initials. 'VM might be Vincent MacLeod,' she said after a minute had passed. I shrugged to indicate I'd not heard of him before, and she identified him as a director. 'Not famous, perhaps, but competent. He works for Warner Brothers. But nothing comes to mind for the others.'

'Well,' I ventured, 'V and Q are uncommon letters and more easily matched. PT, ET, and AL are harder. Hey, doesn't Steve Quinn work for Warner Brothers too? And Lila worked there. Maybe that's the connection! Maybe the others are with Warner. Maybe that's how Lila met them. I know a script girl at Warner – I can ask her.'

Mary Pickford gave a slow smile and reached for her

telephone. 'Let me handle this,' she said, and then, to the operator, 'Get me Warner Brothers, please.' Rob and I waited for the call to be put through to the rival studio's switchboard. 'Jack Warner's office, please,' she said. Then, to his secretary, 'Jack Warner, please.' She listened, nodding. 'I understand. This is Mary Pickford. When he gets out of his meeting, please tell him that I called – yes, yes, of course, thank you, I'll hold. Hello, Jack, dear. How are you? And how is Irma?'

Jack dear? I shuddered. Only Mary Pickford could get away with addressing the tyrant of Warner Brothers in so casual a manner. Rumor had it the man had come by his crude ways growing up in a tough gang in Youngstown, Ohio. I once heard an actor say that studio boss Louis B. Mayer was a monster and Harry Cohn was a son of a bitch, but only Jack Warner was mean for meanness sake.

Once she'd accomplished the pleasantries, Miss Pickford held the receiver an inch or two away from her ear so Rob and I could hear both ends of the conversation.

'I wanted to ask you about one of your former employees, Lila Walker,' she continued.

'Lila, the dead girl? Yeah, she worked here. What d'ya wanna know?'

'She was your secretary?'

'One of three or four, yeah. For about two years.'

'And you fired her a few months ago?'

'Wish to hell I had. After she left, we discovered she'd been skimming off petty cash. Ten, twenty bucks each week. Not much, but I don't like being stolen from.'

'I don't blame you.'

'Yeah, a sly little minx, that one. I wish I'd broken her neck myself. Is that what you wanted to know?'

Miss Pickford's eyes met mine. She knew what had just flashed through my mind, and she shook her head.

'Not exactly. I have a parlor game for you. Do any of your people have the initials ET, AL, VM, or PT?'

'ET or— Hell, how do I know? What the hell is this?'

'A simple question, Jack.'

'Why?'

'I've become interested in Lila's death. There was no police investigation—'

'A waste of time. That Glynn woman did her in, make no mistake.'

'Perhaps. But others may have been involved. Men with the initials ET, AL, VM, or PT.'

'PT . . . PT . . . hell, I don't know, Mary. Let me give this to my office gals and see if they can come up with something.'

'Thank you, dear. I need the information quickly. In a few hours, if you don't mind.'

'What the hell's going on?'

A shrill bell sounded. The lunch break was over. Rob Handler stood up. 'Oh my, Jack,' said Miss Pickford, 'there's that dragon Beaudine calling us back to work. I'll fill you in on all the details next time we talk, when your girls have come up with some names for those initials. ET, AL, VM, and PT. Write them down, dear.'

'Yeah, yeah. I got it. But there better be a good story to this.'

'There is, Jack. I promise you, there is. My love to Irma. Bye.'

Setting the receiver in the cradle, she turned to me. 'I know what you are thinking but no, Jack Warner could not have killed Lila.'

'They say he grew up pretty tough in Youngstown . . .'

'I know. And he has a mean streak. But he's too smart to get involved in murder.' Or smart enough to hire someone to do it, I thought.

The cameraman and the star returned to the set to continue with the hospital scenes. I scurried over to Douglas Fairbanks' office to earn my pay. He'd agreed to release me for sleuthing duty, but I couldn't afford to press my luck. If he found he could do without me, he just might!

Douglas's upcoming film, *The Black Pirate*, was one he was writing himself, although he was keeping that quiet for the time being. Donald Crisp was going to direct, but he and Douglas had started off on the wrong foot so people were snappish. No wonder – it was a hugely difficult and expensive undertaking, the first Technicolor movie ever filmed. Douglas always liked to be out in front of everyone else. Sure, someone had filmed a few scenes of *Ben Hur* and *Phantom of the Opera* in two-color Technicolor, but no one had yet done a whole picture that way. Filming was scheduled to start as soon as Douglas finished the script and technical problems were solved. After that, the only time I'd have for investigation would be the middle of the night.

At four thirty, a boy stuck his head inside the office where three of us girls were sorting files and said, 'Miss Pickford asks you to her dressing room, please, Miss Beckett. Right away.'

I ran out the door and arrived just two minutes later, missing only the first part of Jack Warner's telephone call. Rob Handler was already there, shifting his weight from one leg to the other.

'No, Jack,' she was saying, 'I need men's names. Vincent MacLeod is fine but Paula Terry won't do.'

'Why the hell not?'

'We're trying to identify certain men who may have wanted to harm Lila.'

'Well, I can think of a lot of women who'd've cheerfully slit her throat. But if you only want men, fine. My gals couldn't come up with any men's names.'

Mary Pickford sighed. 'Thank you, anyway, Jack, we'll keep—'

'Did you hear the news? It's in the afternoon papers. The judge sentenced Ruby Glynn to hang.'

Rob paled and swayed on his feet. Thinking he was going to faint, I moved toward him, but he steadied himself against the wall. Mary nearly dropped the receiver. 'No, I haven't seen the afternoon papers yet. Thank you for telling me.'

'If you're trying to get her another trial or something, you'd better hurry.'

'Thank you, Jack. Goodbye.'

Rob straightened up and turned around helplessly. There were tears in his eyes. Mary Pickford and I stared at each other for a full minute before I broke the silence.

'There are two possibilities that I can see. One, that the

names don't all come from Warner Brothers, in which case
we need to consider all the men in the Los Angeles area.'

'That's looking for a black dog at midnight,' said Rob.

'Not necessarily. The telephone directory or the city
directory might be good starting places.'

'What's the other possibility?'

'That the names aren't all men after all. Maybe some of
them *are* women. And in that case, maybe Lila wasn't selling
sex. Maybe she was selling silence.'

'You mean blackmail? She was blackmailing those people?'

'For a certain sum every month. A lot of people in Hollywood
have secrets. As one of Mr Warner's secretaries, Lila might
have read things in letters or overheard conversations she
wasn't meant to hear.'

Miss Pickford took no part in our conversation. She had
withdrawn deep into her own thoughts, leaving Rob and me
to work out the next step. I had the impression that turmoil
bubbled just beneath her calm surface, but such an accomplished actress would never show her feelings in her face.
Suddenly she turned and spoke.

'I think we've done all we can. You are to be commended,
Rob, for your jury service and you, Jessie, for the past day's
efforts.' When neither of us had a response, she continued, a
little defensively. 'Even if we can identify all the initials, what
does that do? We could be making a huge mistake. No doubt
dozens of people have these initials. How are we to determine
which one Lila meant? We don't even know for sure if it was
blackmail or prostitution.'

'We could present this information, this theory, to her
lawyer,' offered Rob. 'He might know what to do.'

'Why don't you do that, Rob?' she said, but I could see she
thought it would lead nowhere.

Miss Pickford glanced at the clock above her dressing table.
'I'm tired. I think I'll tell Beaudine to wrap it up for today.
Try to get some sleep tonight, Rob. Maybe take a sleeping
powder. You did all you could.'

SEVEN

On the Red Car going home that evening, I told myself Miss Pickford was right. It was too late. The task was overwhelming and time was evaporating like a puddle in the desert. Still, her sudden change of heart surprised me. Ruby still had several weeks, at least, before her execution. If Mary Pickford had been the sort to give up when things looked bad, she wouldn't be in the position she was today, the richest, most popular actress in the whole world.

The two-tone Packard Phaeton parked at the curb in front of our rented house was a none-too-subtle clue that someone very rich had come a call. My favorite roommate, Myrna Loy, danced out to intercept me as I came up the walk.

'Jessie, Jessie, you'll never in a million years guess who's on the patio waiting for you.' And without giving me time to guess, she announced with breathless wonder, 'Ricardo Delacruz!'

The actor stood as I came on to the patio, his hat in his hands. 'Señorita Jessie Beckett? I am Ricardo Delacruz.' That an actor of his magnitude, who would be recognized wherever he went in Hollywood no matter what hat, scarf, or sunglasses he wore, introduced himself by name was a tribute to his modesty, and it made me like him at once. He was as handsome as his pictures – something you couldn't say about many stars – with a rich southern California suntan and dreamy dark hair and eyes, dressed in white flannel trousers and a crewneck sweater. But this evening his forehead was creased with worry and those coal-black eyes were swollen and red. Before I could speak, he made a slight bow from the waist, took my hand, and brought it to his lips. 'I am at your service, señorita.' I'd never in my life had my hand kissed, and here it was happening for the second time in one day.

'I have come to thank you from the bottom of my heart—' and here he put his hand on his chest for dramatic emphasis – 'for trying to help my poor Ruby.'

'However did you know about that?'

'I went to Ruby the moment her lawyer called me with the terrible news. I was beyond grief, but I needed to be with my beloved, my jewel.' His rich baritone voice held the lilting cadence of a foreign accent, Spanish I presumed, or Cuban, if that was different from Spanish. This was one actor who would make the transition to talkies, if talkies ever came.

'Please, sit.' I gestured toward the chair and took my place opposite.

'Ruby told me you had come to see her today. She said Mary Pickford was concerned for her. I will take my thanks to her also. Have you any success? Anything at all?' he begged.

'I wish I had better news for you, Mr Delacruz, but all I have been able to do in one day is investigate Lila Walker's life during her last few months. You knew her well, isn't that so?'

He nodded morosely. 'There was a small romance between us. A few times I did escort her to parties. I helped her get small parts in some films. She was very pretty, but it was only on the outside. After I met Ruby, there was no other woman for me, forever. Without Ruby, I have no joy in life.'

'So Lila was jealous of you and Ruby?'

'For a week or two, perhaps so. But she found another man and another after him, so I am not important to her any longer.' I doubted that Ricardo Delacruz was quite that easy to replace.

'Did you ever know Lila to go with men for money?'

He looked shocked. 'No, never. She was a woman of the world, you understand me, but she would not sell herself for money.'

'Where did she get her money, then – to pay her rent, to buy nice clothes, to live?'

'She worked for Warner Brothers. She also had small parts in films, but she wanted big parts.' He shook his head. 'You see, she did not have the talent. A pretty face, yes, but talent, no. She was not liked by directors.'

'Why not?'

'She would push for bigger parts and argue when they refused. I myself saw it one time. And a director once told me she tried the old trick on him, where the young woman is

alone with him and says, "give me this part or I will cry
rape and ruin you."'

It was an old ploy, indeed. Still, it happened. How often,
no one would ever know. Had Lila made that work for her,
or had her screen roles come honestly?

I had an idea. Reaching into my handbag, I took out the
vaudeville program. Unfolding it, I passed it to the actor. 'I
found this among Lila's belongings. At her sister's house.' A
puzzled frown creased his brow, then it disappeared. He looked
up at me. I read the question on his face.

'I don't know what it is either. It may be nothing but a
keepsake, but it was with her address book and it begs for an
explanation. Lila was never in vaudeville according to her
sister, or in Ohio.'

He shrugged his shoulders and returned the program. 'It
means nothing to me.'

'Mr Delacruz, do you know anyone with the initials ET?'

He thought for a few moments, and said no. 'Why? Is it
important?'

'Probably not. What about AL or PT?'

A longer pause followed, then he said, 'Paula Terry?' That
was the second time I'd heard that name.

'They are people who were giving Lila money. I'd like to
know why. It probably has nothing to do with Ruby. Do you
know Steve Quinn?'

'Naturally. The cowboy.'

'Do you know why he would send Lila one hundred dollars?'

'Ah, you think she is being paid for her favors?'

'Or for her silence.'

'Most devoutly I wish otherwise, but I have no idea. Will
you find out?'

'I hope so. I'll try. Mary Pickford asked me to investigate.'

'And you are skilled at such things?'

I smiled at his polite skepticism. 'Evidently I am. More so
than most, at least. So I'll do my best.'

'I hired private investigators before the trial. They found
little that helped my Ruby.' His eyes were dark twin pools of
pain and worry. 'Please, Miss Beckett. Please do not give up.
Ruby is innocent. I know this for certain. She is a gentle soul.

Even a spider is safe from her. You must believe she is innocent. I think you do believe, or you would not be trying to
help her. I can help you. Any money you need . . .' and he
reached in his breast pocket for his wallet.

'No, thank you, Mr Delacruz. I don't need your money.'
But he laid a hundred dollars on the table – more money than
I'd ever seen in my life.

'Promise me you will ask for my help or more money if
you need either,' he continued.

'I-I promise.'

'And say that you will tell me about your progress? Even
a small hope is precious to me. To us both.'

'I will.'

'You have an automobile?'

'Uh, no.'

'I will lend you one of mine.'

'Oh, no, thank you, I could never—'

'And a driver, of course. You have only to telephone.' And
he handed me a calling card with his telephone number.
'Please,' he begged, in a voice that cracked with emotion.
'Please prove my Ruby is innocent.'

EIGHT

Seems it was our evening to impress the neighbors. No
sooner had Ricardo Delacruz's fancy Packard purred
away from the curb than a cunning yellow roadster I'd
never laid eyes on before claimed its spot. I had, however,
laid eyes on its driver before. And lips. My heart beat a little
faster as David Murray climbed out of the sports car. No, I
corrected myself, he was David *Carr* now. Once Portland's
bootleg king, David had trailed me from Oregon to southern
California and pried his way into the film industry's aristocracy
with money he'd made smuggling hooch from Canada. The
transformation from crook to film collaborator required a name
change to keep the feds at bay. Nothing unusual about that

– Hollywood was full of reinvented people. Some were more open about it than others, but everyone, myself included, seemed to have a stage name, an alias, or a shortened version of a foreign tongue twister.

'Hi, kid.' David greeted me with his lopsided grin. Hands pushed into the pockets of his moss green, pleated knickers, he planted a peck on my cheek. Tilting his head toward the roadster, he asked, 'How d'you like it?'

'It's swell! When did you get it?'

'Bought it last week. It's a Kissel. Cost me eighteen hundred buckarinos. I came to take you for a ride.'

All at once, I forgot how fagged out I was from the day's events. I probably should have been coy and made him coax me, but David was so monstrously good-looking that I couldn't hold out. Especially since I hadn't seen him in nearly two weeks.

'Let me run and get a hat and sweater.'

The little car was a dream, with soft leather seats and an engine with a hum so gentle I could hardly hear it. We turned left on Sunset Boulevard, passed Paramount Studios, and headed toward the hills where the big Hollywoodland sign dominated the crest. David must have sensed I needed to relax, for we drove in that comfortable silence that comes from long acquaintance. I left Ruby Glynn, Lila Walker, and Ricardo Delacruz behind and lost myself in the beauty of the empty landscape, rugged, parched, and dotted with splashes of crimson and yellow from flowers that seemed to sprout from the rock. It was about seven o'clock, and the sun looked as if it had stalled above the horizon. After a dozen miles, we circled south and headed back to town. I wasn't paying particular attention to our route until David turned into a narrow street where the red clay roofs and arched doorways told me we were in ritzy Whitley Heights.

'See that house? That's where Valentino and Natacha live,' David said. We drove on a bit further and he gestured toward a pleasant bungalow on Iris Circle. 'That was Charlie Chaplin's house before he moved next door to Pickfair. And there's Harold Lloyd's place.' It was a lovely, hilly neighborhood of homes owned by Hollywood's most successful 'movies' –

that's what the natives originally called the people who worked
in the motion picture industry. Most of the houses were
built in a Spanish or Mediterranean style with tile roofs and
balconies, and I was admiring them as one might admire the
castles of Europe when David pulled over to the curb on
Whitley Terrace and turned off the motor.

'What do you think?'

'Who lives here?'

'I do.'

The house gripped the hillside, three levels of milk-white
stucco clinging to the slope like a frozen waterfall. I stared at
him, open-mouthed.

'You're pulling my leg.'

'I moved in last week. Come on, have a look. Scandalize
the neighbors by entering a bachelor's house unchaperoned. I
double dare you.'

'Are you serious? Honestly, David, you actually bought
this?' I glanced around a bit anxiously, as if cops might jump
out of the bushes and arrest us both, but the house was screened
by shrubbery on one side and a bend in the road on the other,
and no neighbors overlooked the front door.

'Sure, I own it. Lock, stock, and barrel,' he replied, and I
remembered the suitcase full of money he finagled a couple
months ago when a drug deal went south. With his hand on
my elbow, he guided me up the steps.

It was a cheerful house with a white tile floor covered by
bright, flat-weave rugs. The furniture was sparse and mostly
wood, with color provided by the sky-blue and sea-green
patterned sofa and rugs. A large picture window overlooked
a walled garden out back. A brand new radio with a large horn
hugged the wall. There was a fireplace in one corner of the
living room – and a dog lying so still on the hearth rug that
he could have been a statue.

'Oh, my gosh, it's Rin Tin Tin!'

David grinned. 'I only wish he was! Did you know Jack
Warner pays that mutt a thousand a week? Meanwhile his
human actors are pulling down one hundred and fifty dollars.
Sad to say, this is not Rin Tin Tin. Meet Rip. Rip this is Jessie.
Jessie, Rip.' The German shepherd lifted one eyelid to see

what all the fuss was about, then heaved a deep breath that looked like a bored sigh and closed the eye.

'New car, new house, new dog . . .'

'Well, Rip's not new. I've had him for about seven years. And I was sick of living in that hotel with Rip cooped up all day indoors. He's too old to take on walks any more, so I needed a yard.'

'I didn't know you had a dog.'

'A friend brought him home from France after the war, just like that fella Lee Duncan brought home Rin Tin Tin. There were a lot of German shepherds in that war, you know, trained as guards, sentries, messengers, even scouts.'

'How did you get him?'

'My friend's wife was scared of Rip, so he gave him to me.' Either my arched eyebrows gave me away or David read my mind, because he explained, 'I know he doesn't look like much now, but Rip was one fierce guard dog back in the day. He's old now. We don't know how old, but he wasn't a pup when my friend got him, and that was eight years ago. When I was working in Portland, I was glad to have a big, tough dog like Rip at my side. He saved my skin on more than one occasion, didn't you, boy?'

Rip continued breathing.

'I don't have any curtains yet, but the neighbors aren't nosy. The kitchen is in here,' said David. 'I figured you'd be hungry. Want some dinner?'

'You cooked?'

'Hell, no. I bought all this.' He gestured to a selection of food spread on the counters.

'I really shouldn't stay—'

He opened a brand new electric Frigidaire and pulled out his trump card. 'But I have your favorite.'

Ah, champagne. My Achilles' heel. Anticipating my response, he popped the cork and began pouring the magical bubbles into two glasses.

'A new house calls for a toast, don't you think?' I asked.

He touched my glass with his. 'To new houses,' he said. 'But let's hold off on the real toast until after you've looked the place over.' Carrying the bottle, he led me up the stairs.

The second floor had three bedrooms – one with a large bed and dresser that was obviously David's – and a modern bathroom in the hall, the sort with the tub, water closet, and sink in the same room. I'd never been inside any place David lived, here or when I knew him in Oregon, so I looked around with interest to see what his surroundings said about him. The answer? Nothing. The walls were stark white and as bare as an artist's blank canvas. The wooden floor had no carpet. The bed was made – he knew I was coming, no doubt – but there was no spread, just a blanket and a single pillow. The wooden dresser opposite the bed had nothing on it but a small basket with some coins, cuff links, and keys. I admired the view from the window. There wasn't much else to say that wouldn't open me up to double entendre. That single pillow made me feel good, though.

The other two bedrooms were empty. And so was my glass. David refilled it. Then we went downstairs to admire a work-room and maid's suite – unoccupied – on the lower level. When my glass was empty, David refilled it again. I was feeling fine as I settled on the sofa and watched him fiddle with his new radio, turning the knob until the static resolved into band music. 'Can't get jazz, but here's *KHJ*. They're usually clear. You know, I haven't been able to hang pictures or pretty up this place like I want, but I thought you could help me with that. Now, a proper toast.' He sat down beside me on the sofa and topped off our glasses with the last of the champagne.

'All right.' I lifted my glass and waited.

'To our new house,' he said.

'To our new house,' I repeated, and did a classic double take. '*Our* house?'

'Yep. I put the house in both our names. It's half yours. Surprised?'

Speechless was more like it. Eventually I sputtered, 'Why on earth would you do a thing like that?'

'Because it was only fair. I bought this place with the money I ended up holding when that drug deal went bad, and I'd

never have known about that if you hadn't put me on to those
crooked cops, so this place ought to be half yours.' He leaned
a little closer and put one arm around my shoulders. 'Besides,
I want you to live here with me. I'm crazy about you, kid,
and my intentions are not honorable.'

The champagne on an empty stomach was making me more
than a little muzzy, but not that muzzy. I opened my mouth
to reply but David inserted his own words before I could get
mine organized. 'Now, Jessie, I'm not looking for an answer
tonight. You just think about it a while, about what a great
place this is and what a swell guy I am.'

'Don't be silly, David. You . . . I . . . we wouldn't survive
the scandal. Look at what happened when Natacha moved in
with Valentino. It almost wrecked both their careers, even
though they eventually got married!'

'Natacha and Rudy are stars. Our lives aren't splashed all
over every movie magazine and gossip column. No one cares
two pins about us. We have nothing to lose.'

'That's not so. You'd never be invited to Pickfair again, and
I'm almost certain Mary and Douglas would break with you
on your investments. And I'd lose my job for sure.'

'Then they're hypocrites. Everyone knows they were
involved in a love affair while they both were married to other
people.'

'Hardly anyone in Hollywood knows that, and Mary guards
her reputation like Fort Knox. Her fans would desert her in a
minute if she did anything immoral. She won't even cut off her
curls for fear of the reaction from folks who think a bobbed
head is sin's haircut. And besides, with your background, you
don't need anyone wondering where all your money came from.'

I knew I had him there.

Without conceding defeat, David stood up and disappeared
into the kitchen. A moment later he brought two bags of food
to the dining table, which was already set with blue-and-white
placemats and white china plates.

'I didn't know what you'd like, so I bought some
hamburger sandwiches and salad and some cherry pie.'

Suddenly I was starving. 'I've never had a hamburger
before.'

'They're better hot, but these are still a little warm from the oven.'

Hot or not, the food tasted good. The champagne had loosened my tongue, so while we ate, I told him about Rob Handler's jury duty and my investigation. David's always been a good listener. He thinks while he listens and doesn't interrupt until you're finished. And he doesn't treat me like I'm an impulsive child who needed minding.

'. . . and Rob Handler is going to get in touch with Ruby's lawyer tomorrow and tell him what we've learned. Maybe it will give him an idea about an appeal or a delay.'

'Maybe,' he said doubtfully, 'but what are you going to do next? Or did Mary tell you to drop it?'

'Not in so many words. I think she just gave up after she heard the judge's sentence.'

'Ruby may not be executed any time soon. This isn't the Wild West when the hanging came ten minutes after the verdict. My guess is it will be a few weeks.'

I brightened. 'You really think so?'

'Ask her lawyer. Meanwhile, if you believe she's innocent, you've got some time.'

'I don't know for certain that she's innocent. I just think there's more to it than came out in the trial. The whole thing smells funny. What I want to find out is why those five people were paying Lila Walker.'

'You know two of the names?'

'Possibly three, but the only certain one is Steve Quinn.'

David frowned. 'I can't imagine a big name like Quinn paying for something he could get for free any night of the week from girls cadging for parts. It must be blackmail.'

'I think I'll go over to Warner Brothers tomorrow morning and see if he's in.'

'He'll throw you out. It'll sound like you're accusing him of having something to do with Lila's murder.'

'Maybe, but I think I can persuade him to answer my questions.'

'Are you planning to eat that last hamburger?' When I said no, he took off the bread and gave a low whistle. Rip picked himself up, stretched, and limped over for a snack, favoring a stiff hind leg. 'Good boy,' David said, rubbing his head.

Taking my hand, he led me back to the sofa. He sat down first and pulled me into his lap. 'Look, Jessie, you know I'm crazy about you. You are one special girl. From the moment we met, I knew we were destined to be together. You and I are made out of the same cloth. We're two of a kind, scoundrels, and we—'

When I drew a deep breath to object, he waved his hand to forestall any indignant protests. 'All right, calm down. We are *former* scoundrels who have seen the error of our ways. But we understand each other. We don't have to hide our pasts from each other.' He kissed me softly. 'I've never known another girl like you, Jessie.' He kissed me less softly. Rip, with a sudden burst of energy, thumped his tail and watched us from the hearth rug. 'You see?' smiled David, 'Rip likes you too.'

I wished I wasn't attracted to David, but I couldn't help myself. He was handsome and manly – and don't think he didn't know it! – and he sure knew how to kiss a girl. I hadn't done more than kiss in several years, and my body's response suggested the drought had been too long. His hands groped their way under my two-piece day dress . . . I made it easier by unfastening the side buttons. In no time I was panting like a girl running up steps. I kicked off my shoes and was about to pull off my stockings and skirt when sense battered its way into my brain. A bastard myself, I knew all too well the life-time consequences of a moment's passion, and not much scared me more than back-alley abortions. I managed to make a protesting noise in the back of my throat.

'No, it's all right,' David rasped. 'We'll go upstairs. I have some sheaths.' I wanted him so badly, I made no further objection. As he lifted me in his arms to carry me to his bedroom, Rip picked up his head and growled a throaty warning. Seconds later there was a knock at the front door.

David swore. I groaned. 'Leave it,' I said.

But he laid me on the sofa where I was blocked from sight and headed to the door, tucking in his shirt and pushing the hair off his forehead before throwing back the deadbolt.

From where I was, I could hear the urgency in a masculine voice, but I couldn't pick out any words. I wasn't even sure they were speaking English. David did not invite the man inside, thank heavens, so I waited impatiently as they exchanged a few terse sentences. The door closed.

'I'm sorrier than you know, but I have to go somewhere.'

'What! Where?'

'You can wait for me upstairs.' He put his hand under my chin and kissed me. 'I'll be back in a few hours. We'll pick up right where we left off. Throw the bolt behind me.'

And he was gone. Like that.

So much for the *former* scoundrel. I didn't know what David was involved in, but he was in it up to his neck. Once again, he'd lied to me. He wasn't capable of going straight. If I took up with him, it would be like this all the time – secret assignations, unsavory companions, dirty money – until a rival operator or some cop ended it with a bullet.

I looked around for a vase to smash, but there were none in sight, so I picked up David's champagne glass and threw it against the front door. I hoped he could hear it shatter from the sidewalk. In despair, I sat back on the sofa and dropped my head in my hands. Something warm and soft touched my foot. 'What am I going to do, Rip?' I asked, rubbing his head. He gazed at me with great blinking eyes. People always think dogs can understand them. Maybe they do. Maybe Rip knew all about this sudden coming and going, this abrupt change of plans. Maybe he was used to it. I was not.

Stuffing all that passion back into the bottle was like trying to gather smoke, but there was no choice. I looked around for a clock and saw none. I sort of lost track of time there for a while, but it had to be somewhere between nine and ten. David would be back in a few hours, would he? Bully for him. I wouldn't be here. The short hike to Hollywood Boulevard would clear my head and give me time to think. I could catch a streetcar there. I dressed quickly, pulled my cloche hat over my tousled hair, threw on my sweater, and left Rip alone to guard the house.

NINE

The following morning, the magic of Mary Pickford's name got me through the front gate at Warner Brothers and into Steve Quinn's dressing room. His latest cowboy picture would start filming next week at a remote desert location, but today he had just finished a prep session with the wardrobe mistress when I arrived.

'I've got a few minutes before a make-up meeting,' he drawled genially, glancing at the clock on his dressing table. 'What can I do for you, little lady?'

Steve Quinn was a strong-looking man, but smaller than he appeared in his pictures. Deeply suntanned from so much outdoor work, he looked out of place in everyday clothes instead of his chaps, holster, and ten-gallon hat.

'I'd like to ask you about Lila Walker.'

His eyes narrowed and the smile straightened to a tight line. 'Lila Walker? The girl who was killed three months back? I didn't know her.'

'I think you did,' I said as gently as I could. 'Mr Quinn, I need some information, but I want to assure you first that I mean you no harm. Nothing you say will go any further, I promise.' When he didn't blink an eye, I went on. 'I'd like to know why you wrote her a check for one hundred dollars on the day she died.'

That was when I realized that Steve Quinn was not a good actor. His every thought traveled brazenly across his face, expressing in a matter of seconds his journey from shock to anger to fear. It was the fear that interested me most.

'How dare you come here with these accusations, you little tramp! Get out of here!'

'I'm sorry, Mr Quinn. I'm not accusing you of anything. But if you won't explain things to me, privately like this, I'm afraid I have no choice but to go to the police and the lawyers and tell them what I've learned. If you tell me what I need to know, the truth can stay in this room.'

His tanned face paled. 'What else have you learned?'

I let him think there was more. 'Mary Pickford has asked me to investigate this murder because she – and others – believe Ruby Glynn did not act alone.'

'I don't even know Ruby Glynn.'

'But you knew Lila. What was the check to Lila for?'

'Th-that was a wager. A foolish bet that I lost. Nothing of consequence.'

'Every month?' I had only my suspicions that he had sent her a check every month, but I threw this out to see his reaction. Although it wasn't something I could verify myself, I was pretty sure the authorities could get hold of Lila's bank records and even more sure that they would show a monthly deposit of one hundred dollars.

The cowboy star crumpled before my eyes, dropping his head into his hands and moaning something unintelligible.

'I'm not trying to injure your reputation, Mr Quinn. Did you know there were others who were paying Lila a certain sum every month?'

He took his head out of his hands and looked at me with astonishment. 'There were?'

'She kept a list. But instead of names, she wrote only initials. I knew who SQ was because of your check. If I could identify these others, I might be able to figure out if any of them were involved in her death.'

'I had nothing to do with her death!' he shouted, waving his hands, flustered as a girl.

'I believe you. You wouldn't have put that check in the mail on the evening she died if you had known she was dead. By the time you learned of her murder, the mail had already gone out. I'm only looking for an answer to my question, Mr Quinn, so please listen to me. Why were people paying Lila? If she was selling herself, then the initials on the list are men. If she was blackmailing you, then the list could include women. If you can help me with that, I don't need to know the details, and I don't need to bother you again.'

Steve Quinn wrung his hands, rubbed his face, and at one point, dropped his head between his legs, gulping deep breaths like a woman warding off a faint. Finally he steadied himself and spoke, keeping his eyes fixed firmly on the ground. 'She found out . . . I don't know how . . . something about . . . something about a man – someone I haven't seen in years! She threatened to ruin me . . . she didn't want much . . . fifty dollars a month, she said. I paid. But you don't buy silence. You only rent it. And the rent kept going up. Still, one hundred dollars is not too high. Not for me. Lila knew not to overplay her hand. She wouldn't kill the goose that laid the golden egg. But it would never stop. I knew that. I hated her.' He straightened and met my eye. 'But I didn't kill her. I kill people by the score in every picture I make, but I could never kill anyone in real life. When I heard Ruby Glynn had murdered Lila, I was overjoyed. I only wished I'd had the guts to do it myself.'

The allusion to another man told me what it was that Lila had learned about Steve Quinn. This tough, manly cowboy would never have paid for sex with Lila or with any woman for that matter. He guarded the greatest secret in the film world, the one that would instantly destroy any man's career. A word so dangerous it was never spoken in Hollywood, not even in jest.

TEN

Later that same afternoon, I sat with Paula Terry on a bench beneath a fragrant eucalyptus not far from Warner Brothers studios. It was a busy area, but the bench sat apart from the pedestrian traffic. We could talk without being overheard.

She had resisted coming, but the same argument that had broken Steve Quinn brought Paula Terry out to meet me. I knew very little about her. She was a couple of years older than I, she had been named a WAMPAS Baby Star a few years ago, and she worked steadily, if not spectacularly, for Warner

Brothers in both historicals and contemporaries. She was a beautiful woman, but today, anxiety robbed her of her best asset.

'I didn't even know Lila Walker,' she protested as soon as she sat down on the bench. Her eyes were red and moist.

'You didn't have to know her. She learned your secret. She threatened you. You paid her fifty dollars a month to keep quiet.'

She twisted an embroidered handkerchief and blotted the corners of her eyes in a futile attempt to preserve her make-up. 'How did you know?'

'I know a lot more than that,' I bluffed.

'I don't know how anyone found out. I've been so careful. It must have been on one of my trips to Fresno. Lila must have followed me and snooped around when she got there. But no one in Fresno knew, unless my sister let it out by accident. But she said she didn't. It's plagued me, wondering who knew, who let on to Lila. I was always so careful. Even my little girl doesn't know. She thinks I'm her auntie. It's not just myself I'm protecting – it's my little girl. I don't want her ever to know. It would ruin her life as well as my career. You won't tell anyone, you promise?'

This stung. Raised by an unmarried mother, I knew all too well the perils of illegitimacy. I understood from an early age that I would never be admitted to polite circles and that a reputable marriage was impossible. When my mother decided to keep me – she could have dropped me off at an orphanage and none the wiser – it sealed her fate as well as mine. I was the reason she could never go home to her family in Ohio. I was the reason we had to stay in vaudeville, where people were judged more on their talents than on their pedigree.

'I would never expose you or your daughter,' I said in the most reassuring voice I could muster. I felt like a heel, but there wasn't any other way. 'I need to know where you were the day Lila Walker was killed.'

'Why? You think I did it?'

'I want to know where you were, and I want proof. Otherwise . . .'

'Nothing could be easier. I remember that day perfectly. I

was on location in Mexico, filming *Dark Rose*. A bunch of us were in a cantina having a drink after a long day, and someone came over and said that Ruby Glynn had killed Lila Walker the day before. It was the hardest acting job of my career, looking like I was sad when I wanted to shout to the sky with relief.' Even now, her lips turned up in a satisfied smile at the memory. She looked me straight in the eye as her confidence increased. 'And you can check that with the studio.'

Of course Paula Terry could have hired a killer to act when she was well out of the way, but for the time being I had to be satisfied with the knowledge that Miss Terry did not *herself* kill Lila.

Dealing with Vincent MacLeod proved harder. I left messages with his secretary throughout the day but the director would not return my telephone calls. There was nothing to do but track him to his house that evening. The City Directory gave up his address, and I hopped a streetcar to the stop nearest his neighborhood.

The sun had just set, but the long spring twilight provided ample visibility. I found his house, an imposing hacienda-style building, large and new, with an expanse of manicured lawn edged by cheerful flowerbeds with nary a weed in sight. Naturally he didn't answer his own door. A Mexican woman in a beige uniform opened it at the sound of the chimes. 'I would like to see Mr MacLeod on urgent business,' I said, giving her my name and a sealed envelope. Inside was a terse message saying I wanted to talk to him about Lila Walker.

'I'll tell Mr MacLeod you are here,' she said, without inviting me in. I waited on the blue-tiled porch for about two minutes before she returned. 'Wait here,' she repeated. After another couple of minutes, a police car pulled up to the curb.

You don't spend twenty-five years on a vaudeville stage without learning how to ad-lib when the script doesn't come off as planned. Instinctively, I slipped into my younger self, the teenage persona that had kept me working half way through my twenties, and prayed the uniform climbing out of the police car wouldn't turn out to be Carl Delaney. Fortunately, I was wearing low-heeled Mary Janes and a simple day dress that, if it didn't make me look younger, at least didn't add sophistication. I ran my fingers across the dusty porch railing and smudged my cheek, tousled my bob, and stepped into the shadows, just out of range of the harsh porch light, as I watched the officer come up the walk.

Putting his hands on his hips, he sized me up and barked, 'Now what are you doing trespassing here, missy?'

I rubbed my nose with the back of my hand and sniffled. I scuffed my toe in the dirt. 'I'm not doing anything wrong,' I said in my young voice, giving it a little tremor. 'I just wanted to see Director MacLeod. I want to be in the pictures, and if he'll just see me, I know he'll give me a part.' I started to cry, not too much.

'What's your name, missy?'

My mother's stage name sprang into my head. 'Chloë Randall.'

'And how old are you, Chloë?'

'Fifteen.' I sniffed again. 'Are you going to put me in jail?'

'Come along now, young lady.' He put one hand on my shoulder and steered me firmly toward the street. 'I think I'd better just take you home and let your mother and father deal with this. Where do you live?'

'I took the streetcar here. I can get home by myself,' I said, stalling for time to think. My own address wouldn't do. He'd only see my roommates, realize I'd played him for a fool, and haul me off to jail for sure. I needed a family and an address. Fast. Of course there were people, like Rob Handler, who could play my father in a pinch, but I didn't know Rob's address. I knew very few addresses. Except one, dammit.

'I think I'd rather take you home and have a chat with your parents. What's your address?'

'44 Whitley Terrace. That's my house.' And it was God's truth – David had said so last night. 'But I don't have parents. Only my big brother.'

The cop nodded as if to say, *Ah, yes, there's the problem – a brother trying to raise a young sister.* He lectured me all the way to David's house on the evils of the film industry and how it robbed a girl of her virtue so that no man would ever marry her.

When we reached number 44, he rapped sharply on the front door with his baton.

'That's my brother, David,' I said when David opened the
door, speaking quickly to forestall any errant remark on his
part. 'I'm sorry, David. I won't do it again.'

David was quick on the uptake. He scowled at me, then
looked at the policeman with an expression of resigned
concern. 'What's she done now, Officer?'

'Trespassing. Bothering an important director at his home.
Wanting to get in the pictures. The pictures is no place for a
movie-struck young girl, sir, if you don't mind me saying so.'

'I don't mind at all, Officer. I've said so a hundred times,
but the little brat doesn't listen.' He glared at me. Then to the
policeman, 'Thank you for bringing her home, Officer. And
don't worry, I'll keep a tighter rein on her from now on.'

The policeman tipped his hat and left. I stepped inside and
leaned against the closed door. 'Whew! Thanks.'

'My pleasure. You look like you could use a drink. If you'll
sit a while and tell me what's what, I'll drive you home.'

'It's a deal.'

Avoiding the sofa and its memories, I sat in a club chair as
David disappeared into the kitchen and began rattling bottles
and glasses. I couldn't see him but his voice came through
clearly. 'What'll ya have?'

'A gin rickey?'

'Coming up.' More rattling and crushing of ice. 'Listen . . .
about last night . . . I know you were mad. I was going to
bring flowers to your house tonight and grovel.' He reappeared
with a drink in one hand and a vase of roses in the other,
looking so contrite I wanted to hug him and tell him all was
forgiven. I managed to restrain myself.

'Thank you.' The rickey was strong.

'This is about the Lila Walker murder, isn't it? Whose house
were you breaking into this time?'

'I wasn't breaking in; I was ringing the bell.' And in a few
minutes, I filled him in on what I'd learned about Lila's scheme.
'Vince MacLeod is probably one of the people Lila was blackmailing. I want to know where he was when she was murdered.
He wouldn't respond to my telephone messages, so I had no
choice but to go to his house.'

'So that didn't work. What's next?'

'It may yet work. I managed to leave a note telling him I was investigating Lila's murder and that I knew she'd been blackmailing him. I said I'd go to the police if he didn't speak to me.'

David sipped his drink. 'But he called your bluff. He called the police himself. There's your answer.'

I shook my head. 'I'm not sure he read my note. Or maybe he did and thought he could ignore me. I'll bet he doesn't sleep well tonight. I'll bet money he contacts me tomorrow.'

David's grunt sounded unconvinced, but he didn't take the bet. 'What's next?'

I shrugged. 'I'll spend some serious time with the telephone book, looking for people with the initials ET and AL. And then there's that vaudeville program. It must have something to do with Lila's list. It was tucked into that same page in her address book. Maybe one of the vaudeville players has the initials ET or AL. Or maybe it has the name of someone new who she was going to blackmail.'

'You're good at figuring things out, Jessie. Just don't do it alone. If Vince MacLeod was involved in Lila's murder, he isn't going to think kindly of anyone trying to prove it.'

ELEVEN

When Vince MacLeod telephoned me at Pickford–Fairbanks Studios the next morning, I took the call on the staff telephone next to the switchboard. In a voice like rough gravel, he spewed obscenities and insults with careless disregard. The rhetoric rose with his voice.

'You're one of those goddamned Roman Catholics, aren't you?'

'Excuse me? I don't know anything about religion, Mr MacLeod—'

'My wife put you up to this, didn't she?'

'I don't know your—'

'Well, you tell Vera that unless she agrees to the divorce, I'm not—'

'This isn't about your wife, Mr MacLeod. It's about Lila Walker who was—'

'Don't you tell me what this is about, you goddamned bitch. I'm not paying you a cent—'

'I'm not asking for a cent, Mr MacLeod. I'm asking where you were the day Lila Walker was murdered.'

He paused. I could almost hear him thinking. Finally he asked, 'Why should I tell you anything?'

'Because,' I said in a condescending tone that risked enraging him further, 'if you don't, I'll go to the newspapers and the police and tell them that Lila Walker was blackmailing you and that gave you reason to kill her. And they'll focus on the blackmail and start asking questions.'

'I didn't kill her. Ruby Glynn killed her.'

'Maybe, maybe not. Maybe someone helped her.'

'Not me.'

'Then where were you that day?'

'At a funeral in Sacramento.'

'Whose funeral?'

'My wife's father.'

'And who might back that up?'

'My wife. My wife's brother, my wife's sister, my wife's goddamned uncle! Who the hell else do you want? The whole fucking family!'

'I'm not trying to cause trouble, Mr MacLeod. Just tell me the name of Vera's father and I'll be done.' There was a pause so long that I thought we had been disconnected. 'Mr MacLeod?'

The stream of profanity that crackled through the telephone wires made me wince. Finally, the torrent subsided and I heard him say in a subdued tone, 'My wife's name is Helen, and her father was Ralph Freestone.'

'I see.' And I did. The Catholic slur had reminded me of a performer I'd known in vaudeville, a friend of my mother who wasn't permitted to divorce his Roman Catholic wife, so he went ahead and married another woman and toured with her in a credible song and dance act. Hardly anyone knew he had

two wives. Vincent MacLeod was another such. He had Helen
and Vera. Vera was Roman Catholic and wouldn't, or couldn't,
divorce him. He was a bigamist. That knowledge would matter
not at all inside the lackadaisical world of Hollywood, with
its casual mores and freewheeling sexual liaisons, but if news
like that spread beyond the city limits to the public at large,
it would kill his career. Pious Catholic and Protestant women's
groups alike would boycott his pictures. He would lose his
exalted position at Warner Brothers and no other studio would
touch him.

'Thank you, Mr MacLeod. Assuming your information about
the funeral checks out, I will have no further—'

He slammed down the receiver.

Being at a funeral would give him an alibi, sure. But I
wouldn't put it past someone as mean as Vince MacLeod to
have hired a man to do the job.

TWELVE

'I need to look very different from myself,' I explained to
Mildred Young, my favorite make-up artist. Ever since
she'd come to Pickford–Fairbanks a few months ago, we'd
been good friends despite the twenty-year age difference
between us. Mildred was prim, plain, and discreet, rare traits
in the world of moving pictures where nosy parkers pried into
others' affairs as a matter of self-preservation. 'I met with
someone a couple days ago who I need to meet again today
and not be recognized.'

'Man or woman?'

'A woman.'

'Hmmm. That's harder. Sit.'

She folded her thin arms and studied my face for a full five
minutes before turning to her mysterious array of bottles and
jars. Using an artist's palette, she began mixing lotions and
colors from one after another, frowning until the concoction
met with her approval. 'In another age, I'd probably have been

called a witch with all these potions,' she reflected as she tested the mixture on my face.

Since she'd broken the silence, I felt free to talk. 'Is all this your own stuff?'

'About half. The rest we buy from Max Factor.'

'Has it been hard changing from stage make-up to film?'

'It's a challenge. I'm learning every day. You know yourself how different it is. Make-up for the balcony and make-up for a close-up camera shot are as different as an artist painting a mural or a miniature.'

Torn between vaudeville's unwritten rule against prying into people's lives and my desire to be friendly, I hesitated before asking, 'So you're glad you gave Hollywood a try?'

She pulled my hair away from my face and pinned back my bangs. 'Very glad. It was a good move for me at this time in my life. How about you?'

'Putting down roots has been a new experience for me. In vaudeville, two weeks was a long stay.'

'I've put down some real roots myself. Just bought a house.'

Astonished, I drew back. 'I didn't know women could do that! I mean, I thought they had to be married.'

She straightened my head to face the light. 'They usually do. But when I first arrived, I asked where Miss Pickford banked and opened an account there. When I went for a loan, the man turned me down. Said I didn't have a steady job. I told him Mary Pickford would be calling him to explain how steady my job was – close your eyes now – and he disappeared into another office. He reappeared five minutes later saying they'd reevaluated my application and I had the loan.'

'I'm glad Miss Pickford set him straight.'

'That's the funny part. They never telephoned her. I asked her the next day. All it took was the threat.'

I was all admiration. Like Mary Pickford herself, Mildred was a woman who refused to let men block her way. As she worked on my wig, she described her new house and its location outside the city limits. 'But I'm just half a mile from the streetcar, so I won't need to purchase an automobile.'

'When do you move?'

'Next week. I'll be glad to leave that noisy boarding house for some peace and quiet.'

'You'll get plenty of that, living alone in the countryside!'

'Oh, I won't be alone. A friend is joining me. It helps pay the mortgage. If I get a third, I can almost live for free.'

A half hour later, Mildred had transformed me into a plump, foreign-looking woman with tan complexion and a brunette wig. I hardly recognized myself in the mirror.

'A miracle,' I said. 'Thanks.'

'Don't mention it. But what about your splint?'

I held out my right hand so Mildred could remove the splint from my fingers – that was something the landlady would be likely to remember.

'Come straight back here and I'll put it back on,' she said.

'Swell. I can't wait until it comes off for good.'

Carrying a satchel full of envelopes I'd addressed earlier, I hopped the streetcar and retraced the route to Lila Walker's boarding house, arriving in the middle of the morning when the house was almost empty.

The house had seven paying residents in addition to the three women who worked there. The maid came in on Fridays, so I could eliminate her – she hadn't been there on Saturday, the day Lila was murdered. I thought I could also eliminate the cook and the landlady – their initials did not match ET or AL and they had a lot to lose by killing off a boarder. Not to mention, a fifty- or one-hundred-dollar-a-month payment would have been far beyond their means. Nor was Emma Lansing, the one resident I met, a match, and frankly, she was such a chatterbox that if she had stabbed Lila, she'd have blabbed it to the police within minutes. That left six possibilities.

I rang the bell, triggering a barrage of ear-splitting yips that grew muffled as the mutt was banished to the kitchen. Seconds later, Mrs DeWitt threw the bolts and opened the door.

'Good morning,' I said in my lower, adult voice. 'I'd like to see Miss Emma Lansing.'

'I'm sorry, she doesn't return from work until six.'

I had counted on her absence, but the news caused me to drop my head with disappointment. 'Might I leave her a message?'

'Certainly.' She waited expectantly but did not invite me inside. Getting inside was critical to my plan. I had to put the envelope in the pigeonhole myself so I could read all the names. I opened my satchel and clumsily rummaged through the envelopes as if searching for one in particular. I took a long time, then pulled them all out in a messy clump and dropped them on the porch, making sure they scattered widely.

'Lordy mercy! Clumsy me!'

It worked. Mrs DeWitt opened the door a bit more and came out to help me gather them up. In the confusion, I edged a little behind her and put one foot across the threshold.

'Here it is.' I waved an envelope in the air and stood, maneuvering by inches until we had more or less switched places, with me at the threshold and her crouched on the porch. 'Your hands are full. I'll just slip this in Emma's box.'

'Number eight,' she said, straightening her bent back with some difficulty. 'Thank you.'

My eyes panned the labels on each pigeonhole until I had examined every name. No one living at DeWitt's boarding house had the initials AL or ET. Thanking the landlady, I gathered up the remaining envelopes and took my leave. Heaven knows what Emma Lansing would think when she opened her empty envelope that night.

But I left DeWitt's uneasy. Where was it written that the person who killed Lila was also on the blackmail list? It was logical, yes, but so was the idea that someone at the boarding house had killed Lila and scuttled back to her room. I couldn't eliminate the residents just because their initials didn't match. There could have been other quarrels or jealousies in play. It occurred to me that the best way to investigate the boarding house was to move in for a few weeks.

After returning the wig and body padding to Mildred Young, I creamed off the extra ten years of make-up and headed to the main office to borrow a telephone directory. An hour later, I was sitting in the antechamber of Mary Pickford's office beside her secretary, poring through the Ls and Ts. Remembering the mind-reading act on the vaudeville program, I looked for Landrieu too, in case there was an A. Landrieu in Los Angeles who tied in with the program. Even if there was

– and there wasn't a Landrieu of any sort – performing in a vaudeville act was hardly a secret to be protected with money. Half of Hollywood had vaudeville connections.

I was feeling pretty glum when Miss Pickford walked in, dressed in rags and looking every inch the feisty twelve-year-old of *Little Annie Rooney*. Nodding to me, she picked up a stack of papers from the secretary's desk and headed into her office, only to pause just inside the door. Turning, she asked, 'Still working on the investigation, Jessie?'

'Without results, I'm afraid. The LA directory has dozens of possible matches for ET and AL. And those are just the men – wives aren't listed, of course. But now what? Do I give them all a telephone call asking if they knew Lila Walker? Anyone who did is sure to say no.'

Mary Pickford leaned against the doorjamb, her face an expression of thoughtful concern. 'You sound like you're at the end of the road.'

'I could say I was doing a survey and ask if they worked in pictures. That would narrow the field.'

She sighed. 'You know, Jessie, I was all for this investigation in the beginning.'

'It was your idea,' I reminded her.

'I was so worried about Rob, I had to try something, even if it was a shot in the dark. I truly appreciate your efforts. But now, well, there's no shame in failure when you've given your all. As you have done.' Sincerity radiated from her huge, round eyes, but I still couldn't believe she wanted me to quit.

'But if Ruby Glynn didn't do it, we have to keep trying.'

'I'm afraid the truth of the matter is that Ruby did do it, no matter how much we wish otherwise. And kind-hearted Rob feels the way he does because he can't face sending a young woman to the gallows.'

I nodded unhappily. 'You're right. I'll get back to work. My real work.'

Thoroughly discouraged, I returned the telephone book to its shelf and walked around the corner to Douglas Fairbanks' office.

THIRTEEN

'**M**r Fairbanks is not to be disturbed,' said his secretary. 'He's working on the pirate script.'

Some people think there isn't anything to writing a movie scenario because there is no dialogue. They think directors just roll the cameras and shout directions like, 'Walk into the room and kiss the girl.' Before I came to Hollywood, I was one of those people. But there wouldn't be any pictures without writers. The big boys like MGM and Universal maintain a stable of writers, men who spend months working on a single script or editing scripts submitted by others. Pickford–Fairbanks, being a smaller studio, had only a few writers and occasionally bought from freelancers. Mary Pickford had written a number of her own scripts in her career. So had Douglas and so had their partner, Charlie Chaplin.

A successful scenario starts out as a storyline with a plot outline and some character descriptions, then a full treatment with scenes, then the actual script, or continuity, where the treatment gets broken down into camera shots – long shots, medium shots, close-ups. Short titles are inserted to convey some dialogue or thought that can't be acted out and the whole thing gets typed up so carbons can be sent to the producer, assistant producer, director, assistant director, the casting director, the various cameramen and the script girl. That last one was me.

'I was just checking to see if he needed me for anything. If not, I'll go back to my desk.' There was always work at my desk.

'Wanda is drowning in fan mail. You might look in on her and see if she'd like some help.'

Boy, did she ever! 'You're a life saver, Jessie,' said Wanda, pushing a pencil behind her ear and tipping her chair back on its hind legs. 'Our bosses get fan mail from four continents, and the letters multiply like rabbits whenever my back is turned. You could sign a couple hundred photos while I open mail.'

I picked up a fountain pen and filled it with blue ink before making myself comfortable at the spare desk. I'd have made a first-class forger – my Douglas Fairbanks forgery was the best in the studio, and I was occasionally called upon to put my skill to use. For the next hour, I scrawled the boss's name across his publicity photos as Wanda and I gossiped.

'Wanda,' I began. 'Tell me about fan mail.'

'What's to tell? Fans write the actors and actresses at the studio. We answer them.'

'You open the mail?'

'Me or someone else.'

'You read the letters?'

'Yep.'

'What if it's personal?'

'I put those aside. But that's rare. People who write personal mail know Mr Fairbanks or Miss Pickford or Mr Chaplin's address and send letters to their homes.'

'Have you ever seen anything really private, or embarrassing?'

She gave me an odd look. 'Why are you asking?'

'Sorry, that sounded wrong. I'm just wondering out loud. I'm investigating the Lila Walker murder. She used to work for Warner Brothers as a secretary, so she probably helped with fan mail.'

'Definitely.'

'Would she have come across information about Warner's actors that might let her blackmail them?'

'I see what you're thinking. But no, not likely. Fans don't know secrets. They're mostly like this one: 'Dear Mr Fairbanks, I just loved you to pieces in *Thief of Bagdad* and think you're the handsomest man in the world!! I would do anything in the world for you. I'm going to be coming to Hollywood in July and wonder if I could stop by your house and say hello in person . . .' and so forth and so forth. She might have seen something private in letters or memoranda that shouldn't be known. Like, say, someone had to go to Mexico to marry his pregnant girl.' Wanda wiggled her eyebrows up and down in an exaggerated manner.

She was referring to Charlie Chaplin, Douglas's best friend and neighbor, who'd recently gotten a fifteen-year-old actress pregnant. We swapped scandals until her telephone bell rang. Oddly enough, the call was for me. The switchboard gals knew where I was.

'Miss Beckett? This is Benjamin Kaminsky. Do you know who I am?'

'I'm afraid not, Mr Kaminsky.'

'I'm Ruby Glynn's lawyer. We need to talk. How about meeting me for lunch?'

His request surprised me. 'Today?'

'Sooner the better. You're on Santa Monica, I'm on Sunset. We can split the difference and meet at the Green Door.'

'I don't know that restaurant. Where is it?'

'On Highland. And it's not a restaurant, it's a gin joint. There's no sign. Keep walking until you see a green door on your left. Just go on in. I'll be there in half an hour.'

I had passed the nondescript green door any number of times without realizing what lay behind it, but then, that was the whole idea of a speakeasy, wasn't it? Someone once said you didn't need anything more than a bottle and two chairs to make a speakeasy, and that was surely my experience. Outside the city limits in West Hollywood, where the LA cops had no jurisdiction, things could be more brazen, but here in town, discretion prevailed.

I knocked on the green door and when no one answered, helped myself to the doorknob. Once inside, I followed the noise and the smell of cigarette smoke down a dank staircase and through two more doors until I reached the bar. Even in this thick haze, it would not be difficult for Mr Kaminsky to find me. I was the only female in the joint. I sat at one of the tables to wait.

The waiter approached my table just as Mr Kaminsky walked into the room. The lawyer was a round little man with a bulbous middle, an egg-shaped, bald head, and circle spectacles on his nose. His ruddy complexion suggested he drank his lunch here often. I liked him on sight. He sized me up just as fast.

'Christ, you're a baby. How old are you?'

'Twenty-six.'

'You look twelve.' Sliding into the chair beside me, he tossed out his order, 'The usual, Mac. And what'll you have, Babyface?'

'A beer.'

'So, you and Mary Pickford are interested in my case. What I wanna know is why.' He lit a cigarette and added to the haze.

I fed it to him straight. Don't ask why, but I knew I could trust him. While I was talking, the waiter returned with my beer and two glasses of a golden beverage on ice. Kaminsky polished one of them off in three gulps and picked up the second before I had finished my tale about Rob Handler's jury ordeal.

'But you've probably heard all this from Handler,' I concluded.

'I like to hear it from you. You learn anything yet?'

'Well, as you know, there was no real investigation, so I started where the cops should have started, at Lila's boarding house. It's unlikely anyone could have sneaked in there with both front and back doors locked and monitored by the cook, the landlady, and an energetic dog, not to mention the residents who were home that day. There were no vines or trees to get up to her window, and the fire escape was too high off the ground to reach without a ladder. So next I went to Lila's sister's house, where I looked through a couple boxes of her stuff. That's where I found the address book and the vaudeville program.'

'Hey, Mac!' he beckoned the waiter. 'Another round and some sausages! Go on, now, tell me about those.'

As I talked, he drew a pencil and a scrap of paper from his inside pocket and jotted down the initials and numbers from the address book. I told him how I'd approached three people on the list, and I mentioned their alibis without revealing their secrets. We all had secrets we didn't want broadcast to the world – I myself was a swindler and a bastard and had spent some time in jail for theft – so I appreciated the virtues of a closed mouth.

'None of the girls at the boarding house had names to match these initials, and searching the telephone book turned up so many possible matches that I got discouraged. Mary Pickford suggested I quit.'

'She your boss?'

'Technically, Douglas Fairbanks is my boss, but . . .'

'Yeah, yeah, I get it. So you gonna quit?'

For an answer, I took a sip of beer and shrugged.

'Don't quit. Look, hon, I know you think you're getting nowhere, and that's probably true, but you're helping me and Ruby even if you don't turn up a thing. I'm writing up an appeal, and the more I can show there was no investigation, how there's evidence that Lila was blackmailing people and lots of them had a grudge against her, the more I can imply there's a whole story out there waiting to be told and others who might have killed her, the better her odds for a new trial.'

'Even when those people have alibis?'

'I don't have to mention the alibis. And some other people might not have 'em. Maybe you're on to something with that vaudeville program. Just keep stirring the pot, that's all I ask.'

'So you're convinced she's innocent?'

'Innocent? Well, innocence is a relative term, isn't it? Let's just say I don't think she deserves to die. Oh sure, rip out my fingernails and I'll say Ruby Glynn killed Lila Walker, clear as moonshine. But with your help, I can muddy the waters enough in the appeal to get her a new trial. If the appeal fails, I'll go higher. Failing that, a pardon from Governor Friend Richardson, or at least the commutation of her sentence. This opens up lots of possibilities, and anything's an improvement over hanging.'

'Ruby seemed so depressed when I visited her in jail. I'm surprised she wants you to pursue this any further.'

'My client wants me to pursue it.'

'Ruby isn't—?' Before the question left my lips, I knew the answer.

'Nope. Her Latin Lover, Ricardo Delacruz, is my client, and the guy's desperate to save her. He's the one who told me about you. If you need money, by the way, he's a gusher.'

'That much I know already. He came by my house and gave me a hundred bucks to help my investigation.'

Mr Kaminsky nodded.

Considering what I'd just learned, I'd be a fool to quit. My investigation was helping Ruby, not in the way I had antici- pated perhaps, but it was helping. And Mary Pickford hadn't actually forbidden it.

I lost count of the number of drinks Mr Kaminsky guzzled that day, but he never slurred a syllable, and when we left the Green Door, he walked away from me in a straight line like a Baptist on Sunday.

FOURTEEN

L ater that same day, Miss Dolly Baker moved into Lila Walker's old rooms on the third floor. I paid Mrs DeWitt fifty Delacruz dollars in advance for the first and last week's room and board, hoping my first and last week would be one and the same, and hauled my suitcase up two flights of stairs. As boarding houses went – and I was an expert on this subject – DeWitt's was the Ritz. My rooms were twice the size of the single I rented in our humble farmhouse on Fernwood. But I'd grown quite fond of my modest lodgings, the first place I'd ever really called my own. It was home and this was not. I'd be glad when the charade was over, and I could move back.

I wasted no time in getting acquainted at the dinner table as the eight lodgers passed around platters of pork chops, boiled potatoes, corn pudding, and tomato pie.

'Where are you from, Dolly?' asked the plain, middle-aged woman sitting across from me. I made a mental note: Clara, a teacher at the Misses Janes School on Hollywood Boulevard.

'Portland, Oregon,' I replied, choosing a far away place that I was familiar with from last year, just in case someone knew it. As bad luck would have it, someone did.

'Oh, Portland!' said the girl on the end with the wild, curly dark hair. Juanita, occupation as yet unknown. She could never aspire to a bob. 'My grandparents live there and we go to visit now and then. Do you know the Russells on Oak Street?'

'I'm afraid not. Actually, I'm from a small town outside Portland, but we often went into the city to shop.' I rattled off enough stores and street names to convince her I knew the place well.

'And what is it you do, Dolly?' asked Rose, a stunning actress about my own age.

'Nothing yet,' I replied, 'but I'm looking for an office job. I can type and file and work an adding machine. I've got good experience. I'm sure I'll find something soon.'

In no time, I had matched names with faces and a few facts. Next, I would pick them off, one by one. No time like the present.

Under the guise of getting to know my fellow boarders, I planned to encourage them to talk about Lila and whatever they had observed on that fateful day. Some of the women had not been present when the murder took place, and I would need to learn which ones so I could eliminate them from my list of suspects. And I hoped to figure out who among the remainder might have nursed a grudge against Lila, or better yet, who harbored some secret that she was using for blackmail.

'Oh, Dolly,' called Emma Lansing as I passed her open door on my way to the water closet. 'Do come in and join Clara and me for tea.'

'I'd love some. I'll be right there,' I said.

When I entered Emma's sitting room, she was pouring tea and chattering away to Clara about how she and I had met a few days earlier. 'I told Dolly all about what happened the day Lila was murdered,' she said to Clara. 'I didn't want her moving in unaware.'

Clara nodded. 'That was good of you, dear. Mrs DeWitt would never have mentioned it.'

'I was much obliged to you for that, Emma,' I said. 'I think your kindness that day was what convinced me to take the rooms.' Emma blushed. She was young and lively, perhaps twenty-two, where Clara was a good twenty years older and prim. I soon learned the two women worked together at the Janes School.

'I came in the middle of the year,' Emma said, 'to take over from a teacher whose health had failed. Clara told me about her own nice boarding house and, well, here I am! Would you like sugar with that, Dolly?'

'Please. I remember you told me then that you didn't know Lila well.' Turning to Clara I said, 'You must have known her better. You've been living here for how long?'

'Almost four years. And yes, I knew her well. I liked her. She came from New Orleans, and I've got family in Baton Rouge, so we had that in common. She was a good friend, sober and determined to succeed. Not scatterbrained and morally bankrupt like so many young girls today.'

'She wanted to be a screen star?' I prompted.

'And she was making progress. She had some credible parts, not just extras.'

'Were you here the day she was killed?'

'I was downstairs in my own room, so I heard nothing until someone screamed. I rushed upstairs.' She set her teacup on the table and gazed toward the window as if looking into the past. 'It was monstrous seeing her on the floor like that, and then carried out on a stretcher. The amount of blood she lost convinced me that we wouldn't meet again in this lifetime, and I was right. I was shaking so badly I could hardly make it back to my room and once there, well, I couldn't sit. I just paced until one of the policemen stopped by to ask me what I knew. He looked around my rooms while I answered his questions. I wish I could have been more helpful. I knew of no one who would want to harm Lila. She was always so pleasant and generous. Later that night, I remembered I still had her caracul coat that she'd lent me the previous week. The pretty gray one, remember it, Emma? Well, the last thing I wanted was for someone to think I'd stolen it, so I crept upstairs to her room and returned it to her closet. And you know what? Someone had been there before me.'

She came to an abrupt stop, like a stage actress who has lost her place in the middle of the play. I waited, but when she showed no sign of continuing, I pressed, 'What do you mean?'

'Only that there were a few items of clothing on the closet floor. Lila had beautiful clothes and she took good care of them. She didn't toss them on her closet floor harum-scarum like an ill-bred schoolgirl. No, someone had been in her room after her death and helped themselves.'

'You really think so, Clara?' squeaked Emma.

The older woman nodded. 'And I've been watching to see if anything familiar shows up on that person.'

'You think it was Rose, don't you?' Rose – she was the pretty actress with the rosy cheeks that matched her name.

'I'm not accusing anyone, Emma, so don't you go repeating that. And I have no proof.'

'But you probably won't see anything. She wouldn't be so foolish as to wear Lila's clothes here where we would recognize them.'

'That's not necessarily true, dear. I've seen Suzie wearing some of Lila's jewelry, which I suspect she stole in the confusion after Lila's death. Of course, she claims Lila gave her those things.'

Emma giggled. 'All I can say is, no one can suspect me of taking her clothes. I'm too short to fit into any of her things. And Juanita's too heavy.'

'It couldn't have been Juanita. She was gone that weekend, remember? She was in San Diego visiting her parents.'

'Oh, that's right. The police searched her rooms and asked me about her.'

I mentally crossed Juanita off my list of suspects while resolving to speak next to Rose. Thanking Emma for the tea, I crossed the hall to my rooms to prepare for bed. Lila's bed.

Twice in my career I worked for off-stage acts, mediums who communicated with the spirit world. These weren't terrible people – well, one of them was – they brought comfort and hope to grieving relatives and a thrill to those who wanted their fortunes told, making pots of money in the process. The basic swindle is the same for all these charlatans: darkened rooms, lots of moaning and a clever patter to cover up any noises, dark threads, luminous paint, and black-clad confederates who sneak into the room under cover of darkness to float objects and ring bells. Sometimes I worked as a shill, pretending to be a skeptic at the table who is convinced by the apparitions and who contributed to the knocks and movements. Other times, my size and agility made me an invisible assistant, entering through a window or secret door. Before these séances, we always collected information about the marks from newspaper obituaries, gravestones and women's pocketbooks.

So I know that contacting the spirit world is hokum. Even the great Houdini says so. Still . . . there have been times that I have sensed things about the dead. I hoped that being alone in Lila's dark bedroom would be one of those times.

Open windows admitted the cool night air but little night noise. The neighborhood was still save for the random dog barking or occasional motorcar. I lay motionless in Lila's bed concentrating on Lila, trying to put myself in her place . . . in her thoughts . . . until the morning sun woke me, and I admitted failure.

That next day was Saturday and Rose was working, so I knocked instead on Nancy's door and invited her to join me for some breakfast cake and orange juice.

Nancy was quick to express her admiration for my modern sensibility in having taken the rooms of the dead woman. 'So many ninnies are afraid of ghosts, when every educated person knows there is no such thing.'

Nancy was a nurse at Community Hospital, which explained her scientific approach to the afterlife – a view I could have changed after a single session with the Hindoo séance swindlers I used to work for. I soon learned that she had been on a long shift the day of Lila's death and hadn't arrived home until the excitement had passed.

'Naturally, I was sorry to learn of Lila's murder,' Nancy said, 'but between you and me, I didn't cry over her casket. My brother Frank took her to dinner once, and when he telephoned again, she told him a girl like her could look higher than a simple hotel clerk. I coulda strangled her myself when Frank told me that. She never met anyone without thinking how she could use them to her advantage. Her all high-and-mighty and what did she do, I ask you? Nothing that I could tell.'

'What *did* she do? For a living, I mean.'

'I never figured that out. Last year she worked for Warner Brothers but she quit, or more likely was fired. Told everyone she was an actress and gonna be a star. Rose says that too, but she, at least, wrangled a contract outta one of the studios. Oh! I just remembered. Ask Rose some time to tell you what happened between her and Lila.'

'What?'

'I never knew the particulars. I just remember one heck of a cat fight when Rose found out Lila had ruined her chances to get some part she wanted.'

'Didn't you ever talk with the police about Lila's death?'

'No, why would I? Mrs DeWitt said they looked through my rooms, I guess to make sure no one was hiding there, but I had nothing to say.'

We chatted a while about my fictional background until Nancy glanced at her wristwatch. 'Mercy, I need to go. I got errands to run today – my one day off after ten on. I'm glad to know you, Dolly. Welcome to DeWitt's. Thank you for the nice breakfast. And if you're looking for an A-1 fella, I'd be happy to introduce you to my brother Frank. Just say the word.'

On Sunday I ran into Suzie, who lived next door to me, as she was coming home from church. I said I'd like to get to know her a little, since we were going to be living so close, and invited her to brunch at a hotel a few blocks away.

'What's a brunch?'

'It's sort of a new thing. A mix of breakfast and lunch foods. I'd love to treat you.'

She said she'd love to be treated, so off we went. I had heard about Suzie's role in the drama from Emma Lansing, and it was easy to persuade her to talk about that day.

'Emma told me what a heroine you were,' I began, 'coming into Lila's room and trying to staunch the blood.'

'I guess it came natural like, since I've got three younger brothers who are always getting cut up and broken arms. I don't flinch at blood.'

'You ought to be a nurse!' I said admiringly.

'What, like Nancy, you mean?' she scoffed. 'Not on your life, sister. All that one does is empty bedpans and give sponge baths.'

'Still, you kept a cool head, and I admire that. I'm sure the police appreciated your testimony.'

Suzie shrugged. 'I suppose. I don't believe I had anything to add to what the others said.'

'I gather you knew Lila pretty well. What sort of person was she?'

'Hard to say. Sometimes I liked her fine. Other times I thought she was a prig. Oh, I know, I shouldn't speak ill of the dead.'

'You won't offend me. I never knew her.'

'Well, she could be lots of fun. Liked to kick up her heels, she did, especially when men were around. She was really clever. She knew how to get what she wanted.' Suddenly, something occurred to her. 'You know how strict Mrs DeWitt is, right?' I nodded. 'Well, a couple times I'm sure I heard a man in her room. Our beds shared a wall, you know what I mean? It was during the day, not at night, and I said something about it once – asked her if she had permission to have a visitor in her room. She just smiled and said she had no idea what I was talking about.'

'How could anyone sneak a man up here?'

'I dunno, unless she was bribing the cleaning girl to look the other way, because I think it was a Friday afternoon, both times. But golly, that was last year.'

And Lila had been killed on a Saturday, which released the cleaning girl from suspicion.

Once warmed up, Suzie was hard to stop. Which was fine; I didn't want to stop her. 'Lila liked me. Most of the time, at least.' She rattled some flashy bracelets on her arm. 'She gave me these. Didn't want them any longer. I think a boyfriend gave them to her and she threw him over so didn't want to see them any more. They're worth something, I can tell you that. She gave me some other jewelry too. Lila was popular with the men; they gave her things. Not just jewelry.'

FIFTEEN

I went to Pickford–Fairbanks studios on Monday morning as usual, pretending to anyone who cared at the DeWitt house that I was going out to look for work all day. That night after dinner, I noticed Dorothy lingering over her coffee, so I hung back with a cup of my own until we were the last two at the table. She was a lanky, outspoken woman with a perpetual squint that made me wonder if her spectacles were strong enough. We chatted for a while about her work at a bank where she was in charge of loans.

'How long have you been there?' I asked.

'Nine years next month. I graduated from high school in Santa Monica and then went to business college for a year.'

'You must like it.'

She shrugged. 'It's a job.'

'But the people who work there must be a nice sort. Sometimes I think I'd like to marry a banker. Someone reliable and smart and stable.'

She snorted. 'Their fancy suits make them look more important than they are, Dolly, believe me. I wouldn't have one of 'em if he came served up on a silver platter with an apple in his mouth. And I know 'em all, believe you me. They give the new men to me to train, then after I've taught 'em everything they need to know they promote 'em over me. And they still come to me when they get in a jam.'

I didn't have to ask why she wasn't promoted. Everyone knows a woman can only go so high, and she'd obviously reached the limit. 'That must be frustrating.'

'Especially when they get paid two or three times what I get. And do less work.'

My recent conversation with Mildred at the studio prompted me to ask, 'Does your bank ever lend money to unmarried women?'

'Why? Do you need a loan?'

'No, not for me. A friend is interested in buying a house.'

'Tell her to get married.'

'Does your bank have any openings for secretaries?' I asked, mindful of my supposed need to find a job.

'Not at present, but I'll keep my ears tuned.' And while I racked my brain for a way to turn the conversation to Lila's death, she squinted at me and said, 'You're one tough nut. Aren't you even a little bit jumpy about sleeping in her rooms? I mean, golly, I almost moved out of the building, and I would have too, but I'd have lost a week's rent.'

I shrugged. 'It doesn't bother me much. Were you here when she was attacked?'

'I was. I'd just finished washing out some underclothes – I take my outer garments to the Chinese laundry – and that's when I heard the commotion. I hurried upstairs and saw what had happened. Poor girl.'

'Were you friends?'

'I guess you'd say so. We didn't have much in common, her all gaga over the pictures and me up to my neck in loan documents.'

'Did you talk to the police?'

'We all did. One of them came down to our floor and looked in all our rooms, searching for what, I don't know. Clues, I guess. Though if you ask me, they missed the biggest clue.'

'What was that?'

She lowered her voice and leaned in, as if there were people trying to listen to our conversation. 'After the police had left and Lila was taken away to the hospital, I was finishing up my laundry, hanging my things on the rack to dry, when Rose came in with some clothes to wash. I could tell she didn't want me to see them by the way she held them close to her chest. She ran the sink full of cold water and added some soap flakes, then started washing out one blouse and one skirt. The water turned pink. I was curious – she usually takes her clothes to the Chinese too – and she said she'd spilled red ink on them.'

'And you think—'

'It was blood. Everyone knows hot water sets bloodstains. She was using cold.'

Her melodramatic pronouncement seemed out of character
for a staid bank clerk. 'Did you mention this to the police?'
I asked.

'They'd gone. And maybe it was red ink, after all.'

Or maybe Rose had tried to assist Lila as she lay dying or
had helped mop the floor, but I said nothing to ruin Dorothy's
ghoulish speculation. I needed to talk with the elusive Rose.
She came to dinner, but there was no opportunity to talk there,
and afterwards she would vanish out the front door, slipping
home just minutes before the eleven p.m. curfew. On Thursday,
I lay in wait for her on the stairs, pretending to be coming
home myself.

'Oh, hello, Rose. Did you have a nice evening?'

She paused, her hand groping for the stair rail and her eyes
focusing on me with some difficulty. 'Tolerable.'

I could smell the liquor on her breath. I wouldn't have to
work hard to get this one to talk. Pulling a pint of gin out
of my handbag, I asked, 'How about a nightcap? This is the
real McCoy, by the way. I've got a lime, and I can snitch
some ice and grapefruit juice from the kitchen if you're
game.'

'Snitch away!'

'Here, take this up with you and get a couple of glasses.
I'll be right there.'

By the time I'd mixed the second drink, Rose and I were
bosom friends, and it took only the slightest nudge to get her
talking about Lila.

'She was a bitch.'

'You don't say!'

'You didn't know her, did you?'

'I'm afraid not. What did I miss?'

'A lying, cheating little whore with the morals of an oyster,
that's what.'

'Clara told me she was nice.'

'That two-faced schoolmarm? She stole Lila's clothes right
out of her closet the moment her body was on its way to the
morgue.'

'No!'

Rose gave a sage nod and lit a cigarette. 'Want one?'

'Sure, thanks.' We puffed in silence for a moment before I prodded again. 'You were here when she was killed?'

'Yep.'

'Nancy said you and Lila had a bit of an argument shortly before her death.'

'We had an argument every time we passed in the hall.'

'Nancy said that last one was a doozy.'

I watched in awe as Rose tipped back her head and blew a beautiful series of smoke rings. I could never do that.

'Lila wanted to be a star. So? Who doesn't in this town? But hers was the old-fashioned, casting-couch technique. Or threats. One director I know told me she threatened to cry rape if he didn't give her the part.'

'Did he?'

'Yes, he did! Men are such asses. He stupidly got into a position of her and him in the same room alone and her half undressed, so he deserved all he got, but . . .' She pursed her lips in a reflexive gesture. 'You know what? She was prettier than I am, but I have talent. She didn't. She had to – you know what she did one time? This really made me see red. Wait 'til you hear this. We were both up for a part – a featured part – at Universal, for a picture about an art robbery. I forget the title. We weren't the only ones, but it was down to three or four. And I was thinking I had a damn good shot at it. Well, the studio said they'd be in touch by Friday, and Friday came and nothing. So on Saturday I called and the studio said the part had gone to Josephine Sharp. Win some lose some, right? I said something like, "Darn it, I thought I'd've been good in the role." And then this person on the telephone says to me, "I thought you withdrew?" and I says, "Huh?" and it turns out that bitch Lila had called the studio pretending to be me and told them I was withdrawing my name from consideration because I had another part that would conflict. Get it?'

I got it. Lila bettered her own odds by whittling down the field. She really was a bitch.

'I went straight to her room, walked in, and slapped her. Didn't say a word, just slapped her hard as I could. You shoulda seen the expression on her face! Ha! I'd of put a lily in her hand right then if I'd had a knife.' Rose crushed her cigarette and lit another. 'It didn't do her any good. She didn't get the part either. But I might have got it.'

'When was this?'

Rose scrunched up her face in thought. 'January. Why?' The month before Lila had been murdered. Had Rose been angry enough to do more than slap her? Was it ink on her clothes or blood from when she'd returned to Lila's room and stabbed her?

'Just curious. So, er, you lost the Universal part but got a contract soon after?'

'Yep.' She blew smoke. 'But not at Universal. I got a contract at Warner Brothers. Ninety bucks a week.'

Warner Brothers again. It was a huge studio, one of the largest in the world, with hundreds of employees, but still . . . Everything seemed to connect back to Warner Brothers.

I had gotten all I was going to get out of my stay. Any dark secrets lurking within the walls of DeWitt's boarding house would have been exposed by the prying eyes of the boarders and spread by their gossipy tongues, making such information ill-suited for blackmail. The only person who'd harbored genuine secrets was Lila Walker. Although I had an earful about how her promiscuous ways paid her bills, not a single boarder suspected she'd been in the blackmail business.

On Friday morning, Dolly Baker packed her suitcase and gave a tearful farewell performance to an astonished audience of Mrs DeWitt, Darla the cook, and Nancy, who happened along as I was saying goodbye. I had had no luck finding a job, I told them. No one had shown any interest in my meager skills except for two men who had made lewd advances. A small-town girl from Oregon didn't belong in a fast city like Hollywood – and yes, I understood she would not be refunding the second week's rent.

I left DeWitt's and caught the next Red Car to Pickford–Fairbanks studios.

SIXTEEN

By the time I'd reached the studio, I'd worked out a new plan. With the old vaudeville program in hand, I went straight to the switchboard girls and asked them to put through a long distance call to Gus Sun, the fearsome impresario of the Small Time vaudeville circuit based in Springfield, Ohio. I brought a stack of Fairbanks photos with me and sat down to autograph until the call went through. I wanted to ask Gus Sun whether he remembered any of the acts listed in the program.

Even those of us who had never worked his circuit knew Gus Sun's reputation as a bully. He had a couple hundred theaters in his circuit, most of them a notch above Small Time but none that could be considered Big Time. Some called it Medium Time or Sun Time, but at any time, Gus was not a low man on the vaude totem pole. My friend Zeppo Marx and his crazy brothers got their start in Sun Time, and Zeppo once told me Gus was so cheap he sent all his telegrams collect, making his clients pay to hear from him when there were bookings or schedule changes. It got so that performers called the Western Union boy on the bicycle 'Gus Sun's Bicycle Act'. But no one dared complain.

After thirty minutes, the switchboard gal came out to tell me the call had gone through. Gus Sun's secretary would give him my message. I went back to my desk to wait for his return call.

And waited. And waited. When nothing had come by the next morning, I pressed the switchboard to try again. Mindful of the time difference, I left another message with the secretary, this time mentioning its importance to a murder trial. When I hadn't heard anything by noon, I tried again, dropping Mary Pickford's name. Still no response. Next, I spoke to the secretary myself, stressing the importance of my questions and offering to reimburse Mr Sun for the return call, but all she would say was that Mr Sun was a busy man. Busy? Face it. There was nothing in it for him. My subsequent calls didn't make it past his switchboard.

I must have looked as defeated as I felt – head down, lost in my problem, trudging across the open lot to the bungalow where my desk lived. The lot bustled with grips hauling equipment, seamstresses lugging costumes, and actors hurrying to the commissary for a quick sandwich. I didn't notice David Carr coming up behind me until his late afternoon shadow fell across mine.

'Everything OK, kid? You look like your dog died.'

My head snapped up. David, looking more like a screen star than any man in Hollywood, melted me with his little boy grin. 'What brings you to the studio today?' I asked.

'Nothing much – a short meeting with the money men about *Little Annie Rooney*.'

'Then I should be asking you – is everything OK?' David had invested a huge sum in that picture.

'Right on target. Mary's pictures always are. When it comes to money, that little lady's got a man's brain in her head.' He caught sight of Douglas Fairbanks coming out of the office building and acknowledged him with a short wave that brought him our way. The two men exchanged firm handshakes.

'You joining us for poker this Wednesday?' Douglas asked and then, before David could respond, he snapped his fingers like he just remembered something. 'Hey, how's that drug store of yours coming?'

David sent him his usual confident smile. 'Everything's great. I'm leading such a charmed life, the cards are sure to run my way Wednesday, so hold on to your wallet.'

'Drug store?' I asked.

David waved the question away as if trivial. 'A pharmacist friend. He was tired of working for others but didn't have enough to buy his own store. I put in a little cash to get him started. A sound investment, I hope.'

'Where is it?' I asked my question at the same moment as Douglas asked, teasingly, 'What do you know about drug stores?'

'As much as I know about the pictures,' he replied to

Douglas. 'But I know enough to know to invest with people who know what they're doing.' He looked at his wristwatch. 'Golly, I'm sorry, you two have to excuse me. Mary's meeting went longer than expected, and I'm late to another appointment. Jessie, I hope to see you soon.' The men shook hands again and David hurried toward the parking lot.

Douglas turned his warm spotlight on me. 'I don't think he heard you, Jessie – it's Hess's Drugs at the corner of Hollywood Boulevard and Wilcox. Small, but a good location. Now, tell me, how's the sleuthing going? You're turning into a real Sherlock Holmes, aren't you? Hey, there's an idea for a picture!'

I couldn't help but smile. Douglas Fairbanks was one of the handsomest men in Hollywood, which was to say in the world, and when he joked, the sparkle in his eye was irresistible. He had just passed his forty-second birthday (although no one dared take notice of it – film stars did not admit to getting older), and while the wrinkles that fanned out from his eyes and furrowed his brow were becoming harder to disguise with make-up, his boyish grin would keep him looking young 'til the day he died.

'I wish I had better news to report, sir. I'm afraid I've hit a wall.'

'Come on, walk over to the gym with me. I've got sword practice with Uyttenhove at four. Tell me what's happening, and none of that "sir" business.'

With some effort, I matched my steps to his. 'The only leads I've got have played out. The unidentified initials, ET and AL, have so many matches in the telephone book – not even counting wives' names, which we can never know – that following up on them is hopeless. I'm thinking that the vaudeville program may have some connection to the people Lila was blackmailing, but it's so old that none of the acts are still in business. I checked in *Variety* and didn't find one. If I could track down one or two of those people, I might learn the names of the ones in the other acts and maybe one of them is ET or AL. The name of one act began with L. Maybe a first name was Alice or Adam.'

'And if it was, what would that tell you?'

'Nothing unless I could track them down. My best chance is Gus Sun, but he won't accept my telephone calls.'

'Who's Gus Sun?'

'Oh, that's right – you wouldn't know Gus Sun. You came up through theater, not vaudeville. He runs the biggest Small Time circuit, a few hundred theaters in the Midwest, based in Ohio. He's really the best of Small Time. He would probably remember some of the acts on that program, and maybe I could find out how they were connected to Lila Walker. But I can't reach him. I tried dropping names but he wouldn't answer even for Mary Pickford.'

Douglas bristled at the insult to his beloved Mary. 'He wouldn't, would he? Why, that miserable son of a gun – if I weren't so busy here, I'd go to Ohio myself and see if he could ignore a punch in the nose. Hey, why don't you do that?'

'Punch him in the nose?'

'Go to Ohio. Make him see you.'

'Well, I—'

He'd stopped abruptly, delighted with his idea. 'Why not? It's only three days to Ohio. You could be there and back in a week.'

'Are you sure?' It was an impossible idea, one I'd never have considered, but I snatched at it happily. Signing autographs and answering fan mail was a dull way to spend the day.

'Sure I'm sure. There won't be any script girl work until I get the blasted script finished.'

'How's it going?'

'Slow. But it's going to be great. It's got at least two big sword fight scenes that I'm working on now with Uyttenhove and an incredible stunt in the ship's rigging that no one has ever thought of.'

'It sounds magnificent. I can't believe you can write, direct and act in the same picture.'

'Well, I don't think I'm going to direct this one. And no one really knows that I'm writing it. Whenever I write a screenplay – and I've done half a dozen – I use my alter ego, my two middle names, Elton and Thomas, in the credits. But I've still got a couple weeks of writing ahead.' We had reached the gym door. Douglas stopped and looked down at me, his arms folded across his chest. 'So, what I'm saying is, there's always plenty of work to be done around here, but for the time being, we can spare you. For a life and death issue, it's only right. Go to Ohio.'

SEVENTEEN

'I'll help you pack,' said Myrna Loy as she traipsed up the stairs behind me. Although still in her teens, Myrna aspired to stardom and had the looks and the talent to get there. Of course, so did hundreds of other girls in Hollywood, so these assets didn't guarantee success any more than a fast horse is guaranteed to win a race. She was my best friend in Hollywood and the most fun of the four gals who shared the old house on Fernwood with me. 'How long are you going to be gone?'

'Just a week if I'm lucky. How did your audition go?' I pulled my valise out from under the bed and opened my undergarments drawer.

'I thought I did well, but you never can tell in this business. I'm hoping Valentino will remember me from that part I didn't get – when he said I was too young for the part, remember? – and maybe he'll put in a good word for me with his wife. She wrote the screenplay and is one of the stars.' She peered into my valise. 'You aren't bringing *that* to match with that skirt, are you? I like your beige blouse better and it is more versatile.'

Natacha Rambova was a vain, unpredictable and headstrong actress whose main talent, as far as I could tell, had been getting married to an international film sensation. Her latest project, *What Price Beauty?*, was already behind schedule, but no one dared look cross-eyed at Rudolph Valentino's wife.

After Myrna's first bit part a couple months ago as a carouser at a Roman banquet, she had snagged a few more roles. Some, like the showgirl in *Pretty Ladies,* took advantage of her dancing abilities; others, like the Roman senator's wife in *Ben-Hur,* hired her for her magnificently expressive eyes.

'If you get good news before I return, send word to Douglas Fairbanks's secretary at the studio – she'll know where I am. And if the rent comes due before I get back, you know where my money is.' I nodded toward the jewelry box on my dressing table. The first place a thief would look, of course, but I wasn't much worried about thieves. Hollywood glittered with targets far more tempting than a backstreet, ramshackle house with peeling paint, a rotting porch, and five young women earning meager wages. And I knew something about sizing up marks.

'Sure. Hey, are you hungry? How 'bout I rustle us up a couple of cowboy sandwiches before you leave?'

We girls had turned the dining room and parlor into bedrooms so each of us could have her own, which left the spacious kitchen as the only indoor gathering place. As soon as I'd finished packing, I joined Myrna at the table and wolfed down her culinary specialty, a fried egg and bacon on bread.

'Do you have any Veronal?' I asked.

'Lemme check.' She ran back up the stairs only to return seconds later empty-handed.

'Never mind,' I said. 'I'll stop at a drug store on the way. I don't usually need anything to help me sleep on a train, but three nights in a row might prove challenging.'

A horn tooted. I stuffed the last of my cowboy sandwich into my mouth and stood. Myrna ran to the front door and peered out. 'Golly, Jessie, is that a cab?' The ladies of Fernwood seldom indulged in such extravagances.

'Mr Fairbanks is paying for me to go first class. Isn't that swell? Thanks for the supper, hon.' I gave her a quick hug and grabbed my valise. 'See you in a week!'

As Myrna waved from the front porch, I clambered into the cab and told the driver which train station I wanted. 'But I need to stop at a drug store first, if you don't mind. Hess's on Hollywood and Wilcox.'

'I don't mind, lady,' he replied. 'You're paying the freight.'

Yes, it was out of the way, but not dramatically so, and I needed some sleeping powders. I also wanted to see this new investment of David's. A drug store. Who could figure that man out? He had boatloads of money, I knew that – heck, he'd put a hundred thousand dollars into Mary Pickford's current picture, so he owned half of it – and I supposed that people with money needed to invest it somewhere rather than let it sit in the bank. Me, I'd be happy to sit some money in a bank and I would, too, as soon as I had some. Then I'd really feel safe.

The taxi drove to Hollywood Boulevard and turned left. Fashionable shops and expensive restaurants lined both sides of the street, competing for the attention of the film industry's elites. This was where stars shopped for the latest fashions and dined with directors and producers, and where would-be actors strolled, hoping to be noticed as they ambled past endless shoe stores, millinery shops, jewelry emporiums, and lingerie boutiques. The modest corner drug store at Wilcox looked out of place among such finery. The driver pulled against the curb to wait while I dashed inside.

A bell above the door jangled as I entered. I took a few moments to look around the shop so I could make some comment to David when I saw him next. I realized, ruefully, that I hadn't had time to tell him I was leaving town. Well, I'd be back in a week, and he'd understand. David was always disappearing too, and usually without giving me any warning. It was a nice drug store. Not new, but very neat inside. The narrow center aisle was flanked by shelves packed higher than my head with gauze, hot water bottles, witch hazel, thermometers, perfumes, soaps, baking soda and all manner of toiletries. The middle shelves held a variety of ready-made medicines and elixirs like Bayer aspirin, Lydia Pinkham's pills, Mercurochrome, Ayer's Sarsaparilla, Luden's Throat Drops, Dr Morse's Indian Root pills, and Vicks Vaporub. A basket of canes and umbrellas stood at the end of the aisle. I quickly located the Veronal and joined the line at the back of the shop.

The line was long. I counted six men in front of me and before I had moved forward one place, two more had queued up behind me. I fidgeted a bit, but the clock on the wall reassured me that there was plenty of time to catch my train. And the line moved quickly. Oddly enough, it was all men, in front of me and behind. Each gave his name, surrendered a large piece of paper that looked like a stock certificate, and picked up his medicine, already neatly wrapped in brown paper and string. The pharmacist rang up each sale.

Then one of the men, who had completed his purchase and almost reached the door, turned around and returned to the counter. 'Excuse me, folks,' he said to those of us waiting in line, 'but there's been a mistake. If you don't mind . . .?'

We murmured something polite – no need for him to start over at the end of the line again – and he addressed himself to the pharmacist without bothering to lower his voice. 'There's a mistake here. I get whiskey, not gin,' he said, pulling a pint bottle out of the brown paper wrapper and setting it on the counter.

'My apologies, Mr Bowers,' said the pharmacist, who calmly made the switch, then turned his attention to the next man in line.

I let out an involuntary cry of comprehension, which I quickly changed to a cough as several men turned to stare. What an idiot I was! What a trusting fool! David was back in bootlegging. So much for his 'investing with a friend'. The drug store was a front for bootleg hooch. And right in the middle of Hollywood Boulevard! It wasn't his arrest I worried about – there was little chance of that with most cops and judges on the payroll. It was getting himself killed by rival gangsters who already claimed the franchise. And he'd promised me he was going straight, the rat!

Grimacing with clenched teeth, I paid the pharmacist for the sleeping powder and turned to leave. At that moment, an obscured side door swung outward and the rat himself stepped into the shop. I fancied I saw a moment's hesitation as our eyes met. But David was nothing if not smooth. He flashed that boyish grin and greeted me warmly. 'What an unexpected pleasure!'

Sure it was. I didn't smile back. 'I can't believe this!' I hissed, moving closer so our conversation wouldn't be overheard. 'I can't believe what you're up to, after telling me you were out of it!'

His smile grew cold as ice. 'And what, pray tell, am I up to?'

'You know very well what. All these men – they're buying hooch! You're bootlegging again.'

His gaze settled on a faraway point over my head. If I hadn't known him so well, I'd've missed the thinning of his lips and the twitch of that tiny muscle in his jaw that told me just how furious he was. I didn't care. He'd lied to me. My mother's words rang in my head, 'Fool me once, shame on you. Fool me twice, shame on me.' With David, I'd been fooled at least three or four times by now, so what did that make me? A complete simp.

'There's no bootlegging going on here,' he replied calmly. 'Surely a sophisticated woman of the world like you knows about the medicinal exemption for alcohol. As long as a person's got a prescription from a doctor or dentist, he can buy legal alcohol that comes from government-bonded distillery warehouses. These men,' he nodded toward the line, 'have valid prescriptions.'

'Bought and paid for, no doubt.'

'And I suppose you don't indulge in illegal alcohol consumption, Miss High-and-Mighty?'

'Well, I— That isn't the—'

'If prescriptions are being obtained illegally, that is for the federal agents to handle. It has nothing to do with our honest little drug store. Now, if you're finished improving my character, I have work to do. All of it legal and above board.'

I stormed out of the drug store. When the eastbound *Atchinson, Topkea & Santa Fe* left the station that evening, I was on it.

EIGHTEEN

No one is from Hollywood. The endless gusher of hopefuls spewing into town come from big cities like New York and Chicago, small towns like Charlotte, North Carolina, and Tupelo, Mississippi, and the farmlands that stretch across states like Missouri and Wisconsin. A lot don't even come from America, but set out from distant lands, lured by the siren songs of fame and fortune. Few find them. Most, like the sailors in that old Greek myth, meet only ruin or death.

When people ask me where I'm from, I tell them vaudeville. It even sounds like a town. But calling a boarding house home didn't make it so, and moving every week or two meant my mother and I never put down roots. The constant in my life was the train.

Entering Los Angeles La Grande Station felt like returning to the ancestral hearth. My nostrils welcomed the acrid smell of burning coal, my eyes automatically searched for the suspended timetable, my ears strained to hear the echo of announcements about delays and track changes. Humanity pitched and swelled in the cavernous station like a turbulent sea, surging first one way, then another, before breaking into rivulets that flowed toward the various platforms, parting not for rocks or islands but for a family clustered here or a luggage cart there. I had no reason to hurry, but my step quickened and my spirits rose. It was good to be home.

After purchasing a first-class ticket on the eastbound train with Fairbanks cash, I sought out the nearest redcap. I signaled, and he hustled over.

'Where you going to, lady?'

I told him. He wheeled my bag through the arched gangway on to the correct platform and the correct Pullman car where he handed me over to the Negro porter who showed me to the correct seat.

'My name is Willis, miss. I'll be your porter. You just let me know when you want your berth made up. The dining car will be open until ten if you haven't had your supper yet.'

I settled into my seat, prepared to watch the city give way to countryside until darkness obscured the view. Ten minutes later, the train pulled out of La Grande and began its journey across the vast American continent.

I could sleep as well sitting up as I could lying down, thanks to the many nights I had spent in second class. Even as a child, I understood that my mother didn't really think Pullman berths were a frivolous luxury but saying so was her way of putting a good face on financial necessity. Sometimes she would pull my head into her lap so I could stretch across two seats, and I would fall asleep to the sound of her humming and the rhythm of the tracks. Often, as I passed through the cars, I had seen the Negro porters pull beds down from the ceiling for the rich folks and make them up with crisp white sheets and orange blankets, so I knew the system quite well. But this was my first time to actually sleep in one. And because there was no one in the seat opposite mine – for the moment, at least – I felt like a queen with an entire section to myself.

The trip to Chicago took three nights and two days. The Santa Fe route headed east from Los Angeles, and after passing through Albuquerque, split in two, the northern route passing through Dodge City, the southern through Amarillo. Stops were brief, with only a few long enough for passengers to climb down for a short stretch at the station. The tracks joined up again at Newton before continuing through Kansas City to Chicago, where everyone got off at Dearborn Station and scrambled to make connections. In Chicago I would hop on an eastbound train that passed through Indianapolis and Dayton before stopping at Springfield, Ohio, a trip of only a day.

That first night, Porter Willis and I learned we had something in common. His brother was in vaudeville.

'Yes, miss, my brother Samuel sings tenor with the Top Hats. He's been on the circuit for seven years now, almost as long as I've been working Pullmans.'

'I don't recall that act. What circuit did he play? My mother and I played the Western Circuit and Pantages, and later I was in a song-and-dance act that played the Orpheum.'

'Top Hats plays Toby Time, the Negro circuit. They tour mostly in the South, some out West.'

I knew all about Toby Time, of course. The name came from TOBA, which cynics said stood for Tough on Black Asses because of the low pay, but it really stood for Theater Owners Booking Association. TOBA booked Negro acts to tour the Small Time, Negro-only theaters in the South. The best Negro acts, like the late Bert Williams, played white and mixed theaters – more than one on a program was never allowed – and toured with Big Time circuits where they made more money.

As the train thundered east through Arizona and New Mexico the next day, the temperature climbed and dust blew in the windows, covering everyone and everything with a powder so thick you could write your name in it. There was no escaping the heat. The men baked in their suits and ties, mopping their faces with damp handkerchiefs. The women fanned themselves listlessly. Few wasted energy talking. Sundown brought relief as we turned northeast, or maybe it was the higher elevation. That night after I climbed into my lower berth, Willis took a whisk broom to my clothing.

By the third night, I was shooting dice with the porters after the other passengers had retired. Willis and I swapped vaudeville stories and soon he was telling me about the house he'd bought in Chicago for his wife and daughter, and how he was determined that his little girl would be the first in the family to go to high school. 'There was no school back in Alabama, where I'm from. No colored school, that is.'

'I never went to school either. My mother taught me to read.'

'Mine too. She wanted her sons to be somebody. She's real proud of me and Samuel, working good jobs like we do, and not in the fields. I'll bet your mama's real proud of you too, from up in heaven.'

I stayed up late that last night, and when I finally went to bed, thoughts of my mother wouldn't let go. Was she proud of me? Maybe she was, now that I had a steady, respectable job that let me stick to the straight-and-narrow. I wanted her approval as much as always, but I'd never know for sure if I measured up.

I took out a paper of Veronal and dissolved the powder in a glass of water. Even so, I slept fitfully, half dreaming, half awake, thinking about her and my job and the errand I was on, when all at once, my thoughts converged on one name like spotlights focusing on a single actor in the center of the stage. I sat up, my heart pounding.

Elton Thomas. Suddenly Mary Pickford's change of heart took on a more sinister meaning. I had thought her discouraged at my failure. I had thought she had lost interest in Ruby Glynn. I had thought she had concluded that Ruby was guilty after all. But no, she had grasped at once what I was slow to see. Elton Thomas. Douglas Fairbanks' two middle names, the ones he used whenever he wrote his own screenplay. ET.

NINETEEN

'Where's a good hotel?' I asked the redcap when I climbed down from the train at Big Four Station in Springfield, Ohio, late Sunday afternoon. His practiced eye sized me up so he could refer me to an establishment that fit both my social status and my pocketbook. 'The Springfield Hotel. I'll call you a cab.'

After nearly four days of being cooped up in a train, a cab was not what I needed. 'Is it far?'

'Not very.'

'Then I'll hoof it, if you can direct me.'

'Go thataway on Washington and turn on Spring Street,' he said, jerking his thumb toward the exit. 'Three more blocks and you'll find it.' I tipped him a quarter, picked up my suitcase, and headed into the cool Ohio spring.

Gus Sun's offices were attached to the Regent, a new Springfield theater on a street that changed names from Limestone to Spring. Both office and theater were closed on Sunday, of course, but I noted their location. Monday morning, I donned my two-piece, beige linen day frock, belted at the waist (it gave me a mature, businesslike appearance) and climbed the stairs to the second floor reception where a dour secretary guarded the entrance to Mr Sun's lair. Although it was early, a crowd of hopeful vaudeville acts filled the waiting room, some who had never spent a minute on stage – those were the eager-looking faces – and others whose weary demeanors implied hard-won experience. The secretary indicated the multitude with a languid wave of her hand.

'He's very busy, as you can see, and there are many here before you.'

I acknowledged the obvious and added that I had just arrived from Hollywood. Hollywood, California, that is, and had come expressly to see Mr Sun about some of the acts he had booked fifteen years ago. 'Might I make an appointment for later today?'

She pretended to look at an appointment book but made no effort to add my name to it. 'Come back tomorrow,' she said in a dismissive tone. It sounded like the two hundredth time she had said those words today, and the day was young.

'And what time does the office open tomorrow?'

This seemed to require some thought on her part, but finally she replied, 'Nine o'clock.'

I washed out some clothes, took in a Harold Lloyd picture, walked from one end of town to the other, and had a fine dinner at the hotel. At eight o'clock the next morning I presented myself again at Gus Sun's office. The door was open. The cheerless secretary was at her desk, wearing the same rumpled shirtwaist and rust-color skirt, sorting mail. I wondered if she had worked through the night.

'Might I see Mr Sun this morning?' I asked.

'He's busy.' Wielding her silver letter opener like an assassin's dagger, she slit envelope after envelope, glanced at the content, and tossed them into a large tin waste bin at her feet.

'Might I make an appointment?'

'What is this in reference to?'

'Mary Pickford has sent me all the way from Hollywood, California, to speak to him, briefly, about some old acts. It is critical that I see him as soon as possible, as this concerns a murder investigation with life-or-death results.'

She stifled a yawn, and I realized my mistake at once. Of course, she didn't believe a word I said. She had heard far better reasons from people far more desperate than I to see her boss, and my stale life-or-death line must have seemed unimaginative. It was a cruel bit of irony that my lies were usually believed, yet when I told the truth I was dismissed as a liar.

'Mr Sun can't help you,' she said, reaching for another pile of mail. 'He doesn't know anything about old acts.'

'He will know about these,' I said, with more confidence than I felt. 'I've come all the way—'

'I know.' She looked me in the eye for the first time, and I thought I saw a glimmer of pity there. 'Everybody here has come all the way from somewhere, dearie. Have a seat. I'll tell him you're here.'

Resolved to outlast every last supplicant in the waiting room, I settled down to figure out how the system worked so I could find a way around it. Gus Sun's reception was as unpleasant as an office could be – purposely so, no doubt – with backless, wooden benches lining the bare walls and windows too small to air out a large room stuffed with men, women, children, and animals. Except for the occasional squawk from the talking parrots beside me or the whining of the dogs across the room, the place was fairly subdued. Distinguishing the performers from the salesmen was easy: the former wore costumes, the latter carried large, black suitcases full of samples. The population of the room quickly climbed to forty where it remained as people came and went every few minutes. When the benches were full, folks stood outside the door in the dank hallway.

The secretary sorted us all with the same ruthless efficiency that she devoted to the mail. It suggested she was not new at her job. 'I'm sorry, Mr Sun isn't looking for monkey acts,' she would say, or 'Thank you, but we don't need new typewriters.' A fortunate few were allowed to wait as she entered their names on a clipboard that she took with her every hour on the hour when she disappeared into an adjacent room. I hovered by the door and caught a glimpse of more desks and more secretaries in that room. The impresario himself could have been on the floor above or the floor below or in the theater next door; there was no way to tell. I considered waylaying him as he left the building but without knowing where his office was, I could not predict which door he'd use. Not to mention, I didn't know what he looked like. And all the while, the secretary never stopped slitting envelopes and throwing the contents in the trash. I thought of Wanda back at Pickford–Fairbanks where all fan mail, no matter how ludicrous, received a reply. I thought of Lila Walker, whose blackmail career probably started in Warner Brothers as she sorted mail and typed correspondence.

After a while, I gathered there was to be a four o'clock audition in the Regent Theater for certain favored acts. It seemed the perfect opportunity to get in front of Gus Sun. I began to plot how I might take part in the audition.

Four o'clock found me sitting in the front row of the Regent Theater with a dozen other acts when Gus Sun strode in, trailed by two assistants. I picked him out at once by the obsequious men around him. He was a well-built man with dark hair combed back from his forehead and dark eyebrows atop penetrating eyes. They say he'd been a juggler back in the day, and his fluid movements did, indeed, suggest the easy grace of a conjurer. As soon as he sat down in a middle seat, the man on the stage directing the audition rapped his cane on the floor for attention.

'Good afternoon, everyone,' he began, reading from a sheet of paper. 'Mr Sun is here so we'll start now with . . . um . . . Flora and Bill Mancato.' The couple walked out of the wings with a degree of hesitation that I knew would count against them, handed their music to the lone pianist, and cleared their throats nervously. Eight bars into their performance of 'Ain't We Got Fun', danced to a lively foxtrot, Gus signaled to the stage manager who rapped his cane again. The pianist stopped mid-measure. The act was dismissed.

'Next up, Polly's Parrots.' And there was the trainer who had been sitting beside me earlier. I thought the talking parrots did pretty well, and they lasted a full three minutes before the stage manager's cane thumped again. 'See Miss Fleet in the back,' he barked. Gus had approved the act. Polly burst into grateful tears. The parrots were unmoved. The act was headed for Sun Time.

'Next up, Spring Trio: April, May and June Fiorelli.' Two slender, dark-haired girls who looked so much alike that I figured them for real sisters handed the piano player some sheet music and launched into a tap dance routine with song. Before they had completed the first verse, the stage manager pounded a halt. Gus Sun's voice boomed out from his seat in the audience.

'Where's the third girl?' he demanded.

'Our sister May hurt her ankle and can't dance for six weeks. We plan to make the act a duo until she returns.'

'Nope. Two's no good. Come back when you have three.'

'But we've got a good—'

The cane thumped on the floorboards and the sisters trudged off stage, their shoulders drooping like war refugees. I wondered briefly what they were going to do for the next six weeks, whether they had any income to tide them over this rough patch. Then the Eight Allisons bounded on stage with the vitality of seasoned performers, and I forgot about the unfortunate Fiorelli girls.

When the last act was on stage, I made my way over to the stage manager. 'Guess I'm last,' I whispered.

'Who are you?'

'Jessie Beckett, song and dance.'

He looked at his list. 'You're not on here.'

'I must've been left off by mistake. The secretary said I was on the list. She told me to be here for an audition. Listen, I played Big Time for years. Gus'll want to see my act.'

My timing was good, and my self-confidence persuaded him. With nothing to lose, he shrugged and motioned me to the piano. I had no music.

'Can you play "The Ship that Never Returned" in G?' The pianist nodded. 'Chorus after second verse.' I stepped to center stage and began the dance routine I had last done ten years ago.

'Now I'll tell you a story 'bout a gal named Ruby,
On a tragic and fateful day.
She discovered her girlfriend with a knife in her belly,
And she fainted dead away.'

The tune was an old standby for vaudeville singers who often adjusted the lyrics for their own purposes, as I was doing now. It had been the work of fifteen minutes to compose the lyrics. I was no songwriter, but the message came across.

'I work for Mary Pickford and I need to ask you
'Bout some acts of yours of years long past.
One was Jessup and Shadney and another was the Landrieus,
They can help us solve the murder real fast.'

I was banking on Gus Sun to be amused, to laugh, to admire my brass enough to give me a few minutes of his time. I figured he'd have a sense of humor and an appreciation for a performer's chutzpah.

I was wrong.

He bolted out of his seat like it was on fire. Making a chopping motion with his hand, he signaled to the stage manager. The music stopped. I did not. Before he and his assistants could exit the row and reach the side door, I'd jumped off the stage and run after him. 'Mr Sun! Just a moment, please. Mary Pickford sent me to ask you about a couple of old acts . . .'

He spun around. His face was blotched red with anger, his eyes glittered in rage. 'I don't know who you think you are, but you will never work a day in vaudeville—'

'I don't *want* to work in vaudeville! I work for Mary Pickford and—'

The door slammed behind him with a solid thud. One of the assistants stayed behind to block pursuit.

It wasn't the first door I'd had slammed in my face, and it wasn't going to stop me. I retraced my steps out the front of the theater and up the stairs to the receptionist's office, where she was still tossing mail and sorting walk-ins. When the last one had been disposed of, I approached.

'Have you worked here long?' I asked in honeyed tones.

'Thirteen years.' She eyed me suspiciously. She didn't go back as far as the date on my vaudeville program, but those acts might well have lasted beyond 1910 into her tenure.

'I'll bet you have a good memory,' I began, trusting that flattery would take me further than guile. 'Maybe I don't need Gus Sun after all. You probably know more about this sort of thing than he does anyway. I'm trying to track down some of these acts to see if they know anything about the recent murder of a Hollywood actress. We found this program in her desk. None of these acts works Big Time vaude today – I've checked *Billboard* and *Variety* – but I hope to find a current address for at least one or two so I can ask some questions.'

She sniffed, but seemed to loosen up a little. 'Questions won't get you answers. Vaudeville's got tight lips, especially when murder's involved.'

I handed her the 1910 program. 'Would you recognize any

of these acts from your earliest years?' I handed her the program and bit my lower lip.

'Well . . . let's see now . . . the Four Magnanis rings a bell. And yes, now there's one I remember! Grace Hazard – she had talent. Yes, I remember Grace. She went on to Keith's circuit.' A frown darkened her long face, and she looked to one side, as if trying to capture a memory. I wanted to ask, 'What is it?' but didn't dare break her concentration. Finally she trained her puzzled expression on me.

'That's odd,' she said, 'but someone . . . I remember someone asking about these same acts . . .'

Unable to hold back, I blurted, 'Who?'

She pouted her lips to say she didn't know.

'When?'

'Around last Christmas, it was. I remember because Grace Hazard used to do a Christmas act, with songs of the season. Very popular.'

'So someone asked you about Grace?'

'Not me, no. Someone wrote asking Gus about Grace and the Four Magnanis and these others. I only remember it because I was fond of Grace.'

'What did you answer?'

'Answer? I didn't answer. We don't have time here for that.'

As I could attest. She had set aside only half a dozen letters all day. 'Yes, I see how busy you are. And yet, you run such an efficient operation, I'll bet you keep old files, right? I mean, files that would contain home addresses for some of these acts.'

She gave that slow consideration. 'Might have. Let me see.' Standing up, program in hand, she disappeared through the door into the adjacent office. I crossed my fingers.

Christmas. It had to have been Lila Walker who wrote, looking for information on the acts in the program, just as I was doing. Her letter had been ignored as were my telephone calls, but we were two hounds on the same scent. Lila knew as little as I did about the acts on the old program. But she knew why she was looking. I did not. Someone on this program fed into her blackmail scheme. All I had to do was figure out who and why. And then find out if that person had killed her. That's *all* I had to do? I gave a single, bitter laugh.

A few minutes later the woman reappeared. 'Sorry, dearie. Files don't go back that far. We don't keep anything on old acts around for more than a year or two, in case they bounce back, and none of these did.'

I thanked her. I had reached a roadblock I could not skirt. How could I learn anything about these acts if Gus Sun didn't have the information? If only I could reach one of the acts – *just one!* – I could learn something about the rest. Vaudeville performers traveling the same circuit got to know the other players pretty well. They ate together, sat together on the trains between towns, shared dressing rooms and bunked at the same boarding houses. They shot dice and drank between shows, made up their faces side by side, and lent a needle and thread to repair a costume. Any performer on this program would know the others. Finding one would lead me to the rest.

But how? I'd failed to turn up a single name on the Big Time circuits today and none still played Gus Sun. It was time to head home. I didn't want to think about Ruby Glynn. Maybe on the long ride home, I'd come up with some new idea that would help her. But for now, I was fresh out.

The clock on the wall said six. Too late to hop a train to Chicago. I decided to find some dinner, cry in my soup and catch the early bird the next morning. I'd report to Douglas Fairbanks that a valiant effort had come to nothing. Mary Pickford would be sorry we hadn't saved Ruby Glynn from the hangman's noose, but she'd be pleased I'd dropped the investigation, especially since she thought Douglas might be ET.

Once I'd had the chance to think it through, I was sure she was worried for no good reason. Douglas was an overgrown boy prone to pranks and outrageous stunts, but he was no murderer. While I didn't doubt a lucky blackmailer could stumble upon some disagreeable episodes from his past that Douglas would rather keep mum, I was pretty sure he'd punch the lights out of anyone who tried to put the squeeze on him rather than pay out. Mary, now . . . Mary was another matter. His wife was his only serious vulnerability.

I'd only lived in Hollywood a few months, but I'd picked up enough gossip during that time to understand that Douglas and Mary had had a long affair whilst married to others. This was some six or seven years ago, and they'd been terrified back then that their secret would come out. Divorce seemed no solution – divorce was just another flavor of scandal, one that had destroyed many a film actor's career. But they were so much in love that they had to risk it. And when their respective divorces went off without a whimper from the gutter press, they were shocked. Fans loved 'Our Mary' so much that her divorce glided past them virtually unnoticed and entirely excused. Her first husband was history. As far as I could tell, Mary had no secrets that Douglas would be honor-bound to protect.

And Douglas? After due consideration, I was as sure as a person could be that ET was not Elton Thomas. Besides, the other initials that we'd identified had stood for the person's full career name, not middle names or nicknames. And why would Douglas encourage my investigation if he was among Lila's blackmail victims?

So deep in thought was I that I tripped over a curb while crossing the street. When I righted myself, I was facing the front door of a crowded diner. Ohioans dined early, it seemed. Having skipped lunch, I was open to the merits of this regional custom. I went inside.

As a waitress led me toward a table for one, I passed a familiar-looking pair seated in a corner booth. The two Fiorelli sisters, looking glum after their rejection.

'Evening, girls,' I said, stopping by their table. 'I'm Jessie Beckett. I saw you at the audition today. Seems we have something in common – being rejected by Gus Sun.' The oldest girl gave me a wan smile, enough to encourage me to continue. 'I believe I may have a solution to our problems. May I join you?'

TWENTY

B efore we'd finished dinner that night, I had become May Fiorelli, taking the part of the sister with the broken ankle who was in Buffalo recuperating with her maiden aunt. The next morning, April and June taught me enough of their routine to let us sail through Gus Sun's four o'clock audition – and, no, he didn't recognize me. I wore a wig.

I'd like to say I had a strong plan, but in truth, it was as unimpressive as the ninety-seven-pound weakling in those Charles Atlas ads. Still, it had potential and, with effort, could mature into a muscleman. Lila Walker had been trying to turn up something on the acts in the old program, which had to mean she was hot on the trail of a blackmail victim. She'd come across someone in Hollywood who had a shameful secret – someone like Paula Terry and Steve Quinn – and the proof was in the vaudeville program. Someone had a past, and the program was the key. Her attempt to wring information out of Gus Sun had failed, as had mine. But I had a ticket she could never get. I could pursue the search into vaudeville. I was one of them. Properly handled, they would talk to me when they would shut out an outsider.

In the telegram I sent Douglas Fairbanks asking for permission to pursue the search for another week or two, I told him it was the only way I could think of to continue looking for the acts on the old vaudeville program. If I could reach just one person who had been in one of those acts, I could probably get to the rest and learn who had interested Lila Walker so much that she kept that old program with her blackmail list. It might let me identify the initials ET and AL. Or maybe there was another reason she'd saved it. It was slim, yes, but we had nothing better to go on.

Douglas replied promptly. NEVER MIND CALENDAR PROCEED WITH INVESTIGATION RUBY GLYNN COUNTING ON YOU. So I proceeded.

As soon as I had Douglas's permission, I sent a long, expensive telegram to Ricardo Delacruz telling him what had transpired and explaining a little about vaudeville. What the heck, he was paying for it! Delacruz, like Douglas Fairbanks, had not come up through vaudeville and would not readily understand why touring with an act would further our aims. I ended with PLANNING TO WORK SAME CIRCUIT & FIND PERFORMERS WHO REMEMBER ACTS ON LILA'S PLAYBILL STOP WANT TO TRACK DOWN & SEE IF ONE CONNECTS WITH LILA WILL KEEP YOU INFORMED. The following day, he wired me another hundred dollars with a brief note thanking me for my perseverance and begging me to keep him informed of my progress. My heart went out to the man.

Gus Sun bought our act for a decent sixty dollars a week. The Fiorelli sisters and I set out two days later for a six-week, twelve-stop, trial tour that started in Dayton, snaked through Indiana, and ended in Toledo. I had no idea if I would finish it, and I'd warned the girls I would not be able to stay that long, but they were relieved to have work regardless of its duration. If we did well, a longer tour of six months or a year was almost a certainty for them.

The girls had read one of those how-to-break-into-vaudeville books, but book learning proved no substitute for experience. I tried to ease their way without being bossy. As eldest sister, April made the decisions for the act and handled the money. I just nudged her now and then.

When I learned that Fiorelli was Italian for 'little flowers', I persuaded them to change their stage name to 'The Spring Flowers: April, May, and June'. The three of us arrived at a seedy theater in Dayton, ready for our split week – a Sun Time innovation despised by all Small Timers. We started with the usual Monday morning rehearsal. No costumes, no make-up, just a run-through to get the orchestra familiar with the music for each act and let the theater manager determine their order for the program. At this theater, the 'orchestra' consisted of a pianist, a fiddle player and a boy pounding away on the drums.

'You gals working in one?' the manager asked. April looked at me, alarmed.

'No,' I answered. He made a note on his clipboard.

'"In one"' means in front of the curtain,' I whispered to April and June. 'We're working "in two", using the full stage. He needs to alternate the acts so they can set up for a flash act or a tab act – those come with their own scenery and props – while the preceding act is working "in one", in front of the curtain.' They still looked confused but we were up. 'I'll explain later. Now, give it your best,' I hissed. I almost added, 'We don't want to get stuck in the deuce spot,' but I figured that's where we'd land, so I kept my mouth shut.

Two colored men rehearsed after us, their tan skin darkened with cork for the traditional blackface look so popular with white audiences. We stuck around long enough to hear a little of their act – minstrel songs with banjo and fiddle accompaniment. Pretty good.

'You fellas are swell,' I said as they exited into the wings, weaving their way through a pack of trick dogs that were gathering for their act. 'You'll get a good spot for sure.'

'Thank you, Miss,' said the taller one in the gentle accent of the Deep South. 'I hope so. I'm Odie Bender, by the way. This here's my partner, Ed Young. We caught part of your act a bit ago, and you gals got some good moves.' We shook hands all around. They weren't old enough to qualify for my plan, but we'd be seeing a lot of them over the next three days, and it was always my policy to start friendly.

It was close to eleven o'clock and the first show started at one. If we were going to eat, it needed to be now. 'We're going to grab some lunch at the corner diner. Care to come along?'

'No thanks, we brung our own.'

'Won't they let you eat at the diner?' I asked with some surprise. Ohio seemed pretty open-minded when it came to Negroes. Even with my short time in the state, I'd noticed that they went to the same schools as white children and at this theater, at least, there were no signs restricting them to the balcony.

Odie grinned. 'Naw, it's not that. We just saving money. Maybe another time.'

April, June and I finished our sandwiches and milk, and

returned to the theater to dress for the first show. I made straight for the list nailed to the wall at the stage door entrance.

'Where are we?' asked June nervously.

'Three!' I was jubilant. 'We follow the Thorvald Trio and come before some act called Hope & Byrne.'

A stagehand pointed us to the basement where two mildewed curtains hung from the rafters, dividing the room for privacy. On the men's side I could hear several acts getting ready. I recognized the voices from the minstrel act and had seen a midget on his way downstairs, but there were others, including a dog act and a juggler. On our side, a mother fussed over the costumes of three children and an older woman in a burgundy gown trilled scales in the corner. Someone had left a bucket of water and some rags on a table and hung an old mirror on one wall, but the dim light made it useless. The vocalist squinted at her music. She looked to be about forty. Just the right age.

'You must be Tatiana Cherkova, first up after Intermission, right?' I asked. 'I'm May Fiorelli. We're number three.'

'Pleased to meet you.'

'We're new with Sun Time. Have you played this circuit for long?'

'About two years.'

No score. She couldn't help me. I needed to find performers who had been playing Sun Time fifteen years ago, which by definition meant people in their mid-thirties and up. Such a person would be likely to remember at least one of the acts on Lila Walker's program, and if I could track down just one, that would lead me to the others. Of course, they would clam up if they knew I was really asking about murder suspects, but I had that worked out too.

Tatiana Cherkova was an opera singer who performed selections from Gilbert and Sullivan operettas, thirty-year-old music that was still popular with audiences. I wished her luck and completed my hair and make-up as best I could. Fastening the buttons of my pale green, beaded flapper dress, I turned to April who was flattening her too-ample bosom with a firm brassiere in order to create the boyish figure. 'How do I look, Sis?' I asked.

'Like a million bucks, sweetheart,' came the reply from a man on the other side of the curtain. April giggled. I rolled my eyes.

'Why, thank you, Mr Byrne,' I said in my most sugary voice, taking a stab at the identity of the flatterer. 'You are quite the gentleman.'

A couple of guffaws told me I'd missed my target. 'Hey lady, Byrne's no gentleman. I'm his partner, the better half of the act, the handsome, debonair Mr Hope.'

The music above us began the overture, a lively bit of Offenbach that gave the drummer a chance to crash his cymbals. The mother sat on the floor with the kids and read to them from an old newspaper. The well-behaved dogs waited patiently – they were the dumb act scheduled for last place. We were in no rush to go up and clog the wings. June was fumbling with her silk flower corsage.

'So, debonair Mr Hope,' I called, 'do you know how to pin corsages on to ladies' shoulders?'

'I blush to disclose, I am an expert corsage pinner. Meet me at the foot of the stairs, my pet.'

With a nod, I sent June over to get his help, while April and I pinned for each other. Finally we donned our ropes of matched pearls and our dangling earrings, and slipped a dozen bracelets over our wrists. With ostrich fans in hand, we were ready at last.

I've always enjoyed seeing the line-up for the first time, and if I made myself inconspicuous, I could usually melt into the wings where I could see the stage. After a couple of days, I'd know most parts as well as the players themselves did, but the first time was always full of surprises. I was laughing helplessly at the slapstick antics of the second act, a midget act called the Thorvald Trio, when I sensed someone behind me.

'June is a lovely month, but I believe I prefer May,' said a soft but now familiar voice. 'Allow me to introduce myself properly. Leslie Hope, at your service, Miss May.'

He was a handsome young man of about my own age, thin, with slicked-back hair and a long, turned-up nose. His sharp tuxedo made him look every inch the wealthy man-about-town.

I didn't know if he could dance, but he sure knew how to dress. 'Ah, the debonair Mr Hope,' I whispered so as not to distract the performers.

'Please, call me Les. Les Hope. Hope-less. Am I hopelessly in love with you?'

'I'm afraid so,' I said, smiling at the corny line in spite of myself. 'I'm only a stand-in until the real May recovers from a broken ankle.'

'I can work fast.'

'I'll bet you can.'

'It's fate – kismet – our act following yours. I'd follow you anywhere.' Another tuxedo interrupted us and Hope was forced to make introductions. 'Miss May, this is my worthless partner, George Byrne. Say how-de-do, George, and scram.'

Byrne could have been Hope's twin – same age, height, build, and tux – except for the shape of that nose. Byrne's was the opposite, a prominent nose like a backwards L. Doffing his hat, he made a short bow. 'Charmed, I'm sure, Miss May. Do let us know what you think of our act, won't you? We're trying out some new material this week. I'm praying it doesn't get us pelted with pennies.'

'New steps?'

'And a few jokes. You'll see.'

'Nice knowing you, George,' said Les. 'See you on stage.'

Unfazed, George ignored him. 'Why he gets top billing, I don't know. I think a name change is in order. "Byrne & Hope" sounds better to me. Hiya, girls,' he said as April and June approached. A stagehand glared at him until he moved away to the opposite side of the stage to get ready for his entrance.

'I've been thinking about that,' said Les Hope. 'A name change. Not the act's name – my own. Seriously. What do you think about Lester? Lester sounds more masculine than Leslie, don't you think?'

'Since you go by Les, I don't see as how it matters.'

'I've been considering others too. Not another last name. Hope is a good English name. I was born in England, you know. Came to Ohio when I was four. But for a first name, maybe something more American, something tougher, would be good, huh? What do you think about Bill or Joe or Bob?'

The midget act had finished. As they took their bows to healthy applause, I tried out the names he'd offered. 'Bill Hope. Joe Hope. Bob Hope. Hmmm . . . I think maybe Bill?'

The emcee stepped on stage to begin our introduction.

'Excuse me. We're on.'

'You're a cool one. Nervous?'

'Not at all.'

'Ladies and gentleman!' barked the emcee. 'The lovely Fiorelli sisters! April, May, and June!' The three-piece orchestra struck up our opening number as we turned on our best smiles and strolled to center stage wearing our floral-colored frocks in pink, lemon yellow, and pale green.

That last response of mine was a lie. Never mind how many times I worked an act or how many years I'd spent on the stage, my heartbeat always quickened and my breathing always turned shallow when I heard my introduction. I was ready, I was confident, but I was definitely nervous.

Our act began with an amusing version of the popular waltz song, 'And the Band Played On', where we sang the words one beat early, so the emphasis was on the weak syllable and the song ended a note too soon. Harmless fun, and it drew moderate laughter. Following that, we sang and tap-danced our way through 'April Showers', then performed a medley of Irish ballads, some funny, some melancholy. We finished with a lively dance to a lilting, new Gershwin song, 'Somebody Loves Me', and exited stage left to polite applause. Room for improvement but not bad for our first time together.

George Byrne greeted me with a thumbs-up. 'I see you're going to be a tough act to follow,' he said generously. He pulled at his cuffs, straightened his bow tie, and sauntered on stage with a cocky lift of his chin. Les Hope loped in from the other side. April and June scurried out of the way. 'I'll be along in a minute,' I whispered to them. 'I want to watch this.'

Two handsome young men in top hats and tails are going to please an audience no matter how weak their performance, but Hope & Byrne possessed a magnetism that pulled the audience toward the stage, making each spectator feel like part of the act. Both were excellent hoofers, and the small amount of singing showed off voices that were clear and musical enough to pass muster. The jokes were nothing brilliant, but Les had an innate sense of timing that highlighted his quick wit and made them sound fresh.

'I just came back from the doctor,' said Les, without pausing in his soft shoe routine.

'Well, how did it go?' said George, keeping up a flawless mirror image.

'He said I'd have to go to the mountains for my kidneys,' said Les.

'That's too bad,' said George.

'Yeah, I didn't even know they were up there,' said Les. He paused for the chuckles, then delivered another in rapid patter style. 'Did you hear about the fella from out of town who stopped at a hotel, and he stepped up to the manager and asked him if he had a room and a bath, and the manager said, "I can give you a room", and the fella said, "I asked for a room and a bath!", and the manager said, "I can give you the room, but you'll have to take the bath yourself."'

They took turns, cracking a joke between each soft-shoe or buck-and-wing. The formula worked. The audience was clearly enjoying themselves.

'So how'd we do?' Les asked as he bounded off stage.

'Dynamite. You killed 'em. Honest.'

His grin put dimples in his cheeks. 'How 'bout you and me get a bite to eat after the last show?'

'I'm having dinner with April and June. Why don't you get George, and we'll all go together?'

TWENTY-ONE

It was a typical week in vaudeville. Someone tossed a cigarette into a wastebasket, starting a fire that scorched the dressing room wall before it was put out with a bucket of wash water; a trick dog bit a town boy on the leg when the lad tried to ride him; our luggage was taken off the baggage car two stops before our next destination and didn't catch up

until an hour after the first show; and a freak summer storm
brought down the power lines to the theater, canceling an
entire day – and pay – for us all. With the first week behind
me, I was no closer to finding a performer who could remember
acts from fifteen years ago. Two telegrams reached me in
Xenia, one from Lawyer Kaminsky and the other from Ricardo
Delacruz, imploring me not to give up, so I didn't. But I'd be
lying if I didn't admit to feeling discouraged. Thoughts of
Ruby in her prison cell kept me going.

A vaudeville line-up doesn't move together from town to
town, but chance had overlapped the Spring Flowers' schedule
in large part with several others, including the Thorvald Trio,
Hope & Byrne, and Bender and Young's Old Time Minstrels.
The good thing about this was the easy camaraderie that
developed between us. The bad thing was that I met only five
or six new acts at each stop instead of seven or eight. To better
the odds, I visited each theater in each town we hit, asking
about older performers who might remember any of the acts
on the old program.

Les Hope and George Byrne were a stitch, and Odie Bender
and his pal Ed Young were sweet, but I gravitated toward
Shorty Thorvald every time. The first time I caught their act,
I laughed until I ached.

It was a dance-and-pantomime routine, done with music and
mime and a little acrobatics thrown in for surprise. There were
three of them: Shorty, Mile-High, and Joe. The gimmick was
their sizes. Shorty was the midget, of course, and Mile-High
must have been close to seven feet tall. Joe was the 'average
Joe', who topped off half way between the two. When they
lined up by height and danced, audiences hooted. For one dance,
Shorty stood on Joe's shoulders to get up to Mile-High's height
and they did a hilarious waltz number, with Shorty and Joe
playing the female part. It was clever, if not entirely original.
Shorty was their leader, even though he seemed young, about
eighteen, I guessed. His was the concept and creativity and,
therefore, the name. They'd been together about a year and a
half. I wondered why they hadn't broken into Big Time. All
they needed was to be spotted by a booking agent trolling for
new clients. They were that good. In my opinion, anyway.

'Where are we jumping to next, April?' I asked after Saturday's last show.

She fished the schedule out of her handbag and squinted at it. 'Circleville. Train leaves tomorrow morning at eight. It's not far as the crow flies, but we've got to route through Columbus and go south.'

'Split weeks are the worst invention ever,' moaned June. I agreed, but silently blessed the chance it gave me to run into twice as many performers. I'd spoken to three in Xenia but none had been playing Sun Time longer than a few years. Each jump shuffled the deck and dealt me a new cast of characters. Maybe my luck would change in Circleville. Fifteen years wasn't such a long time to work vaudeville. Heck, I'd been working twenty-four before I'd settled down in Hollywood.

'One thing's good about this circuit,' I said as we made our way back to our fleabag hotel after a demoralizing meal at the diner. 'We'll save money.'

'What do you mean?'

'Small towns don't have anything to do at night after the last show, and most don't have speakeasies like the cities do. And the shopping? Main Street's all hardware stores and feed stores. Never mind,' I added, as June's face fell in dismay. 'We'll make our own fun. And there are a couple of real cities on our tour, aren't there, April? What comes after Circleville?'

For an answer, April handed me a creased sheet of blue paper. Someone from Gus Sun's office had scribbled theater names and dates in the blank spaces – twelve towns listed for the six-week run. My eyes ran casually down the list to the bottom of the page, paused for me to absorb my shock, and returned to the town below Circleville. It was the one place I thought I would never, ever see in my lifetime.

'What's wrong?' asked April.

My lips parted but no sound came out.

'Are you all right? You look bad all of a sudden.'

'I . . . yes. Fine. I just . . . my stomach. It's fine now.'

'Yeah, that special was more grease than meat. Tomorrow when we get to Circleville, let's find a bakery and buy us some nice bread and then get some fruit at the market and . . .'

But I wasn't listening. After Circleville came Chillicothe. The small town with the long, funny name. An old Indian word. My mother had mentioned it only a couple of times, but it wasn't something I'd likely forget. We were not welcome there, my mother and I. It was no coincidence that we had never played Sun Time or for that matter, any other circuit that toured Ohio. And I'd soon be there.

On Sunday morning we hopped the milk run for Columbus and then on to Circleville. There were some familiar faces on the train and one particular couple I'd never seen before. No matter, I could tell at a glance they were vaudeville. For one thing, here in the Midwest where Gus Sun's split-week ruled, entertainers made up a healthy percent of the train passengers on Thursday and Sunday mornings. But aside from that, they had a look about them that I recognized at once. Presumably they saw the same in me, because as soon as they'd settled into the empty seats across from me, the man nodded in a friendly way. 'Good morning, miss. Fred Sweeney's the name, conjuring's the game. The little lady is my wife, Nan.'

They looked to be in their forties. Hope springs eternal.

'How d'you do, Mr Sweeney, Mrs Sweeney? I'm May Fiorelli with the Spring Flowers. Song and dance.' And I served up an innocuous remark about the weather that I could gradually massage into subtle inquiries about their vaudeville history. Turns out, I needn't have bothered with subtle.

Mrs Sweeney, a vapid woman with an ample bust, said not one word during the entire trip. Her role was one I understood very well from my own experience as a magician's assistant some years back. She served as the sidekick who distracted audience attention away from the conjurer's sleight of hand. The silent partner, on stage as well as off. Mr Sweeney, with his well-oiled hair and handlebar moustache, had more than enough to say for the both of them. His no-holds-barred monologue left me little to do but nod and thank my lucky stars they were getting off at Columbus. They were no help, having played Sun Time for only four years.

Trains that traveled short distances and made frequent stops seldom included dining cars, since even small stations had counters with coffee and sandwiches, or boys selling apples. At one of the ten-minute stops, I jumped off to buy myself something to eat. I was paying for a banana and a pickle when I heard a commotion of young voices behind me on the platform. I looked out the window to see Shorty in the midst of a clutch of boys, none who looked older than fourteen. They weren't asking for his autograph.

Stuffing my food into my skirt pockets, I moved quickly toward the door. Before I could get to the platform, one of the jeering boys had shoved Shorty to the ground. Another gave him a mean kick. Riveted by their bullying, they didn't notice me until I grabbed the kicking boy by the collar – he wasn't much bigger than I was – and flung him across the platform.

'Hey, you little weasel,' I said, making a fist, 'why don't you pick on someone your own size? Think you could handle a girl?'

One boy scurried off. The others looked around nervously, noticing the handful of passengers on the platform who were now watching the scene play out. The kicking boy got up and brushed off his pants. 'My dad would whop me if I hit a girl,' he mumbled.

'But he'll give you a medal when he hears about you beating up on someone smaller than you, huh? Go on, get lost!' They glared at me and for a moment, I thought I might have a fight on my hands, but as an older couple at the far end of the platform moved our way, the boys exchanged nervous glances and skedaddled.

'You all right, Shorty?' I asked as he straightened up. The older couple veered aside and boarded the train. The conductor leaned out of the passenger car, looked directly at Shorty and me, and shouted the all-aboard.

Shorty didn't seem to see me. He never answered my question or met my eye. Limping over to the train, he struggled to reach the bottom rung of the ladder, but he managed. As I watched, it dawned on me what I'd done, and my heart plunged to my stomach. I hadn't stopped to think. I should have minded my own business instead of rushing over to play the heroine. Better a few bruises than being rescued by a girl. My thought-

lessness dismayed me. I'd have swallowed a box of tacks
before I hurt Shorty's pride.

Nothing I could say would erase Shorty's humiliation. All
I could do was keep my distance for a few days and hope he
would forgive and forget.

We rode the milk run out of Columbus for less than an hour
before Circleville's small station hove into view. A dozen other
performers piled out of the train when we did, and most of
us made our way down Main Street with suitcases and boxes
like straggling refugees until we came to a row of tatty boarding
houses where the owners answered 'Yes' to the question 'Do
you take show people?' Ours had the usual gritty floors, grimy
windowpanes, and greasy upholstery, but at least it had freshly
laundered bedsheets and clean towels beside the washbasin.
To save money, the girls and I usually took one room and let
a coin toss determine which two shared the bed and who slept
on a folding camp bed or a pallet on the floor. That night, I
lost.

During our stint in Circleville, I ran across three acts that
matched my criteria: husband and wife hypnotists who looked
to be in their fifties, two brothers who played the piano and
sang, and a headlining tenor whose cheap toupee and girdle
made him seem even older than he probably was. I approached
the three acts with questions designed to be both flattering
and nonchalant.

'Smooth act,' I said to the hypnotists. 'You perform like
you've been doing this for years. My sisters and I are new to
Sun Time. Have you been playing long?'

They had joined the circuit only ten months earlier. The
brothers were newcomers too.

I waylaid the tenor as he exited his dressing room and posed
the same question. 'Well, little lady,' he grinned a mouthful
of gold teeth at me, 'you gals are the prettiest tomatoes I've
seen in a month of Sundays, and it looks like we'll be spending
some time together for the next couple jumps. Me, I've spent
most of my career as a Broadway star and am only doing this
to kill time 'til my agent calls with my next show. What say
we get a bite to eat after the last show and go for a stroll? I
could give you some tips on improving your voice.' He accom-

panied the invitation with what he no doubt figured was a
come-hither wink and put his arm around my shoulders, but
I parried his advance with a quick excuse.

In spite of the long spring daylight, it was dark by the time
we'd finished our last show. April and June had already
gathered up their satchels and make-up cases and headed back
to the boarding house. I was about to follow when Les Hope
and George Byrne bounded off the stage. Les made his way
to my side. 'Hang on for ten minutes,' he said quietly, 'and
I'll walk you home.'

A cloudburst had washed the streets clean and left the night
air feeling cool and clammy. A breeze rustled the leaves of
the elms that arched overhead, spattering us with raindrops as
we dodged the puddles along the sidewalk toward 'boarding
house row', analyzing our fellow performers as we walked.

'That Bender and Young act is going places,' said Les. 'Odie
plays a mean banjo. They need an agent. Someone who could
go after Big Time gigs. Of course, it would cost them five
percent, but it's worth it.'

'They've tried. No interest. I think minstrel acts are fading.'

'You could be right. D'you know George and I used to do
a little minstrel? The first time we put on blackface, we were
so green, we didn't know enough to use burnt cork. We used
black greasepaint.' I gasped and he chuckled. 'Yeah, and you
know how that story ended. We were in McKeesport then, and
had the chance to do the "Blackface Follies", so we slathered
on the greasepaint. The stage manager took one look at us,
and all he said was, 'My, you look glossy.' After the show,
we tried everything to get that stuff off – lye soap, cold cream,
even considered a blowtorch. But it sank in instead of coming
off. I think I still have some of it in my veins.'

We arrived at my boarding house after just a few minutes.
One light still burned. 'Thanks for walking me home.'

'Aw, shucks. My hotel is in this direction.'

'Liar.'

'Well, I overheard you talking to that tenor with the Roman
hands and Russian fingers and figured you might appreciate
an escort. I heard you asking him how long he's been working
Sun Time. You asked the same question to the hypnotists, and

back in Dayton, you asked Miss Cherkova too. Mind if I ask what it is you're looking for? Maybe I can help.'

Swallowing my chagrin at having been so obvious, I gave him the phony explanation I had worked up back in Springfield. 'Gee, thanks, Les, but you're not old enough. I'm looking for someone who played this circuit fifteen years ago. Whenever I find a person who fills the bill, I show them an old program from that time and ask if they remember any of the acts. You see, I found that program in my mother's trunk after she died. She was a singer, a real headliner in her day, but I don't know anything about her family. She never talked about them, and she died when I was twelve. I believe she kept that program for a reason. Someone on that list was a friend of hers, or maybe even a relative. Someone knows something about her family background. Maybe her hometown. I'd like to find my kin. I want to know who my people are.'

'And finding a friend of your mother's is likely to lead you there?'

'That's my hope.'

'I'm the best Hope you've got, lady!' I laughed again. Then he turned serious. 'I'll keep my eyes peeled for old-timers. If you tell me the names on that program, I can ask for you whenever we play different cities.'

'That's very kind of you, but I'm sure I'll find someone soon. Perhaps at our next stop. Are you heading to Chillicothe too?'

'Yep. Are you catching the nine o'clock?'

'I'm not sure. April makes the arrangements, I just follow her lead.'

'But you're the pro; they're greenhorns.'

'I'm the substitute, remember? It's their act. And April may be green, but she needs to learn. I won't be around for long. Fortunately, she catches on fast.'

'Well, I'll be seeing you in Chillicothe, then. Goodnight.' And he gave me a peck on the cheek before he took off down the street, back the way we'd come, whistling a jaunty tune I couldn't quite place. As nice as it was having a handsome admirer, I knew better than to get involved. As soon as I'd found someone who knew one of the 1910 acts, I'd be gone.

And it couldn't happen soon enough. My thoughts were never far from poor Ruby.

TWENTY-TWO

The scarcity of old-timers was beginning to panic me. Sun Time didn't seem to hold performers as long as the Big Time circuits I'd grown up in, maybe because the good acts moved up and the lousy ones washed out. A telegram from Douglas Fairbanks's secretary told me that Mary Pickford had finished filming *Little Annie Rooney* and had succumbed to Douglas's sudden desire to take an ocean voyage to South America, raising the eyebrows only of those who didn't know Douglas's impulsive ways. They would be gone a month. Not much work could be done at the studio without those two, implied the secretary, so I needn't be concerned about returning at a particular time.

The other news from Hollywood made my spirits sag: Ricardo Delacruz sent another heartbreaking telegram begging for a good report. Ruby Glynn was growing skeletal with despair, and he was praying for a miracle. The account I sent him was not going to raise his morale. The burden of being Ruby's 'only hope' was weighing me down.

Shorty kept his distance now, so on the jump to Chillicothe, I sat on the train opposite Odie Bender. He liked to talk, and the effort it took to be a good listener calmed my jittery nerves. He told me about his family, his piano-teacher mother and his cotton-farming father who preached on Sundays, and about how they wished he'd come home and settle down with a nice girl. 'But me and Ed, we're gonna keep on with this minstrel act as long as we can and keep sending money home 'til we have enough to buy us something. Me, I'm gonna get a little business, a restaurant maybe, one that would serve colored folk. My sister Annabelle is the finest cook in Oktibbeha County, and she would go in with me. With her help, I can't lose!'

In Chillicothe, June and I trailed after April as she hunted up a suitable boarding house. The first door she knocked on didn't take in show people, but the woman was kind enough to point out a once-elegant mansion down the street where a recent widow had started accepting in paying guests. 'Mrs O'Rourke can't afford to be particular,' she said. Mrs O'Rourke happily agreed to take us in for four nights.

'I'll walk back to the station,' I said to the girls, 'and tell the porter where to bring the bags.' I was feeling very queer here in the town that had seen my mother's childhood, and I found myself looking for family resemblances in every face that passed me on the street.

My mother had grown up in Chillicothe. At seventeen, she'd defied her father and left for New York City with nothing in her pocket but the few dollars looted from the Mason jar her mother kept on the windowsill. She left word that the family could write her at the YWCA, but only her younger sister ever did, and she only twice. The second letter was the last, she had said, because their father had disowned his eldest daughter and forbidden anyone to mention her name again. Apart from that skimpy account, my mother had never spoken about her family.

I hadn't decided exactly what to do about this. After sternly reminding myself that not deciding was deciding, I turned to the burly stage manager at Thursday morning's rehearsal and asked, 'Have you ever heard of a family named Pearson here in Chillicothe?'

He gave my question a few seconds thought before answering. 'Nope.'

Later I posed the same question to the piano player. Same response. So I figured the Pearsons had died out or moved away ages ago, and I heaved a sigh of relief that I'd sidestepped the whole issue. Until a young voice piped up, 'You mean Old Man Pearson?' An earnest-looking lad of about thirteen was groping about on hands and knees, laying electrical wire inside the pit. He stood, brushed his hands on his pants, and looked at me with solemn blue eyes.

'I don't know,' I replied. 'All I know is the last name. Pearson.'

'There's a Pearson farm about two miles out of town on the south road.'

'Have they lived there long?'

'I guess. All my life anyway.'

'What's the family like?'

'Well, there ain't much family that I know of. There's Old Man Pearson who goes to our church, 'cept he had a fight with the pastor and doesn't come any more. And there's his daughter, Widow McKenzie, who lives with him.'

The piano player chimed in. 'Oh, Widow McKenzie, to be sure, I know her. When you said Pearson, I didn't remember that she was a Pearson. She comes to town to shop 'most every Saturday and usually takes in an afternoon show. Why'd you ask?'

'Well, I'm not sure they're the same Pearsons, but if they are, they're friends of my family. It's not important . . .' I looked at the boy. 'Maybe on Saturday afternoon, you could point out the Widow McKenzie, if she's in the audience.'

'Sure, miss,' he said, and went back to his wiring.

I sat down to think. Four shows a day doesn't leave much time for eating, let alone walking two miles to look at a farmhouse where I wasn't likely to get a brass band welcome. I made up my mind to waylay Widow McKenzie on Saturday and see if she had a sister who ran away to the theater. I'd have all day Sunday to decide how to deal with her response.

I'd always fancied Chillicothe as a squalid little town full of self-righteous, mean-spirited hicks. I soon understood it was not the town itself my mother despised; it was her own family. As far as I could tell, this was a friendly community laid out in clean, neat squares, where farmers came to buy feed and supplies, and cornfields and cow pastures butted up against the fences at the edge of town. The people I passed on the streets and in the eating-places seemed welcoming, much like people everywhere. By Saturday I was quite myself and even looked forward to seeing whether this widow was, in fact, my aunt. For someone who had grown up with no relations except a mother, the idea of an aunt and a grandfather intrigued me.

After Friday's second show, I waylaid a gruff, gray-haired

monologist on his way to his dressing room and asked if he'd
played Sun Time for long.

'You're mighty nosey, aren't you, girl?' he said, glaring at
me through his spectacles.

I trotted along beside him, uninvited and unwelcome, and
recited the story I'd dished out to every other vaudeville veteran
in my quest for information about the 1910 line-up. 'I found
this program in my mother's belongings after she died,' I said,
holding out the flimsy paper. 'I'd like to find her family, if she
has any left, and I figure she saved this because someone on the
program was a relative or a friend. I'm not nosy. I'm just looking
for people who played Sun Time back around 1910 who might
remember one of these acts. If I can track down one or two of
them, I might learn something about my mother and her kin.'

He stopped and gave me a hostile look before snatching the
paper out of my hand. He squinted at it for a long time before
passing it, wordlessly, back to me. Disappointed, I forced a
smile and turned to go. 'Thanks, anyway.'

I had gone a dozen steps when I heard him clear his throat
in an affected way. I turned around and waited.

'I was working a monkey act in 1915,' he began. 'So I got
to know all the animal acts on Sun Time. I knew the Jock
Howard on your program there. Howard's Ponies and Dogs.
Jock died around that time. Train accident. Killed the ponies
too. Not the dogs.'

'That's mighty sad to hear, but I appreciate the information.
I take it the others don't ring any bells?'

'Nary a one.'

Well, at least that was one name I could cross off the list.

TWENTY-THREE

Saturday afternoon's first show passed without comment
from the stage boy. The four o'clock found me backstage
as soon as our act finished, searching again for the lad.
Two acts later, I found him. 'Is she here?'

He nodded. 'I seen her for you. Row six, one in from the side aisle, gold sweater.' His eyes popped when I slipped him a dollar. Peering out from the wings, I counted the rows. There she was, gold sweater, a homely, silver-haired woman who looked much older than my mother – but heck, my mother had died a dozen years ago, so that was no disqualifier. I raced back to our dressing room, wiped off my stage make-up, swapped my costume for street clothes and made for the exit, ignoring the puzzled looks from some of the other performers. I stationed myself at the theater entrance until the music for the cyclists signaled the final act.

'Mrs McKenzie?' I called, when I spied her. 'Excuse me, Mrs McKenzie?' She stopped and searched for the voice. When she had found me, she looked me over, head to toe, a wary frown wrinkling her forehead. I did the same. No one looked less like my mother. I was certain I had made a mistake, but here she was, so I asked, 'Might I speak with you a moment, please?'

When she had stepped to the edge of the exodus, she looked at me without recognition. Waiting for me to explain myself.

'I'm Jessie Beckett from the Spring Flowers,' I said, fully aware that the name would mean nothing to her. 'Did you have a sister who left home about thirty years ago for the stage?'

She stared at me for several long seconds as if I were speaking some odd foreign language, then her right hand clutched her heart and she swayed a bit on her feet.

'Rachel?' she ventured. 'No, you're too young to be Rachel. You look . . . who are you?'

'I'm Rachel's daughter.' The name did not come easily to my lips – my mother, the acclaimed Chloë Randall, glamorous, talented, fêted by everyone in vaudeville, had been given a gratingly plain, Biblical name like Rachel. It didn't fit her at all. No wonder she had created something more suited to her profession.

I eased Mrs McKenzie through the crowd to a diner I'd eaten at earlier. Once inside, I ordered tea for two. She sat in the booth, twisting a handkerchief in her lap, unable to meet my eyes, so I waited quietly until the tea had arrived and she had taken several fortifying sips before I spoke again. 'Mrs McKenzie, are you my mother's sister?'

Without looking up, she nodded miserably. After a giant swallow of tea, she managed to meet my gaze for a brief second. 'And how is Rachel?' she asked timidly.

'I'm sorry to tell you, she passed away thirteen years ago.'

Mrs McKenzie froze, teacup in mid-air. Two large tears escaped and trickled down her cheeks. Her mouth puckered and her lips moved. Maybe they said, 'Rachel, Rachel.' I'm all respectful for grief and such, so I waited a few moments, but when she showed no sign of focusing on the present, I pressed a little.

'I was only twelve when she died.' Funny how that seemed like yesterday and forever at the same time. 'Could you tell me a little about her? Why she left? You wouldn't have any pictures of her, would you?'

The silence was so long I wasn't sure she would ever break it. At last, she did. 'No. No pictures. Our father says pictures lead to vanity. Did Rachel tell you about . . . about us?'

'Not a word.'

She took a deep breath that seemed to compose her a little. 'Well, then, I'm Esther. There were five of us. Samuel was the oldest; your mother was second. Then Joshua. Then Daniel. I'm the youngest.'

She was loosening up . . . I poured more tea into her cup and soaked up her words as she continued. 'Our parents were, well, difficult. Or Father was, at least. Rachel was even more stubborn than him.' Here she smiled, as if remembering some antic of my mother's. 'She quarreled with Father from the time she learned to talk and walked out the door soon as she finished high school. Said she was going to New York to be an actress. That was the worst thing she could have said to a devout Presbyterian like him. He forbade us to speak her name ever again, said she'd shamed the family beyond reconciliation. Said she was dead to us. Then, some months later, Samuel left. Sweet Samuel, the dearest of brothers. He joined the Army when they called for volunteers for the war in Cuba. A few months later, we got a letter. He . . . he died of typhoid fever in training camp. Never made it to Cuba at all, poor boy. Father said it was the Lord's punishment on him for leaving home. Mother died not long after that. Of a broken heart, I know. Joshua and Daniel lit out as soon as they could, after Father refused to allow Joshua to marry his sweetheart. He took his sweetheart and went west to California with Daniel. Like with Rachel, we didn't hear from them again, so I can't say for certain.'

She fell silent. I prodded her a little. 'But you stayed.'

'Me?' She looked startled that anyone had any interest in her own life story. Perhaps no one ever had. 'I married Ed McKenzie. That was before the boys ran off. Otherwise Father would never have let me marry. Ed McKenzie was a fine man.' She smiled at the recollection. 'He was a butcher with a shop in town, right around the corner, a block west of here. We were happy. He died five years ago last February. The day of his funeral, Father said it was my duty to come home to care for him and the house, since I was his youngest and the Lord had seen fit to give me no children. I didn't want to, but the Bible says honor thy parents.'

While she talked, I studied her. Drab clothes, wispy hair pulled back into a bun, a wrinkled face older than its age. She had broken away, but Fate had dragged her home again. Tradition decreed that the youngest daughter forego marriage to care for the elderly parents, so perhaps she counted herself lucky to have married at all. Sadly, she had been the weakest of the five children, too feeble to stand up to the tyrant.

'Tell me something about my mother when she was young.'

A dreamy look fell across her face as she considered the possibilities, and soon she overflowed with recollections about the award Mother had won at school for spelling, how the pastor said she sang like an angel, and how she'd let Samuel's pet turtle go free in the river. 'She was good with her chores, except she disliked cooking more than anything. And she didn't like green beans, no matter how they were fixed.'

'That I knew!'

Esther finished her second cup of tea. I asked if she wanted something to eat. She glanced at the clock on the wall and straightened. 'Land sakes, no. I got to run put on the roast for dinner. Father'll wonder what's become of me and I don't

want . . .' She trailed off. 'He would raise Cain if he knew
what I was up to every Saturday,' she said, looking around
the diner furtively as if worried she might see someone who
would tell tales. 'I say I'm going into town for shopping and
a church meeting, but I always stop at the theater for a show.
I always thought maybe I'd see Rachel on the stage. It never
happened, did it? But I met you.' She smiled at last, and I
caught a heart-twisting glimpse of my mother in her expression. 'I'll tell him the church meeting went long. Tell me quick
about Rachel. It'll be something to think over in the days to
come, after the sun goes down.' She sounded hungry now, and
I knew it wasn't for food.

I exaggerated. I didn't know if Esther would pass the details
on to her father – she might be unable to come up with a plausible story about how she found out – but in case she did, a
wonderful success story would help avenge my mother and give
Esther something to sustain herself throughout those long, dreary
evenings. Her eyes grew wide as I described Chloë Randall as
the toast of Broadway, the queen of vaudeville, a performer
who toured with her own railroad car full of glamorous costumes.
I embroidered a fairy tale that came complete with a handsome
prince, a husband who was also deceased. I made no mention
of our hard times and my own illegitimacy – it would only have
propped up Old Man Pearson's belief about God's wrath.

'I knew it,' she sighed. 'I always knew she would be a
headliner. She sang like a bird.' After another glance at the
clock on the wall, she met my gaze. It was time.

'Tomorrow's Sunday. I'm off,' I said as she stood. 'I'd like
to see the farm. Can you tell me which street to take—?'

A look of genuine alarm crossed her face. 'Oh, no. You
mustn't. He won't see you. He'd be furious. He'd find out I'd
been to the theater. You mustn't come.'

'I only meant to walk past, to have a look at the place. I
wouldn't stop.'

But she didn't seem persuaded, and I noticed that the directions she gave me didn't match what the stage boy had said.
When we parted, I started to give her a hug, but she sensed
it and drew back. I watched her back until she was out of
sight.

Early Sunday morning, while the air was still cool, I set off walking south, out of the city. After about three-quarters of an hour, I came to the Pearson farm. It was as the stage boy had described, a white house with a green tin roof and a windmill at the side, next to a modest barn. I knew my aunt Esther would be at church, which meant my grandfather was inside alone. I stood in the road a long while, wondering what he looked like, hoping he would walk out on to the porch, and aching to have a moment's contact with him or even a glimpse, until I was forced to admit to myself that I had inherited some of Esther's weakness. As much as I wanted to meet my grandfather, I knew I wouldn't approach the house. The pain of rejection would be more than I could bear.

Finally, I turned to go. My mother and her brothers had walked away from the Pearson farm. I summoned the strength to do the same. The place meant nothing to me.

TWENTY-FOUR

While I was traipsing along country roads, April and June slept late and enjoyed a Sunday breakfast of fried potatoes, oatmeal, bacon and strong coffee. I met them at the station, where April slipped me a roll with bacon before purchasing three tickets on the Norfolk and Western south to Portsmouth. The Thorvald Trio had our identical schedule, but Hope & Byrne and Madame Cherkova bypassed Portsmouth for a longer stay in Cincinnati.

June sighed with envy. 'A whole week in one spot! Aren't you the lucky ones!'

Luck had little to do with it, I thought. The better talent was being shifted to the larger cities for longer runs. Spring Flowers put on a decent show, but the applause was lukewarm, and I didn't kid myself that the sisters were destined for Big Time any time soon. Still, it usually took months, if not years, to hone an act. Eventually I hoped that an agent would catch their act and get them a contract and a route on one of the Big Time circuits like the Orpheum or Keith Albee. It wasn't that far-fetched.

'Just be thankful we aren't on the Death Trail,' I told them.

'What's that?'

'Every day a different town, and towns you never heard of. As many as five shows a day in theaters with benches and roughneck audiences. Split weeks don't seem so bad to people who've played that sort of route.'

Mark Twain could have been thinking of April and June when he titled that travel book of his *The Innocents Abroad*. Raised by strict immigrant parents in Cleveland, those babes-in-the-woods had been nowhere, seen nothing, and knew less about life than girls half their age. After two weeks with chatterbox June, I knew everything about the Fiorelli family and what had driven the sisters into vaudeville. Their father had passed away a few years ago, leaving their mother to support them, barely, by giving music lessons, until she died too, leaving nothing but debt. They took some advice and a loan from a well-meaning neighbor, worked up a few songs, and went to see Gus Sun. While the girls could read and figure well enough, they needed an education in life if they were going to survive vaudeville. I couldn't stay with them forever, and I hated to see Small Time grind them up into sausage.

They were so innocent, they didn't believe me when one day I said that you could still buy legal booze.

'Where do you think your priest gets his wine for church?' I asked April. She hadn't considered that. 'Didn't you ever see those shops where they sell sacramental wine to Jews and Catholics? Right out in the open, with big signs to advertise? Of course, it's supposed to be only rabbis and priests who buy it, but just watch the door, and you'll see that just about every man in the city is a rabbi or a priest.'

'Why aren't they arrested?' June wondered.

'Most of the police are bought off. If not and the case makes it to court, the judges are bought off. Or the juries won't convict. There's too much money to be made for anyone to stop these sales. D'you know, back in Los Angeles, there's a hospital that used to order a gallon of alcohol every month for sterilizing operating instruments. Now they order it by the boxcar, turn it drinkable, add juniper flavoring, and presto! Gin.'

I pointed out the station window to a corner drug store. 'See there? You can buy legal booze with a doctor's prescription at any drug store. Or a dentist can write them, or even veterinarians.' I told them about David Carr and his new drug store collaboration. 'The doctors get a few dollars for each prescription; the drug store makes a big profit; the government collects the taxes; the customer gets his whiskey. Everybody's happy.'

June shook her head in wonder.

I wondered too. The Fiorelli girls were lookers. How was it that there weren't any men in all of Ohio smart enough to snap up three girls with good looks, talent, and kindly dispositions? Vaudeville men would be far quicker to notice their attributes. I predicted it wouldn't be long before the girls got husbands, and the Spring Flowers broke up.

'We'll miss the pretty scenery you gals provide,' Les Hope said when we saw him in the train depot that day. He quickly compared his schedule to ours. 'Looks like we meet up again in Cincinnati and again in Indianapolis. Meanwhile, don't take any wooden nickels!' Tipping his hat, he swung on to the passenger car as the conductor called the all-aboard.

When we boarded our train a half an hour later, we found the passenger cars nearly empty. Toward the rear of our car, I spotted a familiar face. 'Look, April, there's "Frances Morton and Her Picks", the headliners from Xenia.' She was traveling with half a dozen pickaninnies who were no more than six years old and a colored woman who minded them. I understood that role all too well, having helped mind the youngsters in 'The Little Darlings' for a few years. And I knew the pickaninny role too, having played similar parts at their age. After singing a few songs on her own, Frances Morton would call in the picks for the finale, and they'd sing and dance up a storm – insurance for a guaranteed sock finish. Some singers used white kids in blackface, but Frances's picks were real Negroes. I gave a wave in her direction and she returned it with a nod. The picks were sprawled across several seats, fast asleep.

Taking advantage of the space, we sprawled too. It was almost possible for everyone to have his own four-seat section, but not quite. Sitting all alone by the window was Shorty Thorvald. No time like the present, I thought, and I plopped down in an aisle seat facing him and propped my feet up on the seat beside his. 'You don't mind my feet up here do you?' I asked, moving my handbag so the seat beside me was vacant. 'Here, you can do the same.'

The moment the words left my mouth, I could have bit my tongue clean off. My face must have showed my dismay. 'Of course, I don't mind,' he said. 'You get comfortable. My legs won't reach that far, but I'm fine as I am.'

'Sorry,' I murmured inelegantly, certain I'd scotched our friendship for good this time.

To my surprise, he gave me a crooked smile and a long-suffering shake of his head. 'You can't win for losing, can you?'

I gave a helpless shrug. Gushing an apology would only further embarrass us both, and I was relieved he was speaking to me at all after the incident on the platform, so I tried to make up for my latest gaffe with an attempt at sparkling conversation. 'So, what did you think of Hope & Byrne's new gags?'

'I liked 'em fine,' he said with a deadpan expression, 'since I wrote 'em. Two, anyway. What about you?'

'I didn't realize you were the one behind the laughs. I'm impressed. They went over pretty good, I'd say.'

'Good enough to get their act straight to Cincinnati.' He looked right into my eyes when he said it, to see if I understood the implication. I did. No more split weeks for Hope & Byrne.

I nodded. 'The difference between good and better isn't all that great. We won't be playing split weeks forever.'

'You're the optimist, aren't you?'

'Gotta be in this business.'

When he pulled an apple out of a large coat pocket and offered me first bite, I knew I was back in his good graces. We chatted our way to Portsmouth, his slow smile and quick wit making the time race by. I wondered about his background, but people didn't ask personal questions in vaudeville; they talked show business or newspapers. We spent the train ride thrashing over possible comedic additions to his act and to the Spring Flowers as well, and before I knew it, we were pulling into Portsmouth where I hoped I would have better luck hooking up with some older performers or, if not there, at our next stop, Cincinnati. A real city. The real May Fiorelli would return to the Spring Flowers in four weeks, and I was no nearer to identifying anyone on that 1910 program than when I left Hollywood. That program was my last hope. Or, I should say, Ruby Glynn's last hope.

TWENTY-FIVE

Cincinnati was a fine city with so many theaters and variety halls that it had earned a reputation as a good theater town. Some were classy, some not-so-much. Sun Timers played the latter. I'm pretty sure every town in America has a theater named the Broadway, and Cincinnati played true to form. April, June and I located our Broadway in an older section of town near the river, where we met a stagehand who directed us to a hotel that welcomed vaudeville clientele. 'The Bailey,' he said with a jerk of his thumb. 'Cheap, clean and thataway.' As soon as we'd run through our numbers with the musicians, we lugged our bags to the Bailey Hotel.

After a quick sandwich, we went back to the theater to dress for our act. The Broadway had two large, poorly ventilated dressing rooms, one for men, the other for women and children. I can't speak for the men's room, but ours was damp and smelled like someone had mixed a dozen different bottles of perfume with equal parts of flop sweat and cigarette smoke, and painted the walls with the concoction. I wriggled into my flapper dress, added the jewelry then looked around for a place to stash my day clothes. Nothing. Escaping into the fresh-smelling hall, I spied Les Hope exiting the men's dressing room, fastening his cuff links. I greeted him warmly, then asked, 'Do you have hooks on your side? There are no hooks on the ladies' side.' I folded my clothes to minimize wrinkles and placed them in my satchel.

Les pointed toward the far end of the hall to a bank of built-in cupboards I hadn't noticed, where another man was stuffing his belongings into an upper compartment. 'Just say you're mine and I'll gladly share my cupboard with you,' Les said. 'Number sixteen. In fact, I'll gladly share my heart with you. And my lips. And I'm certain there are several other body parts I'd be glad to share if only you'll say the word . . .' He delivered the line with a twist of his invisible moustache and such an exaggerated leer that I burst out laughing. Before I could think of a witty rejoinder, the other man had crossed the hall and was standing beside us, glowering.

'What's so damn funny?'

'Excuse me?' I asked.

'You're pointing at me and mocking me, and I've had about enough of it.'

'Cool off, friend,' said Les. 'I was pointing at the cupboard, not at you.'

'Oh, yeah?' He gave Les's shoulder a none-too-friendly poke. 'It looked to me like you were pointing at me.'

I was pointing at the cupboard, not at you.

'Well, I wasn't. But if you want to meet me behind the theater after the last show, we can discuss your bad manners in a less civilized fashion.'

'Oh, yeah? I'll be there, buster.'

I was pointing at the cupboard, not at you.

'Hunky dory. Before you go, you might want to ask my partner what I did for a living before I went into vaudeville.'

'Oh, yeah?' He threw me a sullen look and stalked off.

All in a rush, I understood the scene at the boarding house. Lila Walker had been pointing at the closet, not at Ruby. *I was pointing at the cupboard, not at you.* Someone had been in the closet. The person who had stabbed her had been in the room all along. The revelation made me forget to breathe.

'Whew! That fella's got a hair trigger,' Les said. 'And a limited vocabulary. Hey, you OK?'

'What? Yeah. Sure.' Quickly I replayed the last few lines of dialog that I'd heard but not absorbed. 'You, uh, you aren't really going to meet him, are you?'

'I'm not the kinda guy to duck a fight.'

'What *did* you do for a living before this?'

Les gave me a thin smile. 'Amateur boxing, lightweight division. A short career: four fights, won three of 'em. And did I mention I have six brothers? Don't worry about me. He won't show. Now, scram, you're almost up.'

April and June joined me and we stowed our clothes in Les's cupboard. There was no lock, but vaudeville liked to think it didn't need locks. We were in the three spot, right after the Irish clog dancers, and this was our first show at the Broadway. I was still reeling from the revelation. Luckily our act was second nature by now. I could have performed it blind.

'I like a small theater,' said April. 'I can see the audience real clearly and I'm sure they can all hear us, even in the back.'

I nodded. She was catching on quickly. 'Yeah, the size of the theater makes a big difference in the audience reaction. That's one good thing about Small Time.'

'What's the other?' she teased.

'Did you see what the last act is?' June asked. I shook my head. 'It's a film. Something called *Lost at Sea*. Have you ever heard of putting a film in a show?'

'Not in the old days, but you see it more and more. A short picture is a good way to start or end the show.'

'I guess it's cheaper,' said June. 'Films don't need hotel rooms or meals.'

'And they cost almost nothing to ship,' added April.

'And they don't argue about dressing rooms, or get sick, or show up late. Come on, that's the end of the cloggers. We're up.'

It wasn't until later that night that I had the chance to work out the details of Lila Walker's murder. She had been stabbed right before Ruby arrived. There had been no time for the killer to escape, so he – or, to be fair, she – had ducked into the closet, hoping no one would open the door. No one did. While there, he'd messed up Lila's clothes. Clara, the schoolteacher at DeWitt's boarding house, had remarked on the disarray when she returned the borrowed coat. Clara thought one of the boarders had helped herself to Lila's clothes and dropped something on the closet floor. I doubted that now. The killer had made the mess.

After Lila was carried out to the ambulance, the room had emptied. How long had the killer remained hidden in the closet? At least an hour or two, at least until all the noise of the police and detectives had died away. Then he'd slipped out. Through the water closet window, perhaps? Down the fire escape to the lowest level where he could jump to the ground? It didn't explain how he'd gotten in to begin with, but it was a plausible theory as to how he got out. Thank you, Les Hope, I thought fervently, as I drifted off to sleep.

TWENTY-SIX

When I was sixteen, I sneaked into a movie theater to watch *Birth of a Nation* and heard for the first time about the Ku Klux Klan and how it started. I liked the flick a lot and figured the Klan for a decent, patriotic organization seeing as how President Woodrow Wilson praised it so highly, though I did wonder, even then, at the sort of grown men who could prance about in white sheets and hoods without mortal embarrassment. It wasn't until a few years later that I understood another point of view from some Negro hoofers who impressed upon me that it was wise to give sheeted men a wide berth, especially if you were colored, Catholic, Jewish, Jap, or immigrant. Which meant most of vaudeville.

So I'd never seen a Klansman up close until that Sunday evening in June when our train pulled slowly into the station at Redfield, Indiana, and we were met by about thirty white-sheeted men lined up single file parallel to the tracks, standing dead silent, arms at their sides like soldiers standing at attention. One of the men broke ranks as the train stopped and jumped aboard our car before we had a chance to stand up. I was in the third row aisle seat that night, sitting beside Odie Bender and across from his partner, Ed. Both men stiffened when they saw the Klansman and dropped their gaze into their laps, as if even meeting his eyes would be fatal.

The Klansman stood so close to us I could have touched his sheet. His pointed hood and white costume covered him from head to ankle, leaving only his eyes and his scuffed, tan oxfords exposed. Out the window, I could see the rank and file standing on the platform as if immobilized by the growing darkness. The one in our car held up his hand for quiet. An unnecessary gesture.

I wasn't afraid, not precisely, but it did cross my mind that I was sitting beside Negroes and across the aisle from April and June Fiorelli, who were Italian and Catholic – and that I was, for all intents and purposes, a Fiorelli too. But we were quite safe on the train, and I patted Odie's arm for reassurance.

''Scuse me, ladies and gents,' the Klansman began with a showy throat clearing. 'A moment of your time, please. Welcome to Redfield. What we have here is a nice, law-abiding, white, Christian community, and we aim to keep it that way. This being Sunday, we know there's lots of you vaudeville folk on board, and we're proud to have you visit us, excepting the niggers. Niggers can just keep on going. We don't want any trouble here. That's all I have to say, so hurry along, folks, and get off if you're getting off, cuz this is just a ten-minute stop. Train leaves at nine sharp.' And he rejoined the long white line.

I looked at Odie but he and Ed were staring firmly at their folded hands. Quietly, almost shamefully, those planning to disembark began gathering up their belongings. A booming female voice from the rear of the crowded car said, 'Well, Martha, looks like we'll be staying on to Indianapolis, like it or not.'

June twisted around from her seat across the aisle to see the source. 'That's Frances Morton,' she said. 'I hope her picks are asleep so they won't be scared.'

As April stood and reached for her bag in the overhead

rack, a white man in the middle of the car spoke up in heavily accented English. 'Me, I don't take orders from no coward in a sheet. I do not get off. Serves them right for their programs to be short.'

'Who's that?' I whispered to April.

'Dunno. Someone who got on a few stops ago. What did he mean, short programs?'

'Theaters need nine acts to make up a typical show. If you take away the Negro acts and ones like his that don't get off the train, the programs will shrink to eight or seven acts, and folks will complain they didn't get their money's worth. The ticket prices might have to drop.'

After a white barbershop quartet announced seconds later that they, too, would refuse to perform in Redfield, a low buzz spread through the car. What decision would each act make? 'How about it?' I asked April. 'I don't like the looks of this place. What say we give Redfield a pass and go straight through to Indianapolis?'

'We can't,' she said with a stone face. 'We can't afford to lose three days' pay. And we have a contract. Come on.'

I understood her point. Any complaints from theater managers could mean getting dropped by Gus Sun.

We exited on to the platform to wait for our trunk and valises to come off the baggage car. It took me a moment to figure out exactly what was wrong – a station is usually a noisy place with people calling out hellos and goodbyes, boys hawking food, and porters shouting, 'Make way!' This evening, though, the air was so still I could hear the hoot of an owl in the distance. The presence of the silent men in white had muffled all conversation. Passengers picked up their suitcases and scurried away. 'Look, April,' I said softly so the robed men couldn't hear. 'What about this – we'll go on to Indianapolis and try to find some last-minute work there, maybe for some canceled act. If we can't, I'll pay the hotel bill out of my share.'

April hadn't spent her life in vaudeville. She hadn't grown up with Indian, Chinese, Jewish, Polish and Negro performers. I didn't know how she felt about the Klan or whether she'd even heard they hated Catholics as much as Jews, and this wasn't the time or place to fill her in. So I was more than a little surprised when she nodded curtly. 'All right, then, get back on board.' Heaving a sigh of relief, I turned to get back into our car.

'Wait!' June pointed toward the back of the train. 'Our bags.' Our luggage had already come off the baggage car and was sitting with others in an untidy pile on the platform.

'Get on board,' I said. 'I'll get them loaded. Here, June, take my handbag.'

'You won't have time!'

'Yes, I will. If it gets tight, I'll jump in the baggage car for the rest of the way. Now hop on!'

Hoofing it toward the rear of the train before the porter could slam shut the baggage door, I felt the eyes of a dozen Klansmen on me. They couldn't help but overhear me call out, 'Please, sir, would you mind? Our luggage isn't staying after all.' I pointed out our trunk and three suitcases, which were mixed in with a few dozen other bags and crates.

'What's the matter, doll? Didn't you understand?' One of the bedsheets stepped out of rank and came a few steps closer, close enough that I could see his eyes gleaming through the slit in his mask. 'You can stay, honey. Just them niggers can't.'

'I understand quite well, thank you,' I said in my frostiest manner. 'We don't feel welcome here. We're going on to Indianapolis.' The porter swung our first two suitcases up into the car.

Two other men joined their friend. 'What is it, Charlie?'

'This dame ain't staying. Says she don't feel welcome here,' he sneered.

'This one's a nigger-lover.' With a sinking feeling, I recognized the voice of the man who had given the ultimatum to our car. 'I saw her sitting next to a young buck. Right beside him she was, putting her hands all over him. Made me sick, I can tell you.'

The porter gave me a frightened glance as he swung the third suitcase into the car. 'I got the trunk next, miss, you can go on.'

'Thank you.' Ignoring the men, I lifted my chin and turned toward the front of the train. By now, several more had gathered, blocking my path. The best way to handle this would be to bluff, walk straight into them, and hope they would give way. 'Excuse me, gentlemen, I have a train to catch.'

Good plan. Bad result.

With folded arms, the men huddled closer. I tried to go around. They only snickered and shifted to block me, first right, then left, toying with me, cat-and-mouse fashion. 'You say she put her hands on a nigger?' said one muffled voice. 'What, like this?' And he reached over and grabbed my bosom.

Without hesitating a second, I aimed a hard kick at his shin. But my foot got caught up in the folds of fabric, and I lost my balance. Rough hands caught my shoulders and kept me from falling to the ground. 'No, like this,' someone said. I fought back, but all that drapery made it impossible to land a kick. My cries for help fell on deaf ears – the station had cleared quickly of passengers, and the only person not wearing a robe was the hapless porter.

'Hey, now,' the skinny man said nervously. 'You leave that young lady alone.'

The Klansmen hooted. 'Mind your own business, Jinks,' said one. 'Go on home now and keep shut if you know what's good for you,' said another.

Jinks knew what was good for him. He skulked away.

Several cars ahead of us, a conductor called the all-aboard. I pushed hard against the man who was holding me and lashed out with both arms, but with so many, it was child's play to pin my arms behind my back and grope my breasts. Hands pulled my shirtwaist out of its belt and squeezed underneath. Other hands held my flailing legs and felt up under my skirt. I screamed to the conductor, but the train's whistle drowned out any sound I made. No one could see me. I had disappeared into what must have looked like a large pile of laundry.

'I think this little slut is disturbing the peace. What do you think, George?'

'Go ahead – call the sheriff!' I spat. 'I'll have you arrested for assault.'

The engine squealed and the train lurched forward with a huff. Still time to jump on to the ladder if I could break free.

There was much sniggering at my remark until someone called out, 'Oh Sheriff!' in a simpering, high-pitched voice. One of the Klansmen standing in front of me pulled off his hood and blessed me with a malicious smile. 'At your service, Bill. Looks like I'm gonna need to arrest someone for assault. Any of you men want to press charges against this shameless hoyden?'

There was a lot of joshing. 'Arrest me too, Sheriff. Put us in the same cell.'

The engineer blew the whistle again. The train chugged forward, picking up speed with every second.

'Good work in apprehending this violent criminal,' the sheriff said. 'I'll take over from here, men. Think a couple nights in the hoosegow might tame the little whore? At least it'll serve as an example to nigger lovers everywhere.'

A round of laughter greeted this witticism. Whoever was holding my arms threw me at the sheriff's chest. His powerful hands grabbed me by the shoulders and shook me 'til my brains were scrambled, then dragged me toward the street, gripping my arm so tightly it went numb. His other hand circled my neck, ready to choke off any call for help I might be tempted to make. The deputy loping along beside us had pulled off his hood too, so passersby would see nothing more alarming than two officers of the law escorting a disheveled young woman to jail.

Such precautions proved unnecessary; we passed no one except other white-robed figures on our way to the jail, just two short blocks away. It was nearly dark. Redfield's population had retreated behind curtains and closed doors. No one was watching. I knew very well how the script would go once we arrived at the jail. They would put me in a cell and take turns.

TWENTY-SEVEN

A single glance took in the sheriff's office. Large room, two cells on one side, a dark hall leading to other rooms or the back door. The floor was streaked with mud, the desks piled with messy stacks of paper. The sheriff shoved me against one of the desks, knocking some of the papers and a stained coffee cup to the floor. The handle broke off. He lifted his robe and unbuckled his belt while his deputy busied himself pulling the shades. The sheriff had just dropped his pants when the deputy hissed, 'Jesus H. Christ, it's Mrs Hoffman!'

Not four seconds later, the door to the jailhouse flung wide and a full-figured matron on a mission burst into the office. The sheriff let go the hem of his robe, covering the trousers that puddled at his feet. He tried, unsuccessfully, to wipe the guilt off his face, but the woman was deep in her own problem and didn't seem to notice anything amiss.

Mrs Hoffman's timing was perfect. My luck had changed!

'Oh, thank God! You're just in time. These men are going to rape me!'

Yanked off her purpose, Mrs Hoffman reared back, blinking hard. The feathers on her beige hat bobbled as her startled gaze traveled from sheriff to deputy to me and back several times.

'Excuse this unfortunate young woman, Loretta,' began the sheriff. 'She's one of them cheap actresses jumped up on drugs and don't know what she's saying.'

'I am not! They dragged me in here—'

'Just look at her, I ask you.' He held up his hands in supplication.

I know what I looked like. Tousled hair, a blouse pulled loose from the waist, and one stocking that had broken off its garter and crumpled around my ankle. 'They tore my clothes at the train station and—'

Mrs Hoffman drew herself up to her full height and glared down at me with all the scorn she could muster. 'For shame, you young hussy! How dare you accuse our sheriff of such a despicable thing! Why, I've known Bertram Purcell most of my life and a finer public servant never walked this Earth.' The sheriff took out a handkerchief and mopped his brow, grinning with obsequious relief at Mrs Hoffman's tribute. 'I only stopped in to see if my husband was here, but as he is not, I'll take my leave.'

Desperate, I tried again. 'Mrs Hoffman, *please* take me out of here. These men are lying to you. They're the ones who tore my clothes and they're going to rape me the moment you leave. Just take me with you!'

She paused with her hand on the doorknob and turned to look at me once more. I could see a flicker of doubt in the back of her eyes; then it was gone. Men in Mrs Hoffman's world simply did not behave in such an unthinkable manner. She straightened her shoulders and marched out with her head held high.

The deputy, who hadn't so much as twitched since Mrs Hoffman's foot first crossed the threshold, was brought up by his boss. 'Go lock the back door, you fool, and get the shades,' he snapped. 'Time we taught this whore some manners.' Holding up his pants with one hand and his robe with the other, the sheriff crossed the room to the front door and threw the bolt. There would be no more unexpected interruptions from either direction. No chance of rescue.

Molten rage coursed through my veins, almost blinding me. But I couldn't miss the sheriff spouting curses as he struggled with his excess of clothing. His pants were around his knees. His arms were tangled in the bedsheet. His face was covered for an instant as he pulled the sheet over his head. With the deputy still in the back, I was alone with the bastard. I saw my chance. The only one I was likely to get.

In that brief moment, my anger erupted, and with strength I didn't know I had, I kicked him in the groin. With his scream muffled by the sheet, he staggered backwards and fell to the floor. As he writhed helplessly, I snatched the white robe out of his hands, grabbed the hood from the desk, and dashed for the door. Before the deputy could make it back to the front office, I had thrown the bolt and run outside.

Anyone following me – and I was certain they would try – would assume I'd gone toward the train station, so I headed in the opposite direction at a dead run. I turned the first corner so they wouldn't see me when they exited the jail. I pulled the Klan robe over my head. The sheriff wasn't a tall man, but I measured only a whisker above five feet, so the hem dragged on the ground. In good light, I'd've looked like someone's daughter playing dress up, but it was night. The pointed hood gave me some extra height. Any Redfield citizen who caught a glimpse of me from a distant window would have seen nothing more worrisome than a public-spirited Klansman heading home.

I forced myself to walk in a casual manner. Nothing would attract more attention than a white sheet running pell-mell along the sidewalk with skirts hiked up. Keeping to the back streets, I avoided gaslights, moving always away from the train station, putting as much distance as I could between the jailhouse and myself. I could circle back later. Somewhere a church bell chimed a tuneless note, marking the half hour. I was stunned to realize it was only nine thirty. It seemed like hours since I had left the station. I would need a safe place to hide while I waited for the eleven o'clock, the last train until morning. I dared not miss it. When the morning light came, I'd be a sitting duck. Trouble was, nobody knew that better than the sheriff. He and his deputy and probably a whole bunch of Klansmen would be waiting to intercept me, watching every corner of the station and the tracks. I needed a plan.

A clump of bushes on the corner of a residential block provided a temporary hiding place. I took off the white robe – too visible in the dark – and balled it up to sit on. The minutes crawled past. A couple of times, I heard noises – footsteps, a cough, an owl hooting, some low conversation – but no one came near me. No one except a small dog that sniffed around the thicket. If he were interested in my peculiar behavior, he didn't bark about it.

Years ago, when I'd been young and on my own after my

mother died, I learned some tricks from a con man who regularly rode the rails for free, tricks that had stood me in good stead more than a few times when my own purse was light. While the church bells chimed ten and then ten thirty, I developed a plan I thought had a decent chance, then worked through every complication imaginable. Finally, I crawled out of the thicket and began to make my way toward the station, keeping to the shadows, pausing to peer around every corner, taking my sweet time. Once I heard someone coming and ducked into a shop doorway, but it was only a man walking his dog on the opposite side of the street. The dog looked in my direction and whined, but his master paid no attention.

When I stumbled on to the railroad tracks, I followed them toward the station, making sure I approached it from the same direction the train would come. I walked along the far side of the tracks ever so cautiously, hugging bushes or buildings. Tramps planning to jump on a train always jump as the train is leaving the station, before it's going too fast. That's what they would expect me to do. But I would jump as the con man had taught me, as the train was slowing down on its way *into* the station, and from a position that put the train between me and the people on the platform.

Crouching behind some steel barrels a hundred yards outside the station, I listened hard for the engine. In the light ahead, I could make out several men milling about at the edge of the platform, waiting. Whether they were passengers or disrobed Klansmen, I could not tell.

The faint sound of the approaching engine grew steadily louder until it drowned out the fierce pounding of my heart. I had to time my move carefully so I could jump on to the moving ladder and hold on. Closer to the station would be slower and easier, but too close and they'd see me. Too far back and the speed would wrench my hand from the railing and knock me down. I would only get one chance.

The train roared in, brakes squealing as it neared the station. Closer and closer. The moment the engine passed me, blocking me from the sight of anyone standing on the platform, I came out from behind the steel barrels and started running. The noise was deafening. Wheels screeched against the track, cylinders pounded, steam hissed. The brass bell clanged to signal arrival.

There was no time to think of the very real danger of losing my balance and falling under the wheels. A ladder on a passenger car went by, but I had to let it go. Too fast. The second car could be my last chance – I couldn't count on there being a third passenger car – so I threw myself on to its ladder, left foot and left hand at the same time. The speed nearly tore my arm from its socket and the whiplash slammed my head against the side of the car, but I reached for the other railing with my right hand and, dazed, pulled myself up the steps. The brakes hissed in protest and moved slower with every second. The acrid odor of the steam cloud engulfed me. On my knees, then on my feet, I climbed the steps and wedged myself into the vestibule between the two cars.

By this time the train was creeping along and men appeared on both sides of the tracks, checking to make sure no one had boarded the train that way, but I was safely aboard. After making sure no one in the seats was looking in my direction, I ducked into the men's lavatory and fastened the latch just before the train lurched to a stop. Anyone searching for a woman would not think to check the men's room. I hoped. Breathing heavily, I sat on the lid of the water closet and collapsed my head into my hands. If there had been any food in my stomach, I'd have thrown it up. A couple of times, the handle on the door rattled, but I made no response. They could go to another car – there was a men's lavatory in each.

In my mind's eye, I could see the sheriff sending some of his men to surround the train while others watched up and down the tracks. Seeing no one who resembled their quarry, they would assume I was still hiding somewhere in town. After the train pulled out of the station, they would resume their search.

I rode all the way to Indianapolis on that lid, partly to avoid the sheriff's men who might have boarded the train to look for me and partly to avoid the conductor. My ticket and my money were in my purse, which I had handed to June just before I ran down the porter, and I knew my excuse would not convince a conductor. So as we pulled into the large, well-lit Indianapolis station and I felt the train stop, I stuck my head out the door and surveyed the stream of people getting off.

It was after midnight. Everyone wore that glassy stare of exhaustion, and not a soul paid me any mind. I tucked in my shirtwaist, combed my hair with my fingers, and stepped off the train.

April was waiting for me on the platform, bless her heart, an anxious crease in her brow. 'Is everything all right? We were worried when you didn't come back to the passenger car, but we figured you were in baggage. And then you weren't.' Her eyes grew large as she took in my disheveled appearance. 'Oh, my.'

I wished I could have spared her the whole sordid story, but that wouldn't be possible. I would have to tell her and June tomorrow, because I had made up my mind to quit the act and return home. Enough was enough. After more than three weeks, I'd learned nothing that would free Ruby. My theory about Lila's killer hiding in the closet would do no good unless I could back it up with a name and some evidence. I was exhausted, badly shaken, and utterly discouraged. My brilliant plan was a bust. No trails led to any of the acts on the mysterious program, and I was convinced now that none would. Small Time circuits just didn't hang on to performers like Big Time did. After a few years, acts either washed out or moved up. If I had made the smallest progress, I'd have stuck it out, but it was a hopeless quest. Time to admit that it was just a program that Lila had stuck in her address book, nothing more. Most likely the jury was right, and Ruby had committed the murder.

'I had a bad time of it with the bedsheet boys. I'll tell you about it tomorrow. I'm sorry, April, but I'm leaving the act. I'm going home.'

TWENTY-EIGHT

That night, I lay awake in bed, unable to shake my despair, testing ways to break the bad news to Ricardo Delacruz. He would be crushed, but his expectations had been oversized from the start. I didn't think I could face Ruby Glynn again. My investigation had always been a long shot. Now it was over. I'd done my best, but I'd flopped. All washed up, as we say in vaudeville. Time to go back to Hollywood and my job, where I would be safe.

The next morning, April and June uttered not a single word of complaint after I'd told them what had happened in Redfield. 'I can't believe there aren't any policemen to call who could bring those horrible men to justice!' said April.

'They *are* the policemen,' I said.

'Well, we don't blame you a bit.'

'You are so brave!' June added. 'I don't know what I'd have done in your shoes.'

'You'd have been smarter than I was and kept your mouth shut from the start. But don't think I'm going to leave you girls in the lurch. I'll stay on until tomorrow, or another day if necessary, so we can modify the routine for the two of you. Luckily the act's name is Spring Flowers, not Spring Trio or anything that would make it look like someone was missing. Like as not, Gus Sun will never hear about the change. You'll be ready by Thursday's show.'

At that moment, who should stroll into our hotel but Hope & Byrne. They expressed themselves so delighted to meet up with us again that nothing would do but a reunion lunch. April aimed a nervous glance at the clock behind the desk. 'Will you have time?' she asked. 'We aren't performing until Thursday, but your first show starts at two.'

'There's a lunch counter right across from the theater,' said George. So we washed up in the hall sink and headed in that direction.

On our way inside, we passed Shorty, Mile-High, and Joe coming out. 'How's the grub?' asked Les.

'Can't go wrong with the chicken salad,' replied Mile-High.

'I hope they serve fast,' I said to no one in particular. 'You don't want to be late.'

We five squeezed into a booth meant for four. Les artfully sandwiched himself between June and me and, after we'd ordered, began his nonstop prattle. 'So, have I told you girls about when George and me had a dance act with Siamese twins?'

June and I responded at the same time with one, drawn-out word and a roll of our eyes. 'Yesss.'

'How 'bout the time we used greasepaint for blackface?'

'Yesss.'

'OK, uncle!' He held up his hands in mock surrender. 'Your turn. Give us a story, April.'

'Gosh, this is only our fourth week. We don't have any stories yet.'

'And if we don't hear from Gus Sun soon about another contract,' added June, 'we never will have any. What do you think, Jessie? You think he'll give us a regular contract?'

'I think so,' I said cautiously. Six-month contracts were standard for this circuit, but even three would have been welcome. 'We've not been canceled once and audiences aren't sitting on their hands.'

'We couldn't have done it without Jessie,' April told the boys. 'She helped us get started on the right foot. She knew how things worked.'

'What will you do when the real May returns,' Les asked me.

That was my cue. 'Well,' I began, letting it sound as if I'd been called back before I'd anticipated. 'I'll be leaving in a day or two, going back to Hollywood and my script girl job. Douglas Fairbanks will start filming his new picture soon, a pirate picture, and I'll be working fourteen-, sixteen-hour days when that starts.'

'Gee, that's a crying shame,' said Les. 'We'll miss you. But it's good to know important people like you,' he teased, 'in case I decide to become a film star.'

'May will be back soon,' said April, 'but she won't be doing
much dancing right away. Jessie's going to help us work up
a routine that will go easy on her foot. Assuming we get a
contract, that is. It's just a shame your time with us didn't get
you any information about that old program, Jessie.'

'Not a thing?' asked George.

I shook my head. 'Nothing that could lead to anyone on
that list. I learned one name on the program had died in an
accident ten years ago, but that's it. It's almost impossible to
find performers still playing Sun Time after fifteen years.'

'And Shorty didn't remember any of those folks?' asked
Les.

'Shorty? Shorty Thorvald?'

'You know of any other men named Shorty around here?'

'But he told me they'd been working a year and a half.'

'Thorvald Trio has been together a year and a half, maybe,
but Shorty's been working Sun Time most of his life. Like
you, he started out as a kid. You mean you didn't know? I
thought you two were thick as thieves.'

'But . . . even so, he can't be old enough . . .'

'Shorty's twenty-seven.'

If I hadn't been wedged against the wall beside Les, I'd've
fallen into my soup. 'Holy cow! I thought he was seventeen
or eighteen!' My face grew hot and, I was sure, red as my
lipstick. I'd made the same, stupid mistake others always made
about me. I'd judged a person's age by his size. Shorty was
small, therefore Shorty was young. Of all the people in the
universe, I should have known better.

'Come on, we'd better hustle over to the theater,' said
George. 'Les and I go on fourth.'

'Fourth? Good for you!' Four was the second-best spot in
any program.

'We'll come with you,' said April, 'and look the place over.'
I beamed with pride. April had done exactly what I'd trained
her to do – check out the facilities in advance of her first show.
I followed. I needed to find Shorty.

On the second floor, there were almost enough dressing
rooms to give each act its own, tiny space – an unexpected
luxury. April and June finished their look-about and left as the

overture kicked in. I held back a little longer, reluctant to say
goodbye to vaudeville now that I was actually leaving. I
watched a few of the acts from the wings, smiling at the now
familiar antics of the Thorvald Trio and the smooth moves of
Hope & Byrne, and tried to find Shorty in their dressing room
afterwards, without any success.

'Have you seen Shorty?' I asked when I saw Mile-High,
but he only shook his head.

I found him after the first show, relaxing with a group of
men behind the theater, smoking and drinking. When I walked
up, someone handed me a jelly jar with an inch of clear-as-
water hooch. I took one sip and nearly gagged. Nothing against
hooch, but this batch had a rubbing alcohol flavor that
suggested it had been just that a few hours earlier. Smiling
through the pain, I held on to the jar and moved into the shade
of the building. Shorty followed.

'Cigarette?' he asked, snapping open a horn case.

'No, thanks.' I would nurse my hooch until I could pour it
out unnoticed. 'I just learned from Les Hope that you've been
in vaudeville all your life. Like me.'

'Most of my life,' he said. 'You were almost born on stage,
you told me. I got started at nine.'

'What sort of acts did you do before the Trio?'

'Acrobats, comedy, a midget theater. How 'bout you?'

'A variety, like you. When my mother was alive, she set me
up in a kiddie Shakespeare act that toured alongside her own
for a while. I was with the Kid Circus, a brother-sister song-
and-dance act, a magician, things like that. Were you on Sun
Time back then?'

'Been Sun Time my whole career. Gus oughta make me
partner,' he said, filling his lungs with cigarette smoke and
letting it out with world-weary sophistication that betrayed his
age. How had I not noticed that he was older than me? It was
so very obvious, now that I knew.

'Did you tour with your family when you were a child?'

He shook his head. 'I was born on a farm in Michigan.
About the time my parents gave up hoping I'd grow, a circus
came through town. The owner offered to take me along. I
was already pretty useless on the farm. Can you imagine

someone my size harnessing horses, driving a tractor, or
stacking bales of hay? I didn't much like the circus freak show
routine so I jumped to vaudeville after a year or so and stayed.
It's a good life. Or as good as life is going to get for me.' He
drew a last, long pull on his cigarette before crushing it under
his foot and giving me a hard look. 'Is this third degree going
somewhere?'

So much for my subtle interrogation skills. Apologizing, I
took the folded program from a pocket and handed it to him
with the phony story about looking for information about my
mother. 'So I've been looking for people who've been in the
business since 1910 or thereabouts and who might remember
some of these acts.'

'Why didn't you just say so?' He ran his eyes down the
list. 'I was only thirteen that year, but Stagpooles I remember.
Australian, like it says here. Three men and two women. Two
of 'em were married to each other; not sure about the others.
They went back to Australia when the war ended – you won't
be finding them. Emilia Frassinese was from Pittsburgh. She
got very sick and went home. May have died. I never heard
anything more about her. And Jock Howard's dead for sure.
Killed in a train wreck. Lesta and Fern Ames were sisters,
funny as hell. They made costumes on the side – they made
some things for me, the best I ever had. I wish they were still
on the circuit, but they saved their money and went home to
Memphis in, uh, let's see, I was about eighteen then, so it
must've been 1916. If I ever work Memphis, I'll look them
up. The Landrieus . . . ha! "Two minds with but a single
thought."' He chuckled and rolled his eyes, remembering.
'Alain was knocked cold when Nanette started sleeping with
a ventriloquist, so I don't think there was much mind-reading
going on between those two. Never heard of the rest.'

'What did you say his name was?'

'Alain. Like Allen but he said it A-Layne like the Frenchies
do. Jerk.'

Alain Landrieu. AL.

There were no Landrieus in Los Angeles but he could have
sent in payments from anywhere. Someone with the initials
AL was forking over seventy-five dollars a month to Lila,

renting her silence, as Steve Quinn had said. Had Lila been digging for dirt on Landrieu when she contacted Gus Sun last Christmas? She must have found what she wanted elsewhere and added him to the roster shortly before her death.

'Do you know where they were from?'

'I've no idea. The Ames sisters might. They were friends of Nanette's.'

It was all I needed to get back in the race. For once, I wasn't ashamed of the reports I sent Delacruz and Kaminsky. At last, I was making progress!

TWENTY-NINE

Once I'd arrived in Memphis, finding the Ames sisters was a snap.

'Why, sure, I know the Misses Ames,' said the desk clerk at my hotel. 'There's probably not a soul in Memphis, man, woman or child, who hasn't bought a Hat Box hat. You're sure to find just what you're looking for, and if you don't, why, Miss Lesta and Miss Fern will make it custom for you.' He gave me directions, and I took off on foot toward the city center.

The irony of my circumstances was not lost on me. For more than three weeks, I'd been searching for performers of middle years and older who could identify any of the people on Lila Walker's vaudeville program, only to find the young man with the answers had been sharing a billing with me the entire time. To my mortification, I, a child performer with a long memory, had ignored the possibility of other child performers with long memories, and to compound my error, I'd judged Shorty's age by his size – an everyday experience in my own life that should have prevented me from making such a mistake. I feared Ricardo Delacruz and Douglas Fairbanks had placed too much confidence in my investigative abilities.

I'd parted ways with the Fiorelli sisters, Shorty, Les Hope,

and the others in Indianapolis. I would miss them all, but that
was vaudeville. You ate with someone every day for weeks
until you felt like family, and then you didn't work with them
again for years, if ever. Getting sentimental with goodbyes
was pointless. Besides, I might see them again one day, and
they all knew they had a floor to sleep on if they ever played
Los Angeles. There's some truth in the oft-repeated claim that
vaudeville was like family. Some, but not enough. I still craved
the real thing.

I had gone to Chicago to catch the southbound express to
Memphis. Before I left Indianapolis, we'd reworked the Spring
Flowers act as a duo and hoped Gus Sun wouldn't get wind
of the change. It was only for a few weeks, and besides, people
do fall ill in vaudeville, and acts have to adjust. As luck would
have it, the day before I left, a telegram from the impresario
himself arrived – collect, naturally – offering the Spring
Flowers a six month route. Our act had made the cut. April
and June were overjoyed. I was proud of them.

The Ames sisters' millinery in their hometown of Memphis
was no run-of-the-mill hat shop – the showroom alone took
up half a city block. There were four sales clerks waiting on
customers, and when I asked if I might talk with either of the
proprietors, one of them escorted me into a brightly lit work-
room where a dozen women were stitching away on hats, caps,
veils, and bonnets. We paused before a round woman with a
puffy red face who was attaching a delicate lace veil to a
mourning hat.

'A Miss Beckett to see you, Miss Lesta.'

Miss Lesta gave me a wide smile and set her work aside.
'And what can I help you with, child?'

Suddenly conscious of my unimaginative straw cloche and
dingy gloves, I introduced myself, pulled off one glove, and
offered my hand. Miss Lesta had a jolly, reassuring way about
her that must have served her in good stead in business as
well as vaudeville. When I told her I had come from Sun Time
and knew Shorty Thorvald, she clapped her hands and beamed.
'Stop! Don't say another word. Let me fetch Fern. She's in
the office. She doted on that boy and won't want to miss a
thing you have to tell.' Moments later, I was sitting in a corner

of the workroom with both sisters, drinking tea, eating oatmeal cookies, and talking about Shorty and his current act.

Fern was the opposite of her sister: thin where Lesta was plump, tall where Lesta was short, and reserved where Lesta was sociable. But their warm Southern manners soon made me feel I had known them all my life, leading me to speak more freely than perhaps I should have. I couldn't seem to help myself.

'Well, now, sugar, you didn't come all this way to tell us about Shorty or buy a hat,' said Lesta at last. 'And while I'm thinking about it, gimme here your nice hat. I have some blue-green ribbon right here that's just the color of your pretty eyes, and there's just enough left to freshen this up, if you would humor an old vaudeville gal and let me do some work while we talk here.'

'You best let her do it,' said Fern. 'Sister gets grouchy if her fingers aren't busy with something.'

Lesta gave a merry laugh. 'Idle hands make the devil's work, I always say.'

Utterly disarmed, I surrendered my straw cloche and began telling the truth about why I'd come to Memphis. I'd repeated the phony story about my mother so many times that the honest truth about Lila Walker's murder and Ruby Glynn's defense sounded in comparison like the script for a bad melodrama. It did occur to me that I should take care about what I revealed in case I was talking to someone who was involved in Lila's blackmail scheme or murder, but it seemed impossible that either of these women could have had anything to do with such goings-on.

'Of course,' I said, 'the 1910 program could have been stuck in Lila's address book by accident and have nothing to do with her blackmail list, but there's a chance that someone on this list knows something about her killer or was even involved in her death.' I wanted to see what they would say before I asked outright about the Landrieus, so I took the program from my purse and handed it to Fern. 'There's your act, first after intermission. I've already learned that Jock Howard and his ponies were killed in a train accident years ago, and Shorty thinks that Emilia Frassinese died, so they can't be suspects.

And the Stagpooles went back to Australia. Do you know anything about the rest?'

UNIQUE THEATRE
Strictly Moral Family Theatre at a Popular Price

Overture
Selections from *Babes In Toyland* . . . . Herbert

FIVE STAGPOOLES
Australia's funniest acrobatic act
EMILIA FRASSINESE
Violinist
JESSUP AND SHADNEY & Co.
Entertainers in Ebony
GRACE HAZARD
Costume novelty, 'Five Feet of Comic Opera'
RALPH CUMMINGS & Co.
Presenting 'The Typewriter Girl,' a one-act play
Staged by Cecil Beck

INTERMISSION

LESTA AND FERN
Novelty Sister Act
THE LANDRIEUS
'Two minds with but a single thought'
HOWARD'S PONIES AND DOGS
Most attractive animal act in the Varieties
THE FOUR MAGNANIS
Musical Barbers
CRYSTALGRAPH, animated pictures

Exit March:
The Stars and Stripes Forever . . . . Sousa

Fern passed the list to Lesta before speaking. 'I recognize all these names, but some I knew better than others. I'd heard about Jock's death but not about Emilia's. Didn't know the

Stagpooles well – they kept to themselves. Grace Hazard was a good friend. We still hear from her from time to time. She married and moved to New York. What's her name now, Lesta?'

'Derby. Grace Derby. Last I heard, she plays in Broadway musicals. She had real talent, not like some of us, eh, Sister?'

'Grace had a sensational act,' Fern said. 'Pantomime followed by some very funny songs. What a voice!'

'Ralph Cummings . . .' mused Lesta. 'I haven't thought about him in years. Who were those gals with him? Julia Branshaw and Sara Somebody?'

'Sara Rutherford. Their one-act play was clever. A murder mystery. Oh! Is that a clue?'

'What was the plot?' I asked, alert for any similarities to the Walker murder.

'It was set in an office,' Fern continued, 'with different characters coming in and out. Those four actors – Sara, Julia, Ralph and Cecil Beck – played two or three characters each. The boss was murdered and the typewriter girl figured out the killer. He came into the office inside a large box. Wasn't that it, Sister?' Lesta nodded. 'Does that sound important?'

I shrugged. 'I don't know. I'll keep it in mind, though. What about Jessup and Shadney?'

Lesta had finished sewing the ribbon on to my hat. She picked up some tiny silk flowers from a nearby table and began snipping and tying them into a colorful flourish. 'I remember those boys. Negroes from Mississippi. Hal Jessup used to talk about Hattiesburg, Mississippi all the time. But I don't remember anyone named Shadney, do you, Sister?'

Fern shook her head to say she didn't remember. 'They had a lively act. Acrobatics and comedy. There were six of them, all young and lean and full of muscles, except Hal who was older but just as lean and muscular. They did some good tricks and some juggling. I think some of them were kin.'

'That's so! Hal Jessup was the uncle of one or two of the boys. They weren't but in their teen years. Nice boys, well mannered. Just come up to Sun Time from Toby Time.'

'What about the Landrieus?' I said, without mentioning what I'd heard from Shorty about Mrs Landrieu and the ventriloquist.

'They followed us here, but we didn't share a billing with them very often,' said Lesta. 'I do know how they did their tricks, though. The words Alain said from out in the audience when they held up some object were code to Nanette who was blindfolded on stage. And that code wasn't easy to do, I can assure you.'

'How did you learn that?' asked Fern.

'Nanette told me how it worked one day. She was very sweet. Then Alain found out she'd spilled the beans, and that's the reason he beat her up that time, remember? He was a mean one.' Realizing what she'd just said, she looked at me and gasped. 'Oh! Maybe he's the one! I wouldn't put it past him, not after I saw how he treated his wife, bless her heart.'

'I think she left him,' said Fern. 'She never said goodbye, but we never saw her again.'

'I hope she did leave him,' added Lesta. 'She deserved better than that bum. Every woman deserves better than that.'

'Do you know where they were from?'

'He used to talk about the bayous,' said Fern.

My heart beat faster. 'New Orleans?' Lila Walker had come from New Orleans.

'I can't say. Don't remember any talk about New Orleans but it's possible.'

Lesta said, 'I remember Nanette saying that the family owned a dry goods store. I expect he went back home to that when the act fell apart.'

'I know who would know!' said Fern with a snap of her fingers. 'Hal Jessup. He owed Landrieu money and with Landrieu quitting vaudeville, Jessup would have to have sent the rest on to him somewhere.'

'And Jessup was from Hattiesburg.'

'Hattiesburg? Where's that?' I asked.

'North of New Orleans, in southern Mississippi.'

I nodded. I could head there next and from there continue on to New Orleans if Hal Jessup said that was Landrieu's home. But something Fern said stuck in my head. Mrs Landrieu had disappeared suddenly, without saying goodbye. Had she left her no-good husband for another man? Or had he killed her? Was that what Lila held over him?

There was one more act we hadn't touched on. 'What about the last act, the Four Magnanis?'

Fern answered first. 'The usual barbershop quartet routine. That style of singing wasn't as popular as it used to be, and I think Gus Sun canceled them. Do you remember anything more about them, Sister? You were sweet on one of them, weren't you?'

'Two were brothers: Ralph and Walter Crutchfield they were.' She rolled her eyes at the recollection. 'And you're right, I was kinda sweet on Ralph, but nothing came of it. The others were Gerald Somebody-or-Other and . . .'

'Paul,' Fern said. 'Paul Peterson. Or maybe Peter Paulson.'

'They got started singing at church,' Lesta said. 'A Methodist church in Spartanburg, South Carolina, where one of 'em's father preached. I suppose they went back there after they washed up.'

She presented me my hat with a flourish of her hand, like she was finishing a magic act. Which in a way she was, having turned my dowdy headdress into a fashion piece that any Hollywood screen star would have been proud to wear. Waving away my offer to pay, she handed me a printed card with their address. 'Now you write us here, Jessie, and let us know if we've been any help to you.' And after a few more minutes of politeness, I took my leave of the Hat Box, feeling as if I was saying goodbye to my dearest maiden aunts.

I was closing in on Alain Landrieu. If I could learn more about this violent man who beat up women, like where he'd been when Lila Walker was murdered, I might make genuine progress. I sent identical telegrams to Kaminsky and Delacruz advising them of my breakthrough. I was finally getting somewhere! Early the next morning, I had an encouraging reply from Kaminsky urging me to keep at it. An hour later, the Western Union boy returned with another telegram, this time from Delacruz. I ripped it open, expecting more of the same. But no. The state of California had set the date for Ruby Glynn's execution. She would hang in two weeks.

THIRTY

Summer seemed to have turned Hattiesburg into a ghost town. The air throbbed with heat. The leaves on the trees hung dusty and limp, undisturbed by the antics of a single squirrel or bird, all of whom I was sure had been roasted in place by the sun. With my white linen blouse and blue serge skirt plastered to my skin, I exited the depot, stepping over a dog that lay in the canopy shade as if dead. A porter followed with my bag as I crossed the sizzling macadam street to the hotel directly opposite the depot.

'Do you have a room?' I asked the desk clerk and before he could reply, I added, 'A corner room would be much appreciated.'

'How many nights?'

'One, I hope, but I may require a second night if I can't get my business done tomorrow.'

'Tomorrow's Sunday. Not much business going on then.' He was fishing. I smiled but did not bite. He examined his register. 'There's a vacant corner room on the ground floor, if you want it, miss,' he said. 'Two dollars. And every room has an electric fan.'

The fan alone was worth the two dollars – with a fan and a cross breeze, the room might be tolerable by nightfall. 'I'll take it.'

Alone in the room, I closed the shades, stripped off every stitch of my clothing, turned on the fan and stood in front of it while I sponged water on my skin. It was so deliciously cool, I actually shivered. I could have stood there for an hour, but there was work to be done.

Refreshed, I returned to the front desk. 'Does the hotel have someone who can launder some things for me while I'm here?'

'Certainly. It usually takes a full day, though. When do you want it?'

'I left some clothes on the bed in my room. If you could

have someone collect them and return them by tomorrow morning, I'd be much obliged and would happily pay the laundress double.'

'Is there anything else, miss?'

'I wonder where I might get a light meal. A sandwich or a salad and a tall drink.' He directed me to a diner on the next block. 'And perhaps you can help me find someone. I'm looking for a man. A colored man who used to belong to an acrobatic act in vaudeville. Name of Jessup, Hal Jessup. I'm told he came from Hattiesburg.'

The clerk's brow wrinkled in thought. 'The name don't ring a bell, but there're about thirteen thousand people in Hattiesburg and a quarter of 'em colored.'

I thanked the man and started out for the diner, too hungry and thirsty to let the heat stop me.

'No, hon, I never heard of him,' said the waitress as she wiped the Formica table clean and took my order for chicken salad and iced tea. 'Maybe you oughta ask some colored folks. They'd likely know him.'

'I haven't seen any since I arrived.' Which was not as surprising as it might seem, considering how quiet the town was. I'd passed only one person on the sidewalk since I left the hotel. And both hotel and diner had *Whites Only* signs posted.

Her eyebrows came together in a frown as she considered my remark. 'Well now, that's 'cause they mostly keep to themselves on their end of town. East Hattiesburg, that is. Come tomorrow morning for breakfast, and you can talk to our colored cook. She'll prob'ly know. Betty knows everybody.'

After another sponge bath and a fitful night's sleep, I took a stroll about town to get a sense of the place while the morning air still smelled fresh and clean. I passed the Air Dome and the Lomo Theaters, both on West Pine Street and both displaying *Closed for the Season* signs as you would expect in the South during the summer months, when the heat shut down theaters of all sorts. Same thing happened in the winter in some northern states and parts of Canada. I peered in the windows of shops that would not open today and listened to the church bells calling townspeople to worship. I reached the diner at nine. A different waitress took my order for toast and coffee, and when I had finished, I asked if I might step in the kitchen and speak briefly to the cook.

'Excuse me, Betty?' I directed my question to a skinny young woman stirring grits into a pan of boiling water. Even this early, the kitchen temperature was hot as Hades. A screen door kept out the flies and most of the air too. Betty set down her spoon and wiped her glistening face with her apron.

'Yes, ma'am?'

'I'm not from around here,' I began, like I was telling her something she didn't know. 'I came to town to talk with a Negro man named Hal Jessup. Used to be in vaudeville. He's probably in his fifties. Would you know where I might find him?'

Her eyes grew round with surprise or fear or both, and she took a step backwards. 'Hal Jessup? What you want with Hal Jessup?'

'Nothing serious,' I replied in my most reassuring voice. 'I only want to ask him about his vaudeville days. Do you know him?'

'I know Hal Jessup. I knowed him real good. He got hisself killed yesterday.'

THIRTY-ONE

By the time I'd reached the Jessup home in East Hattiesburg, the porch and front yard were filled with folks murmuring in hushed tones and milling aimlessly about like people do when they wish they were someplace else. It was mostly men on the porch and women inside, with a few solemn youngsters standing near their parents, restless, trying to behave. One little girl had slipped away to the bottom step where she sat content to pet a calico cat. I stepped over both of them and made my way up to the house. I was the only white person there. Heads turned. People stopped talking. I felt their curiosity.

A bent-over old man, reading my awkwardness, pointed out the newly widowed woman sitting in an overstuffed armchair in the cottage's front room. As I approached, someone handed her a glass of lemonade. 'You know you need to drink up on a hot day like this, Louise,' she urged. I waited my turn, and after people had cleared a little, crouched on my heels beside the chair so I could look her straight in the eye.

'Hello, Mrs Jessup. My name's Jessie Beckett. I'm very sad to hear of your husband's passing.' She took a sip of the lemonade and gave a listless nod without giving me more than a glance. Her other hand held a crumpled handkerchief, but her dull eyes shed no tears. Grief had taken her far away.

Betty at the diner had told me the bare bones. Hal Jessup worked for a big lumber company, cutting pines and loading logs on to big eight-wheel wagons for the trip to the mill. A hard job, but he was a big man with powerful arms, even at his age. A rope had snapped and the logs had rolled off the truck and crushed him. A tragic accident.

Cold logic said his death had nothing to do with me. My intuition screamed in protest. I'd argued it out with myself on the taxi ride to Mobile Street. How could this possibly be a coincidence, coming as it did the day before I was to have called on him? Coincidence be damned. Someone didn't want him talking to me.

But no one knew I was coming to see Hal Jessup except the dear Ames sisters. In my telegrams to Lawyer Kaminsky and Ricardo Delacruz, I described my progress and what I had learned from the Ames sisters, but they were on my side! They were desperate for me to find anything that would help poor Ruby's appeal. Delacruz even offered to wire me more money. Who else knew where I was going? The ticket seller at the Memphis train station? I shook my head in frustration.

But even granting that those people were above suspicion, there was always the possibility that an offhand remark or an innocent comment might have alerted someone else. Who? I might never know. But if that had happened, how could anyone possibly have arranged to murder Hal Jessup so fast? And so 'accidentally'?

It had to have been a coincidence.

Mrs Jessup was in no condition to talk, so I accepted a glass of lemonade from a tall woman with big teeth and a welcoming smile who seemed to have taken charge of hospitality. I introduced myself. 'Will the funeral be held soon?' I asked.

'Tomorrow. This time a year, they like to get 'em in the ground quick. Will you be wanting to come, then?' I could hear the underlying question – who in heaven's name *are* you? – but she was too polite to ask.

'Yes, I would.'

She told me the name of the church and pointed to the reverend on the porch who would officiate. Every person in that room was watching me out of the corners of their eyes, and when I crossed over to introduce myself, Reverend Buford was ready for me. Unlike the lemonade woman, he did not hesitate to ask the question on everyone's mind. 'What brings you to the Jessup house today, Miss Beckett?'

'I never met Mr Jessup, but I came to pay my respects to the family. I got into town yesterday, intending to look him up and interview him, to ask a few questions about his vaudeville days. Some friends of his in Memphis, the Ames sisters, told me about him and his act, "Entertainers in Ebony."'

'That's a disappointment for you to miss him like this.'

I nodded. 'Indeed it is. Does he have any other family? Any children?'

'No, Hal and Louise married 'bout ten years ago, too late to be blessed with children. But Hal, when he was younger, before he married, before he went off to vaudeville, he help raise two nephews, children of his sister who died and their father in prison. He was good as a father to those boys. A fine Christian man. Never touched a drop.'

Ah, two of the boys in the vaudeville act. I could hear my mother say, 'There is more than one way to skin a cat.' I looked around the room full of women. 'Are they here today? On the porch?'

'One's in Detroit, and he ain't gone get here. Other one, now, he's in Chicago but we 'spect him for the funeral. His name is Ray Pigram. A good boy, Ray. He'll look after his uncle's wife.'

I wasn't leaving Hattiesburg until I got what I came for. Someone didn't want Hal Jessup to talk to me. I don't know how they staged the logging accident, but they did. I couldn't make myself believe it had been a genuine accident. I was determined to find out what Mr Jessup would have told me, if not from Mr Jessup himself, then from one of the others in his act.

As I left the house and passed through the men clustered on the porch, it occurred to me that I might have brushed past the person who'd arranged the accident. Whoever it was must have been a logger too, or he wouldn't have been at the site. He must have known Hal Jessup. He would surely attend his funeral – it would look odd if he didn't. It also occurred to me that someone who had killed one man and gotten away with it might not mind killing a nosy young woman.

THIRTY-TWO

When I left California five weeks ago for my 'one-week trip', I didn't pack my go-to-funeral clothes, so first thing Monday morning, I went searching for something respectful to wear to avoid scandalizing the mourners. I managed to spend some of Ricardo Delacruz's money on a two-piece, black cotton dress with a white lace collar and a modest ruffle on the hem of the skirt and on the bottom edge of the overblouse, plus a matching felt cloche and gloves. My black Mary Janes would get me through the day.

Funerals are always somber affairs, but this one was different from any I'd ever attended. The church was so full that some people were left outside, huddled around the entrance. Ladies dressed in white greeted people at the door to usher each mourner to a seat and urge those already seated to squeeze a little closer together. Once the service began, the mourners wailed, and 'Amened', and sang spirituals about going home to Jesus, then the pallbearers hoisted the pine coffin on to their shoulders and walked it out back to the cemetery where they laid Mr Jessup six feet under. A fitting coffin for a lumberjack who cut pine forests. After more singing and praying, the preacher announced that the widow would be receiving at her home, where the ladies of the church had prepared a hearty meal for all.

The Jessup's small house was packed that day, as was the yard. The dining room table was so laden with food that someone had put boards over two sawhorses in the front yard and covered them with a crisply ironed, linen tablecloth for overflow. Sliced ham, fried chicken, slaw, biscuits, cornbread, pickles, fresh sliced tomatoes – every delicious food you could think of had been provided by the churchwomen. Eagle-eyed young girls snatched up plates and forks the moment someone set them down and spirited them into the kitchen to be washed, dried and set out again. I hadn't eaten so well in weeks. Months.

Louise Jessup stood outside today, so as to greet mourners more easily. Someone had placed a chair beside her in the event she felt faint, but she was a tough woman and chose to stand. She never shed a tear, not that I saw, anyway. Hovering close beside her was a younger man. The nephew from Chicago, I judged from his solicitous manner and his appearance – he had the lithe body of someone who had been a dancer or acrobat. People spoke their condolences to him as well as to the widow.

I wasn't the only white person in attendance today, at church or home. I watched the crowd part as a thin white man with a toothbrush moustache approached the widow and nephew. A step behind him was another white man with a big belly. I guessed they represented the logging company. I moved closer and strained to hear the conversation. The fat man, I took him for the owner or some high-up boss, began to talk.

'. . . sincere condolences, Miz Jessup . . . one of our best men . . . twelve years . . . sorely missed . . . horrible accident . . . do the right thing by you . . .' Then he gestured to Moustache Man to continue.

This one spoke a little louder, thankfully, as I was not the only one trying to catch his words. Most people near me stopped talking and developed an all-consuming interest in their food as they pretended not to listen.

'. . . such a sad loss . . . thorough investigation revealed the rope snapped . . . no one's fault, no one can be blamed. There was no one around when it happened . . . a terrible, freak accident.'

No one around except the murderer.

I figured I knew how it really happened. It was absurd to think someone could have persuaded Jessup to stand still beside the wagon while they cut the rope and tumbled the logs on him. I figured the murderer knocked him in the head, laid him beside the wagon and then cut the rope. Any head wound would have been chalked up to damage from the logs.

Moustache Man was saying something about a local bank. 'First thing tomorrow morning, I'll be there to open up an account for you and deposit that sum into it. We know very well that nothing can compensate for your husband's loss, but that should lessen your worries about financial difficulties.' She nodded. I could tell she didn't care, but perhaps she would later. It was a kind gesture on the part of the logging company. Most would have sent flowers and patted themselves on the back.

I paid my respects to the widow and was introduced to the nephew, Ray Pigram. 'I came to town too late to talk with your uncle,' I told him. 'I was intending to ask him about his vaudeville days. You were with Jessup and Shadney, too, weren't you?'

'I was,' he replied, helping his aunt into the chair. 'Now you sit right here, Aunt Louise, and I'm gone get you some of this nice food the ladies made, and don't you go saying you ain't hungry 'cause I know you gone eat it for me 'cause you love me like a son and that's the end of that.' I followed him to the groaning board and stood next to him as he fixed her a plate.

'That was generous of the logging company,' I remarked, to get the conversation going.

'And they paid for the funeral too. They decent folks.'

'About your act . . . "Entertainers in Ebony". I like that name. I take it the act broke up about a dozen years ago?'

'Yeah. That's when Uncle Hal came home and started working for the lumber company.'

'What caused the break up?'

'Well, see now, there were six of us to start, all pretty good acrobats. Uncle Hal was older and so strong, he did the main lifts and juggle. We could all juggle a little, but man, he could juggle like no one else! He learned when he was in the circus, back a long time ago.' He set down the plate, picked up three walnuts and proceeded to show me his skill. A ripple of fond chuckles traveled through the crowd. 'He trained us, me and my brother Frank, and three others. But training takes a long time, and when one would leave, it was hard to replace him, so we just got smaller.'

'Why did they leave?'

'We boys was all originally from these parts. Or mostly. First we toured Toby Time in the South for a coupla years, then Sun Time. When we got up to Illinois, Michigan, Ohio, and such parts, we saw how things was, how they was good factory jobs for colored folks that paid real good and decent schools for colored children. No way we coming back to Mississippi.' He put a whole ham biscuit in his mouth and made the 'Mmmmm' good sound.

'So the act just fell apart?'

He nodded and swallowed. 'Frank, he older than me, he found work in Detroit at Fords. Uncle Hal, he understood. He thought it best for Frank, but he had to fix the act for five. Then another left in Akron to work in a tire plant but he died later. Then I found a good job in Chicago, and it was time to quit. Uncle Hal coulda gotten a job up North too, but he too old to change, or that's what he said. He came home, got married to Louise and got work at the logging company.'

'Do you remember a husband-and-wife team that shared your Gus Sun billing called Landrieu? Mind readers?'

'Yeah, sure I do.'

'I'm trying to track them down too. I don't suppose you know where they were from?'

He ate another ham biscuit while he stretched his memory back a dozen years, then said, 'No, but I might know where to look, after folks have gone.'

'Thanks. I'll stick around.' And then, to be friendly, I asked, 'Who else was in your act? Besides Hal and your brother, Frank.'

'Well, they was Buck Watt, TD Wistar, and Sam Jeter.'

Unfamiliar names, and unimportant. But I was being sociable, building trust, so I said, 'These men, they must be in their thirties now, right? Do you know what became of them?'

'Well, I told you about Buck – he's the one died in Akron. And TD joined the army and got sent to France for the war and never come home.'

'Oh, I'm so sorry.'

'No, no, he didn't die. He just never come home because he like it so much better in France than here. And I never saw Sam again, not since we broke up, but he was a smart one so I bet he got hisself a good job somewhere. 'Scuse me, Miss Beckett, while I get this plate to Auntie. I'm gone get some food in her stomach if it's the last thing I do.'

Clinging to the hope that Ray could tell me where Alain Landrieu was, I watched him tend to his aunt. The crowd was starting to thin. Folks were heading home.

'Miss Beckett?'

I turned. Ray was standing beside his aunt, motioning to me. She wanted to talk to me. I hurried over.

'Ray tells me you came all the way to Hattiesburg to talk to my husband about the old days.'

'Yes, I did, Mrs Jessup. I wanted to ask him about his vaudeville act. I'm very sorry I never had the chance to talk to him. Ray filled me in pretty good, though.'

She looked up at Ray, smiled, and patted his arm. 'My Hal loved this boy, and his brother Frank too, like they was his own. He loved talking 'bout those years when they traveled around the whole country doing their juggling and acrobat tricks. Lor', he was fond of them!'

'How long did they tour?' I asked, just for something to say. I pretty well knew the answer.

'About five years, wasn't it, Ray?'

He nodded. 'Started in Toby Time in oh-eight. Got to Sun Time two years later.' That would have been 1910, the year on my program. 'We were young kids when we started, thirteen, fourteen, and wild like kids are. But Uncle Hal, he had no trouble keeping us in line. Kept us busy practicing hard.'

'Who was Shadney?'

'Oh, that was made up. Uncle Hal thought it sounded better than one name.'

'Do you want to see a picture of Hal back then?' Mrs Jessup asked, and without waiting for my reply, turned to Ray. 'Go get that picture on the mantle, son. You know the one.' Ray hustled inside and reappeared a moment later with a large framed picture that he handed to me. It was a photo of the whole act, all six of them, and the boys looked pretty young so it had to have been taken at the beginning of their career. I recognized the style right away – a professional shot taken for their publicity, with the boys carefully posed and Hal standing in the middle with his juggling clubs. The quality was sharp, the details clear.

I was looking at Hal, the man I almost met, the man whose death I probably caused by my meddling, when Ray reached over with one finger to name the boys, one by one. 'That's me here, I's real skinny back then, and Frank with the hat, and this here's Buck Watt, Frank's best friend who passed ten years ago. Old Buck played a joke or two on us in his day. This one's Sam Jeter – stubborn as a mule, but not from these parts – and this one's TD Wistar. He the youngest and lightest so he always on top . . .'

Ray went on about the boys in the act, but his voice faded to a soft buzz, like an insect in my ear, as I looked, and looked again, and looked *again*, at the face of the one he'd called Sam Jeter. A handsome, light-skinned lad of about sixteen with arms more muscular and a chest broader than his years would suggest. He'd changed in the years since this photo was taken, but I recognized Sam Jeter. I knew him.

People changed a lot about themselves when they came to Hollywood, and so had Sam Jeter. He'd changed his name, his nationality, his family history and his race. There could be no doubt. Sam Jeter was Ricardo Delacruz.

THIRTY-THREE

A s the mourners dispersed and the church ladies finished up in the kitchen and dining room, washing the dishes and distributing the leftovers, I pulled Ray to a corner of the sitting room for some quiet talk. The only men still at the Jessup house were outside breaking down the makeshift table and carrying the borrowed chairs back to their owners. I didn't know if any of those worked for the logging company. I wasn't feeling too trusting of logging company men at present since one of them had killed Hal Jessup, no doubt in my mind. And I didn't want that person, if he was still around, to see me talking to the only other member of the vaudeville troupe in case he got any ideas. Ray and I were alone in the parlor where no one would notice us.

'I'd like to get in touch with one or two of the others, if you know an address for any of them.' It never seemed to occur to Ray to wonder about my interest in a long ago, washed up, vaudeville troupe. If he'd asked, I had a story ready about an article I was writing for *Variety* – pretty feeble, but the best I could do on short notice. Fortunately, he wasn't the suspicious sort.

He gave me Frank's address. 'Like I said, I don't rightly know where Sam and TD are. Uncle Hal woulda known.'

'You said all the boys were from around here except one. Sam Jeter. How did he get in the act?'

Ray smiled at the recollection. 'Sammy, he come to Hattiesburg from Jacksonville, Florida. He used to talk about Jacksonville where his family from. But he didn't have any family left but an old lady cousin here, so that's why he came here.'

'And the cousin? Is she still here?'

'Oh, she old back then and happy to let Hal take him off her hands. She dead by now, for sure. You know, that Sammy, he used to make us cigars. He knew how to make 'em. Real Cuban cigars. Whenever we'd see a tobacco field, he'd snatch

some leaves and dry 'em in the sun for a few days, and roll
us all cigars like he learned back in Jacksonville when he a
kid, rolling cigars for some Cubans. They were mighty fine.
I don't never smoke a cigar or cigarette that I don't think back
on those days.'

For form's sake, I asked a few questions about the others,
but I'd learned what I needed to know. Ray offered to search
his uncle's desk for the Landrieu's address, and I said 'Sure,'
but it wasn't in my sights any longer. When he came back
with the news that Alain Landrieu lived in New Orleans, I
thanked him sincerely. I left the Jessup house with my emotions
in turmoil, triumphant that my hunch about the vaudeville
program had proven correct, thrilled with the information I'd
learned, and horrified at its cost.

I checked out of my hotel the next morning and took a taxi
to the train station where I would buy a ticket to New Orleans,
a short distance to the south. From there I'd ride to Houston
where I could board the Atchison, Topeka, and Santa Fe line
north to where it hooked up to the westbound line to Los
Angeles. I didn't need to track down Alain Landrieu. I didn't
need to puzzle out the people behind the initials ET and AL.
Those marks, whoever they were, had nothing to do with the
murder of Lila Walker or Hal Jessup.

Ticket in hand, I stopped at the Western Union office to
send three, carefully composed telegrams.

> NO LUCK IN HATTIESBURG JESSUP DIED RECENT ACCIDENT
> STOP WIDOW KNEW NOTHING ABOUT VAUDE DAYS STOP
> HEADING NEW ORLEANS TOMORROW TO FIND LANDRIEU
> LAST HOPE THEN HOME NEXT WEEK VERY SORRY NO
> RESULTS YET DISCOURAGED JESSIE BECKETT

After sending this to both Delacruz and Kaminsky, I wrote
another, honest one to David Carr.

> HEADING HOME FROM MISSISSIPPI ARRIVING FRIDAY NOON
> PLEASE MEET ME STOP DONT TELL ANYONE STOP SHOCKING
> NEWS JESSIE

'Wait for a reply, miss?' asked the clerk.

'No, thank you.' I paid him and went out on to the platform to sit on a bench, tapping my foot with impatience as I waited for the train to New Orleans. Less than two weeks before the state of California hanged Ruby Glynn. I had a lot to accomplish and very little time. I would not be stopping in New Orleans to look for Landrieu. There was no need. I knew why Lila Walker had saved that 1910 program. Revenge.

THIRTY-FOUR

The hypnotic clatter of wheels on rail allowed my thoughts to dwell on Ricardo Delacruz and his connection to the murder of Lila Walker. But I wanted to be alone. I turned to the too-friendly man sitting beside me and asked if he had an extra handkerchief as the motion was making me feel sick and I might throw up at any moment. He handed me his handkerchief and moved back two rows. Undisturbed, I stared out the window and tried to untangle fact from supposition. All I really knew for certain was that Sam Jeter had changed his name and his race, and that meant he had something to hide. Something big. Something that Lila Walker could blackmail him for.

No sooner had Delacruz muscled on to the silver screen five years ago than he was compared to Douglas Fairbanks for his manly physique and daring acrobatics. Everyone at Pickford–Fairbanks Studios knew Douglas didn't like him, but we also knew how jealously the 'King of Hollywood' guarded his status as America's foremost athletic hero and how he belittled upstarts who threatened his prominence. Now that I knew something about Delacruz's background, I understood how he had achieved his agility and physical strength. After several years of rigorous acrobatics plus who-knew-what after the act had folded, it was no wonder he was closing in on Douglas.

Delacruz was also nipping at the heels of that international
star, Rudolph Valentino, the Latin Lover whose bedroom eyes
and smoldering expressions caused women to swoon and men
to forbid their wives and daughters to see his films. Roles that
Valentino and Fairbanks judged beneath their notice were
inevitably offered to Delacruz, who snapped them up, using
each one to narrow the distance between himself and his rivals.
He was no household name – not yet – but he was on his way.

They resembled one another, Valentino and Delacruz, with
their coal black eyes, dark hair, and swarthy complexions
attributable to their foreign birth and the relentless southern
California sun. But where Valentino hailed from Italy, Delacruz
claimed Cuba and a fictional pedigree he'd created from his
childhood in Florida. I figured I knew how it happened.

A light-skinned Negro boy from Jacksonville falls in with
some Cuban immigrants of similar appearance. There is a
friend his own age perhaps, or an older man who takes an
interest in the child. The Cubans make cigars for a living. The
boy watches and learns. He spends his days with his immigrant
friends, picking up a smattering of Spanish. He makes them
laugh as he mimics their accented English, never imagining
that one day he would put these trifling skills to use in changing
his life.

But with no family – did they die or desert him, I wondered
– young Sam moves to Hattiesburg in his early teen years,
sad to leave his Cuban friends, but grateful for an elderly aunt
who will take him in. In Mississippi he meets other boys and
falls in with Hal Jessup, a former circus juggler who trains
him along with his own nephews and takes them touring
through the cities of the United States courtesy of the glamorous world of vaudeville. An adventure beyond imagination!
When the act washes up, Sam finds work in the North, or
joins a different act, or the circus, or goes on stage. He moves
frequently and works with no one who knows his background.
At some point, someone mistakes him for a white man or
comments that he could 'pass'. He realizes that his skin is
light enough to let him make it in the world of white enter-
tainment, a life more lucrative and far less restricted than the
one he has. But to be successful, he needs a backstory

explaining his dusky features. The Cuban persona must have seemed heaven sent.

He dares to go west to California, to Hollywood, where his acting talents and athletic prowess propel him into minor roles in adventure films. He doubles for some famous actors, then gets parts in his own name, now the exotic-sounding Ricardo Delacruz. He squires around ravishingly beautiful young hopefuls, eager to sleep their way up his ladder on their way to stardom, and his studio arranges phony romances for him to titillate the fan magazines. Lila Walker is one of these.

So what went wrong? In a word, love. Ricardo met Ruby Glynn, an actress of modest success, and fell in love. He discarded Lila. Furious, she created as much commotion as possible before giving up. She realized he wasn't coming back.

For Lila, revenge replaced remorse. She'd guessed Ricardo's secret. Perhaps he let his guard down for an instant or tossed an offhand remark that made her suspicious. Maybe she realized he didn't know Spanish beyond a few phrases. Maybe, as one of Jack Warner's secretaries, she overheard a rumor. Never mind how she knew. She knew. And believe you me, a Negro passing as white would not have been swept under the rug, not even in Hollywood. Lila's discovery would have blocked any chance Ricardo had of marrying Ruby. California, like every other state, had laws prohibiting white people from marrying colored. He'd have lost Ruby.

Somehow, Lila came across an old program from Ricardo's vaudeville days and made the connection. I wondered about that. She must have seen it either at Delacruz's house when they were romantically involved, or at the Warner Brothers office. She must have approached him, demanding payment, just as she had blackmailed her other victims. Everything was clear as gin so far. But this was where the hooch clouded up.

How did the murders of Lila Walker and Hal Jessup occur? How come none of the initials on Lila's blackmail list matched Ricardo Delacruz's initials or even Sam Jeter's? No RD. No SJ. If she had been blackmailing him, why wasn't he on the list with the rest? I couldn't help Ruby unless I could answer these questions.

So Delacruz decided to kill Lila instead of paying. But why

would he do that? Everyone else paid up. Lila was a sensible girl, not too greedy. She made certain that the amounts she demanded were small change compared to the salaries of her targets. That was the key to her success. Why would Ricardo take such a risk when he could well afford fifty or one hundred dollars a month?

Because he had more to lose than the others. For Steve Quinn, Paula Terry and Vincent MacLeod, exposure of their secrets would have destroyed their careers. God-fearing citizens all over America would have boycotted their films and their studios would have canceled their contracts if word had leaked about homosexuality, illegitimate children, or bigamy. But for Ricardo Delacruz, the consequences would have been catastrophic. He'd lose Ruby, the white woman he loved, when she found out he was a Negro, but worse, he'd likely be lynched. Here was a man who had been performing romantic scenes with white women. He'd kissed them in close ups on the silver screen. Magazines had run articles featuring him dining with white women, playing tennis in white country clubs, and sporting on yachts with white tycoons. The truth about Ricardo would not just kill his career, it would kill *him*. He'd be recognized everywhere and safe nowhere from the fury of the Ku Klux Klan. Something I understood all too well.

So he had to kill Lila to protect himself. Fine. How did he do it?

He sneaked into her boarding house, knifed her, then sneaked out again. Easily said. But I couldn't have done it myself, and I'm pretty good at getting where I want to go. Was he trying to set Ruby up? Surely not. His love for Ruby was genuine or I'd eat my hat. He wouldn't harm her on purpose. But accidentally? Did he know Ruby was on her way to Lila's boarding house? How could he possibly have timed his visit to end minutes before her arrival?

Ruby's honest manner made me doubt she had known in advance that her beloved was going to kill Lila. Could she have helped Ricardo get into Lila's rooms and out again? Maybe, but how? I closed my eyes and tried to picture the scenario. Could she have opened a window and heaved Ricardo inside so he could kill Lila? Without Lila noticing? Ricardo was athletic, but even an acrobat can't climb walls if there is no trellis or thick vines. Was he capable of leaping up to the fire escape ten feet off the ground and pulling himself up? Had he done it before? Was he the man Suzie heard in Lila's bedroom that time, months earlier? If so, he knew where the fire escape led and which rooms were Lila's. Did Ruby know he was hiding in the closet? Was she covering up for him? I had trouble believing they were in it together. For the life of me, I couldn't be sure about what had actually occurred in that boarding house the night Lila was murdered. And I had not the faintest shadow of evidence.

I recalled Delacruz's face when I showed him the vaudeville program. He hadn't so much as batted an eyelash. A good actor, that one. I remembered when he visited me at my house and begged, 'Please prove my Ruby is innocent.' What he did *not* say now seemed more significant than what he did say. He did not say, 'Please find the killer,' as others would have said. No, he said, 'Prove Ruby is innocent.' Two very different requests.

Now I knew why he'd come to see me at my home in Hollywood. He must have been aghast to learn I was going to investigate. He couldn't prevent it without giving himself away, but he could at least keep tabs on my progress if he pretended to be helping me with money and encouragement. All those telegrams hadn't been designed to boost my spirits, or his. They were to find out how close I was getting to the truth.

Guilt must have motivated him as much as fear. He'd gotten off scot-free while his beloved languished in prison, looking forward to the drop in just two weeks. He wanted someone, anyone, to find her innocent, but without finding him guilty. A tricky proposition. She, on the other hand, wouldn't bend so far as to link her lover to the murder, if indeed she knew. So he must somehow save her. That's why he'd hired Lawyer Kaminsky to work on the appeal.

But there was still the unanswered question about Hal Jessup's death. Surely it was murder. Delacruz was the only one, other than his lawyer, who knew where I was going. Well, the Ames sisters knew, but they were too sweet to have anything to do with murder. Weren't they? Surely all that treacle wasn't a ruse! I'd told Delacruz and Kaminsky in the telegram from Memphis that I was heading to Hattiesburg to learn the whereabouts of AL, Alain Landrieu, and that I'd eliminated most of the other acts.

Why would Delacruz take the risk of murdering Jessup? He must've figured Jessup would rat on him. But why would Jessup suddenly speak up after all these years? What made me think Jessup even knew Delacruz was passing? He could have recognized him in a film, sure, but maybe the man didn't go to the theater. Were there any colored theaters in Hattiesburg? And Delacruz wasn't a huge star like Douglas Fairbanks or Charlie Chaplin, names everyone knew, even if they didn't go to the pictures. Maybe Jessup hadn't seen any Delacruz films.

It had been fifteen years since Jessup had seen Delacruz. Who's to say he'd even recognize him in a film? Then again, I recognized him from the publicity photo. He looked pretty much the same, just older. And it wasn't just Jessup who might recognize him. There were others in the act. Ray Pigram and his brother Frank probably went to the pictures now and then. But TD Wistar lived in France and Buck Watt had died in Akron. That left just the Pigram brothers and Hal Jessup who might – might! – see one of Delacruz's films. If they did, surely they would notice the resemblance between the screen star and their old vaudeville comrade. But perhaps not, if the connection between the 'Cuban' actor and Sam Jeter was so outrageously unlikely as to be unthinkable.

Even supposing Jessup or the Pigram brothers had recognized Delacruz in a film, what would they gain by exposing him? From everything I'd heard, Hal had doted on those boys and wished them every success, even when they left him. Seems like he'd've kept his mouth shut tight if he suspected such a thing. As would the Pigrams. They knew all too well what horrors awaited Delacruz if word leaked.

Maybe Jessup didn't know. Maybe Ricardo just worried that he did. And was low enough to kill him just in case. Was he going to kill Frank and Ray too? I breathed a sigh of relief when I realized he couldn't know where they lived. They didn't know where he was either. But he knew where Jessup was, because I had tracked him to Hattiesburg.

However, the problem of timing troubled me. How could Delacruz have done it from the other side of the country? He couldn't possibly get to Mississippi and back that quickly, even if he hired an airplane. Delacruz couldn't have done Jessup in himself, but he could have hired a killer. He got the telegram I sent him on Thursday, when I'd blabbed about learning that Hal Jessup had gone home to Hattiesburg, and Jessup was killed on Saturday. I didn't know how he could accomplish that in such a short time, but it could have happened if Delacruz had known someone living in Hattiesburg who worked for the logging company or knew someone who did, and one of those people agreed to murder for hire. With his money and connections, Delacruz could get anything done quickly. But I didn't know how. Nor could I prove a blasted thing.

And there matters stood. I'd reached an impasse. I had plenty of theory and not a whisker of evidence that Ricardo Delacruz was responsible for the murder of two people. I could certainly accuse him of passing as white, and I could prove it with that photograph at the Jessup house. That would scotch his career and probably kill him, but it wouldn't clear Ruby Glynn. The arguments swirled around in my brain until my head ached. I dozed in my seat, comforted by the thought that in three days I'd be in Los Angeles with David. I could trust David to help me figure it out.

THIRTY-FIVE

Traveling from Mississippi to Los Angeles took longer than going in the other direction. Eager to be home, I chafed at every delay – and delays were conspiring against me. I arrived in Houston too late to catch the last Atchison, Topeka and Santa Fe train north and had to stay the night in a hotel. Even a cool bath didn't make up for that. The next morning, I was on the first train to Wichita where I would hook up with the westward-bound train to Los Angeles, the same line I'd taken east to Chicago back in May. It had been hot then. Now late into June, Texas was unbearable yet bear it we all did, baking in that car like cookies in a rolling oven. The open windows admitted a fine dust that powdered our clothes and the olive-green upholstery, and turned to grime on our perspiring faces and necks. Ladies fanned themselves with silk fans; men blotted their foreheads with white linen hand-kerchiefs that came away brown. I wore my gray cotton day dress because its drop waist style meant a loose fit, but the fabric stuck to my skin regardless. While no one was looking, I rolled my stockings down to my ankles and then, in an act of defiance, pulled them off entirely, trusting that my fellow passengers would be so wrapped in their own misery they would never notice a young woman's bare legs, let alone become more overheated at the view.

If I hadn't been in such a hurry to get back to Los Angeles, I'd probably have booked a hotel room in Wichita and taken the following morning's train, but I was keen to get home to David. A plan to bluff Sam Jeter into admitting he'd killed Lila Walker was forming in my head. A confession was the only thing that would save Ruby. I needed to talk it through with someone. David was the person I trusted most. And least.

That night, the railroad in its magical efficiency uncoupled my Pullman car and a few others and hitched them to the train bound for Los Angeles. Tucked into my upper berth, I hardly noticed the gentle jolts. By breakfast, we were leaving Kansas, and the temperature threatened to bust yesterday's record. At every stop, the dining car took on fresh ice so we had cold beverages on demand, but the sticky heat wilted my appetite. I wet the corner of my napkin in my iced water and blotted my face, imagining how wonderful it would feel to pour the entire glass over my head. I drank orange juice and iced tea for breakfast and tried to escape by burying myself in a newspaper.

A minor commotion toward the front of our car caught my attention. Two porters, their heads bent together, were talking in low, anxious voices. They peered out the windows on both sides of the train. So did I. In the distance, I saw the cause of their concern – a very dark cloud. A tornado?

'Is there a storm coming?' I asked as our porter worked his way through the car, closing each window with a practiced snap.

'Yes, miss. But don't you worry.'

'Perhaps the rain will cool us off a little,' I said hopefully.

The porter shook his head. 'Not that kinda storm, miss. This a dust storm. I never heard of 'em before last year. We didn't used to see 'em at all but nowadays, once in a while when there's not enough rain, the wind kicks up a lot of dirt. No one knows where it all comes from or where it all goes, but it don't last long.'

I felt the train's rhythm slow.

Dust storms. I imagined I knew what one was like. I was wrong.

The wall of darkness roiled toward us. It reached higher than a house and moved like a giant muddy waterfall, tumbling and churning over rocks, billowing toward our train as we raced to meet it. When we collided, I felt an actual crash. Several women screamed.

The porters tried to calm us. 'It's all right, now, ladies. No need to fret.'

Plunged into the brown void, we sat blind while the beast rattled us so hard I feared our car would be torn off the tracks. There was no telling how deep the storm was or how long it would last. Our car shook like a toy in the hand of an angry child. I couldn't make out if we were still moving forward or if the engine had stopped. I lost all sense of time.

Despite the closed windows, dirt as fine as expensive dusting powder found its way through the cracks. I took refuge in my handkerchief, but even so, the dust got into my nose, mouth and throat. Some passengers began coughing. Our porter managed to keep his balance as he carried a tray of water down the aisle. No one complained about the brown film floating on the top.

I didn't know if we were in Oklahoma or Texas. The dust storm didn't care. It battered us with bits of branch and desert

trash picked up from God knows where, and then gave up as
suddenly as it had attacked. Once I could see outside again,
I realized our train was still moving, though very slowly. When
the porter said it had been just thirty minutes, I was stunned.

'Here you go, miss.' He handed me a damp towel and a
soft brush to take the dust off my clothes. I glanced over at
the woman across the aisle, with her dirt-streaked face and
dusty hair and hat, and burst out laughing.

'I beg your pardon, ma'am,' I said, but she waved off my
apology.

'I know what I must look like, looking at you,' she said,
and soon we were all chattering back and forth, giddy with
relief at our escape.

The day grew hotter. At six thirty our porter mopped his
face and rang his four-note chime. 'Dinner is served in the
dining car to the rear,' he announced with more enthusiasm
than I would have thought possible. My appetite had been so
deadened by the temperature, I had skipped the last two meals
in favor of cold drinks, but now I needed food. As I made my
way to the dining car behind our first-class Pullman, I hoped
there would be something cool and wet to eat. Melon, perhaps,
or custard pudding.

So efficient was the dining car crew that it looked as if the
dust storm had never happened. The tables had been spread
with snow-white linens, gleaming china plates, and silverware
so polished you could see your face in the handles. Someone
had put fresh pink flowers in crystal vases and placed one at
the center of every table. The boutonnière in the waiter's white
jacket matched. Below his flower, stitched in black on his pocket,
was his name; Suddeth. 'Right here, miss,' he said in a rich,
deep voice that would have sounded good on the radio. He
indicated a table for four where a goblet of iced water waited
for me. A timid-looking, gray-haired couple was already seated
there. The man rose slightly in his seat as I took my place.

'Dr Montague Jones,' he said as he scooted his chair an
inch farther away, 'and my wife, Mrs Jones.' They reminded
me of a pair of skittish mice. We exchanged the expected
remarks about the heat and the dust storm before I picked up
my menu and they returned to their silent meal. I marked my

selection on the order form for fruit cocktail, deviled eggs, rolls with butter and iced tea, then handed it to our waiter.

Moments later, Suddeth brought another diner to the fourth seat at our table – a single man sporting an eyepatch. Oddly, I noticed that he had come from the back of the dining car where the kitchen was located. This seemed peculiar because on a long train like this with two dining cars, one is usually positioned near the front for the regular passengers and the other – the one where I was sitting – at the end near the sleeper cars for first class. Our dining car was evidently not the last car after all.

His brass-buttoned, navy blue jacket resembled a uniform in its cut, but his bearing was not that of a soldier. When he spoke, I recognized the broad vowels and the language of a man raised on the tough streets of Chicago. He said his name was Jack Stubbs, but somehow, I knew it wasn't. Dr Jones introduced himself and his wife, who gave the newcomer a timid smile.

'You a doc, huh?' Stubbs began and once he'd begun, he never stopped. 'Well ain't that a coincydince? I'm in the medical business myself. Medicinal whiskey, to be precise. Purely legal and above board, but you'll know all about that, eh, Doc?'

The couple's expressions made such a profound shift from polite to horrified that I suspected Dr Jones was a doctor of divinity. Jack Stubbs continued, oblivious to their nervous glances. Judging from his sloppy behavior, he'd been dosing himself with some of that medicine.

'Me and the boys got a whole office car full of medicine bottles,' he said, pulling a pint from his vest pocket and setting it proudly on the table. Old Grand-Dad. *Bottled in Bond*, the label read. *Unexcelled for Medicinal Purposes.* 'Go ahead, take a swig. Care to write yourself a prescription first? Ha ha! This is the real stuff. None o' that bathtub gin. Lotsa people wanna get their mitts on this sorta medicine, that's for sure.'

The Joneses shook their heads in unison. I was curious, but declined. For the moment, anyway.

'Suit yourself,' he said, handing his dinner order to the waiter. As he slipped the bottle back inside his jacket, I caught a glimpse of a gun strapped to his chest. 'And be quick about it, boy,' he snapped. 'I don't have all night.' Turning his attention back to the Joneses and me, he said, 'We've been minding this shipment since Louisville. Me and my boys. Picked it up at a distillery warehouse a coupla days ago.'

'What does that mean, "bottled in bond"?' I asked.

Stubbs wiped his mouth with the back of his hand. 'That's a warehouse for legal whiskey. They're patrolled night and day by armed guards like me,' he thumped his chest, 'and watched by a government gauger. That's the taxman. Nothing goes outta there without him taking count. Except once,' he lowered his voice conspiratorially and leaned forward, 'once I heard of this fella who ran a thin hose through a crack in the wall into one of the casks of whiskey and siphoned off all the hooch before the gauger noticed the barrel was empty.' He slapped his palm on the table and grinned with such pride I wondered if he'd done it himself. 'So the gauger, he takes count of the stock each month, adds up the ones going out and makes sure the arithmetic matches last month's numbers. Medicinal whiskey hasn't been taxed yet, and it don't get taxed until it gets bought. That's when the drug stores, or hospitals, or whoever pay the tax.'

My stomach was getting a nervous feeling with all this talk of medicinal whiskey, what with David Carr and his newfound interest in drug stores. So I couldn't help what I said next. 'Um, Mr Stubbs, I'm wondering . . . how far are you going with this shipment? To Los Angeles?'

'No, liddle lady, not that far.'

I sighed. David wasn't involved. Although there was nothing illegal about it, so why was I relieved? He must have done something similar when he bought bonded whiskey for his drug store. Mr Stubbs was talking again, happily slurring his words.

'. . . and we loaded it, all of it, ourselves, just the three of us. They brought up two office cars but we was able to fit everything into one. Piled to the ceiling. Less work keeping track of one car, you see?' He tapped the side of his head with one finger to show his smarts. 'That way we can take turns in the dining car and getting some sleep.'

The waiter came with my meal, handing Dr and Mrs Jones the excuse they needed to take their leave. The doctor muttered something unintelligible as he departed. Mrs Jones said nothing but cast me an anguished look that conveyed more clearly than words her dismay at leaving an innocent child like myself in the clutches of this reprobate. I swallowed the last of my iced water and pushed my glass over toward Mr Stubbs. 'I still have some ice left here, Mr Stubbs. Might I have a sample of your medicine now?'

'Certainly, certainly, liddle lady. That enough? Now, where was I? Oh yeah. Not every state allows medicinal whiskey, but most do. Here's the thing. Some states let it be legal but the stuff can't taste good. I ask you, what's the point in that? Damned fool politicians!'

I took a sip. Jack Stubbs was right. This was the real McCoy. Went down like a cold flame, smooth and sharp. I accepted his offer for another swig and let him talk about how he lost his eye in France in the Great War while I dug into my food.

Moments later, the waiter served Mr Stubbs his order, a sizzling steak and steaming fried potatoes. He tore into the meal like a man who hadn't eaten in days, packing in bite after bite without seeming to chew before he swallowed. I understood his hurry when another man stopped beside our table. Like Mr Stubbs, he too wore a navy blue jacket with brass buttons and he too had come from the back of the dining car. Without speaking to either of us, he made the scram motion with his thumb, then helped himself to a seat across the aisle.

That's when I knew Jack Stubbs was not the boss of the three guards. With no hesitation, he picked up his plate and scurried out the back of the dining car. He couldn't excuse himself with his mouth full, so he said nothing to me at all. It would have been funny if I hadn't sensed the underlying menace in the boss and in Stubbs's abrupt response. The boss man was fearsome to look at. His mouth was nearly covered by an overgrown moustache, and he wore his long, dark hair slicked back behind his ears with brilliantine. He shot a threatening stare at anyone who dared meet his eye. I didn't do that twice. I finished my cold meal, returned to my seat in the first class car, and rode the train into New Mexico, glad I didn't have to deal with such Neanderthals anymore.

THIRTY-SIX

'**M**ake up your berth, miss?'

A visual sweep of the car told me that my berth was the only one still closed. Although nearly dead from boredom, I was too wakeful to sleep. 'Yes, please.' I gathered up my newspaper and handbag. 'Are we in Arizona yet?'

He pulled his watch out of its vest pocket. 'We usually in Arizona by this time,' he said.

'I'm going to the dining car for a little while.'

'They closed now, miss.'

'I don't want anything to eat. I just want to sit up a while longer.'

The dining car was nearly empty when I entered. Two late diners, female and middle-aged, stared out the window into the nighttime desert as they stirred listless circles in their cups of tea. Four men were nursing their drinks – after-dinner medicinal whiskey, perhaps. The outside air smelled clean and the temperature had dropped along with the setting sun. Clattering from the galley told me the cook was still cleaning up. The waiter busied himself setting tables for tomorrow's breakfast. He spotted me and gave a welcome wave of his arm, 'Take any table you like, miss. May I get you something to drink?'

'Suddeth, isn't it?' He nodded. 'Some water, please, and a spoon. With ice, if there's any left.' It had been hours since our last stop, and I imagined any ice had melted by now. Rummaging around in my handbag, I found a packet of Veronal. As soon as Suddeth brought my water, I dumped in the powder and stirred until it disappeared. I'd sleep soundly tonight.

I finished my newspaper as I sipped the bitter sleeping

potion. The four men retired, leaving me alone with the two women, Suddeth, and the cook, who remained hidden from sight in his miniature kitchen. I studied the women. Their identical freckled complexions made it easy to guess they were sisters. One was about ten years older than the other; both seemed wrung out by the storm and the heat. Loyal to the fashion of their youth, they wore ankle-length dark skirts, starched shirtwaists, and high-button shoes. The dust had ruined their hats, but propriety valued a dirty hat over a bare head. I imagined they were going to visit family, or perhaps they'd already been and were returning home. The day's tensions drained away. I'd be home tomorrow. I began to feel drowsy.

The train slowed, then jolted to a stop. Through the window I saw a tiny station with a sign lit by a single electric bulb. Navaho Springs. The town must have been located some distance from the tracks, for I could see no indication of life. This would be a good time to wash my face and get ready for bed, I thought, without the motion of the train jostling me. But just as I reached the Pullman car, I saw that someone else had the same idea. A young woman slipped into the ladies water closet at the rear of our car. I returned to my table to wait my turn.

Suddeth finished laying out silverware and started folding napkins at the table next to mine. While he worked, we chatted a bit about nothing. After a decent time had passed and the train had still not started up, I made my way back through the dining car. The water closet would be empty by now. Opening the dining car door, I started to cross the vestibule into the Pullman only to see . . . nothing.

Far in the distance, a light from the vanishing train grew smaller by the minute.

'Suddeth,' I called in alarm. 'I think something's gone wrong with—'

Angry shouts erupted on the platform beside the office car. Five men were facing off in a furious shoving match. When I recognized Jack Stubbs and his brilliantine boss, I knew at once what was happening. Someone was stealing the whiskey.

THIRTY-SEVEN

'They've uncoupled the last two cars,' I said in an urgent voice. 'The train's gone. We've been left behind.'

Suddeth froze midway through folding a napkin. The freckled women looked up, too astonished to speak.

Outside on the platform, an argument raged. The voices came into the dining car as clearly as if the men had been sitting beside us. The light was dim but it was enough for me to recognize one-eyed Jack Stubbs and his surly boss. A third man, a hefty bruiser with no neck who wore an identical navy blue jacket, had to be the other guard. The two newcomers must have been the ones who'd uncoupled our cars and were fixing to steal the hooch. One was slender with a badly pockmarked face and one ear partially torn off. His partner wore his stringy blonde hair in a bowl haircut. That one kept looking behind him, pulling on his scraggly beard like his nerves were giving out, as well they should, since he and his pal were outnumbered three to two. Anticipating a gunfight, I dropped into my seat so I could hit the floor if need be.

'You goddamned fool, Roscoe!' The snarl came from the boss. His back was to me so I couldn't see his face, but I knew what it felt like being on the receiving end of that deadly glare. Then it struck me like a hammer blow; he knew the name of the would-be thief. These guards weren't defending the cargo – they were in cahoots with the two men who had uncoupled the cars. And all five were falling out in royal fashion in front of our eyes. We were in the thick of a robbery, in great danger, and I needed all my wits about me.

And I had just swallowed a packet of Veronal.

Horrified, I snatched one of the newly folded napkins and stuck my finger down my throat. No need to panic, I tried to reassure myself. But what little I'd eaten for dinner several hours ago had left my stomach, so the sleeping powder had been quickly absorbed. I vomited almost nothing. All I could do now was steel myself to fight off the effects.

The arguments outside escalated. 'How the hell was I supposed to know—'

'Who's the jackass who unhooked two cars?'

'Who you calling jackass?'

'I'm looking at him! What, you can't see there ain't two office cars? You blind or something? You sons of bitches don't have one brain between the pair of you!'

'You can't talk that way to him.'

'You keep outta this.'

'I'm warning you—'

Enraged, Bowl Haircut lunged clumsily at the boss, who landed a strong punch to his belly, doubling him over. Pockmark took up for him, and Stubbs grabbed him around the throat to hold him back. Those two fell to the ground in a scuffle. No Neck started kicking the one who was down.

'I don't take that from nobody!' Bowl Haircut backed off unsteadily, still clutching his belly while reaching inside his coat. Horrified, we all watched as he pulled out a knife and lunged.

The boss wasn't the boss for nothing. Faster and unencumbered by any qualms, he sidestepped Bowl Haircut's attack. 'So, I can't talk to him that way, huh? Well, talk to this.' The crack of a gun split the air. I gasped.

The shot brought the cook out from the galley, his eyes bulging with fear. 'What's going on?'

'Get down on the floor!' I hissed to the women. The cook and waiter did not need to be told. 'Shhhhh. They're stealing the whiskey. Someone will hear them and call the sheriff.' I spoke with more confidence than I felt. I had seen no town nearby, only the depot, and that appeared deserted.

'You shouldn't'a killed him,' someone said.

'He come at me first. Besides, he ain't dead. Just wounded. Look.' I peered over the windowsill and saw one of the men kneel and tie a handkerchief around Bowl Haircut's leg.

The man screamed in pain. 'I'm gonna die! Curse you, Joe! Damn you all to Hell!' Someone took hold of his arms and dragged him to the edge of the platform.

Someone else said, 'Shut up, Roscoe!'

The gunshot drew notice from inside the depot. A man's face appeared at a window. He ducked when the crooks saw him, but too late.

'Go get him,' the boss said. 'Quick! Before he can get off a telegram.'

Stubbs and Pockmark dashed into the depot and dragged the stationmaster from his office. The hapless man was thin as a boy, and for the space of several heartbeats, in the dark, I thought he *was* a boy, but his cap got knocked off, revealing a balding head. I hoped he'd had time to send a telegram to the nearest authorities. Wherever they were.

'Anybody else in there?'

'Just him.'

'What are we gonna do about them?' I exchanged a long look with Suddeth. They meant us. We were witnesses to a theft and, if Bowl Haircut died, a murder.

'Shut up and lemme think.'

'Ain't nobody in there but two Pullman niggers and some women.'

'Go see.'

I pulled away from the window just before Jack Stubbs climbed the steps to the dining car and looked through the door. Without entering, he took stock of the five of us crouching fearfully on the floor. Meanwhile, the argument about the wounded man continued.

'He's bleeding pretty bad.'

'Well, I'll be sure to send a doctor as soon as we get to California!'

'He sure as hell isn't going to be any help if he bleeds to death. We got a lot of loading to do.'

'Bring up all the trucks.'

'That's all of 'em. Two's all we could get.'

'Jesus! How the hell we gonna get all this loaded on two dinky trucks? And holy shit, they're not covered! How we gonna get away when everybody and his brother sees we're hauling whiskey?'

'It was mighty hard getting those.'

'Cry me a river.'

'There's three women in there and the two niggers,' Stubbs

reported. If he'd recognized me, he didn't say, and I thought it possible he didn't remember me at all. He'd been pretty drunk at our earlier meal.

'Look, we can't stand here all night. How do we move this car to the siding?' demanded the boss.

Silence.

'I said, how do we move this goddamn car to the siding?'

The stationmaster's tremulous voice squeaked, 'Me?'

'Who you think I'm talking to, faggot?'

'Y-you can't move a car. Not without an engine.'

'Whaddya mean, we can't just roll it?' Stubbs asked.

'They don't roll, sir. Not without an engine.'

'Christ, you idiots never thought of that? How long we got 'til the next train comes in?'

'I-I d-don't know, sir,' said the stationmaster.

'The hell he don't.'

'This help you remember?' Another gunshot sounded, making me jump because I didn't see it coming. The sisters stifled screams. I heard no accompanying yell so assumed the gunman had fired a warning shot. It appeared to do the trick.

'F-f-four hours. Maybe five.'

'Christ, don't kill him, Joe. We need all the help we can get unloading these cases.'

'Get the niggers, then. They can work. And get those damned women out here where we can keep an eye on 'em. Hurry up, we don't have all night.'

THIRTY-EIGHT

At first, Jack Stubbs stood guard over us, brandishing a gun like we were desperadoes itching for a shootout at the O.K. Corral. After a few minutes, the absurdity of the situation sank in – three women cowering against the weathered depot siding – and he figured we weren't going to flee into the desert night. He pocketed his gun and went to help with the loading, leaving a threat to hold us in place.

'You even think about moving, and you'll get a bullet in you just like him there.' 'Him there' wasn't moving, and I suspected that, if the young man hadn't bled to death yet, he soon would.

'Don't worry,' I said quietly, hoping to calm the petrified women. 'We'll be fine.'

My intuition had been right, they were sisters. 'We're going home to Flagstaff from our father's funeral in Santa Fe,' the older one said softly. 'Our name's Vandergrift. I'm Eleanor and this is Pamela. I'm worried about her. She's never been strong.'

'Nonsense, Eleanor, I'll be fine. No need to be concerned about me.'

'It's her heart,' she continued, ignoring her sister's protestations. 'I was just going to get her medicine when you said we'd been left behind. She needs that medicine! And it's miles away by now. Oh dear, and we almost made it to Flagstaff. What are we going to do?'

'We're going to rest right here until help comes. Or until these men finish loading the whiskey and leave.'

'Why hasn't the train come back for us?'

'I expect the engineer hasn't noticed yet that he's missing a dining car. After all, it's dark and the track runs straight. As soon as he reaches Holbrook, the next stop, everyone will know something went wrong, and they'll be right back for us.' I sounded pretty confident, I must say. In truth, I figured we were at least an hour's ride from Holbrook. And what would happen then? Once railroad officials realized two cars were missing, would they send the sheriff or another engine to get us? That would depend on whether they thought there had been an accidental uncoupling or a theft. If they knew what the office car was carrying, they'd suspect theft, but I wasn't sure if railroad officials were privy to what was inside a private car.

The single bulb kept the desert blackness at bay, leaving us inside a circle of dim visibility. A thick swath of stars stretched across an enormous sky, and a cool breeze stirred up a mix of earthy, pungent smells that a city girl like me couldn't begin to identify. A mysterious, quavering cry repeated itself periodically, making me wonder if coyotes or bobcats roamed the wilderness. The dangers of the nighttime desert were not lost on me, but I would risk stumbling over a snake or cactus rather than wait patiently to see what the boss had in mind for us. Slipping into the dark would be fairly easy for me alone, and I would do it right now but for the helpless Vandergrift sisters. They couldn't move, and I couldn't just leave them.

The exact details of this whiskey heist were murky, but I understood the basics. It was one of those foxes-guarding-the-henhouse cons, where the men hired to protect the whiskey had judged that greater profit lay in helping themselves. They'd arranged in advance with two others to uncouple the office car at the semi-deserted station of Navajo Springs so they could make off with the whiskey before anyone noticed the cars were missing. If they'd brought two large, covered trucks, they could have loaded it up and disappeared, none the wiser. The plan wasn't supposed to include a dining car with passengers and crew to watch.

Meanwhile, the stationmaster, the two colored men and the four thieves transferred the whiskey, case by case, to one of the open trucks, working steadily for a quarter of an hour – I could see the depot clock through the window – until the truck bed tilted alarmingly to the right.

The boss wiped his forehead on his sleeve. 'Now, here's what's gonna happen. You—' he looked menacingly to the exhausted stationmaster – 'You're coming with me. And you too—' he pointed to the cook – 'and we're going to stash this whiskey somewhere safe. Where is up to you.' He gestured again toward the stationmaster. 'So if you want to see tomorrow, you be thinking of a nice, safe, empty warehouse or barn or shed someplace nearby. While we're gone, the rest of you load up the other truck. We'll run the two of 'em back and forth a few times until we've gotten all the whiskey stashed. Got it?' The men nodded. 'Then let's vamoose.'

Pockmark loped into the shadows and a moment later, I heard an engine start. As soon as the boss had driven away, he brought the second truck up on to the platform and they resumed loading.

Pamela Vandergrift was looking worse. She sat on the wooden platform, leaning against the depot wall, her face a chalky white and her breathing short. Her sister fanned her and murmured soft encouragements.

The crooks talked in low tones as they worked. The night was silent and the air clear. The way the depot sat behind us and a rocky hill blocked one side made a sheltered space that acted a little like an amphitheater, carrying every word the men said to our ears like we were the audience to a play. So that they wouldn't hear us and realize how well the sound traveled, I whispered to the Vandergrift sisters to keep very quiet.

It was a calm-looking, mundane scene being played on that outdoor stage: men loading a truck, women sitting to the side. I knew we were in danger, but I couldn't prevent that damned Veronal from dragging me down. I fought it as best I could, making myself stand when all I wanted to do was lie flat on the platform and give in to sleep. Eleanor Vandergrift threw me an anxious glance as she fanned vigorously, wondering no doubt which of us she was going to lose first. Her sister showed no sign of improvement.

The men had finished loading the second truck as full as it would get, and the boss had not returned. Making no sudden moves, I eased over to the truck, past Suddeth, who was slumped on the ground with his head on his knees, to where the three crooks stood, shifting from one foot to the other, their cigarettes glowing in the dark.

'Excuse me, Mr Stubbs,' I began with all the politeness of a Sunday afternoon social. 'You remember me. I'm Jessie Beckett, from dinner.'

He squinted, taking stock of me for the first time. 'Yeah, right. Whaddya want?' He seemed a bit taken aback. I pressed my temporary advantage.

'The ladies there are the Misses Vandergrift, sisters traveling home from their father's funeral.' It couldn't hurt for Jack Stubbs to know our names. It made us more human, less easy to shoot. 'The younger Miss Vandergrift is gravely ill. Her medicine is in the Pullman and, of course, she can't get to it now. I remember your kindness in sharing some of your medicinal whiskey with me at dinner and wonder if I might impose on you for a little for her?'

His face showed his surprise. Without answering, he reached inside his coat and brought out the bottle of Old Grand-Dad.

'Thank you kindly, Mr Stubbs,' I said, returning to my place against the wall. 'Here, Miss Vandergrift, take some of this.'

'Oh dear, Miss Beckett,' whispered Eleanor. 'We took the pledge. We could never touch liquor.'

'What was the name of your medicine,' I asked Pamela.

'My medicine?' Confused, she turned her eyes to her sister for an answer.

'Anglo-American Heart Remedy. A restorative for the heart.'

'Well, everybody knows all those restoratives are mostly alcohol, so this is probably a lot like . . .' I trailed off. Judging from their horrified expressions, there were at least two people not included in the group known as 'everybody'. 'Look here. This label says, "Unexcelled for Medicinal Purposes". It isn't really liquor; it's medicine. You need something, and this can't hurt.'

'It's *whiskey*.' Eleanor whispered the word as if it were blue.

'Only if you like it. If you don't, it's medicine,' I said.

The sisters exchanged a long look. Then, without further protest, Pamela reached for Jack Stubbs's bottle and took an unladylike swig. She grimaced as it went down. 'Another,' I urged. She swallowed three gulps before handing back the bottle. I took it over to Stubbs, planning to engage him in further conversation, but at that moment, the faint hum of an engine reached my ears, and I spotted headlamps in the distance. Better I return to my spot against the wall than the boss catch me chatting with his men like an old friend. He'd been gone about an hour. Moments later he pulled his empty truck beside the loaded one and jumped out.

'OK, OK, let's trade off here,' he said quietly. 'No time to lose. We found a place about seven miles west of here on the south side of the road, an empty shed. It'll do. You—' he gestured at Pockmark – 'you come with me this time. We can work faster with four. The rest of you, shake a leg. And,' here he looked over at us,'if you need more help, put them women to work.'

THIRTY-NINE

I stood with my back against the depot, shifting my weight from one foot to the other, struggling to keep my eyelids open while I listened to Jack Stubbs and No Neck grumble as they lugged whiskey. Suddeth toiled silently alongside them, sending me nervous glances every now and then. I watched the clock. With four men to unload, it would be less than an hour before the boss returned this time. I told my dull brain that I needed a plan.

'How many times you think we gotta do this?' No Neck was saying.

'I figure four truckloads'll get all of it. Maybe five,' said Stubbs.

'Wish we had bigger trucks.'

'Whose fault is that?'

'His.' Good strategy, I thought, blaming the dead man. 'What are we gonna do with him?'

'Dunno. Take him with us and dump him in the desert probably.'

'How long you think it'll take for the railroad men to get here?'

'You do anything but ask stupid questions? How the hell do I know? Forget about it. We'll be outta here by then.'

I was considering that very issue myself. By now the train would have reached Holbrook. The engineer would have noticed that he was missing two cars. Did he know what the office car was carrying? Did anyone in Holbrook know? If so, they would instantly understand what was going on and send for the sheriff. If not, they might think some sort of accident caused the uncoupling. The railroads used Pinkertons sometimes – maybe they would be called in, but how quickly? Where were the nearest federal prohibition agents? Would any kind of lawmen be awake this time of night?

And how long would it take for them to get here by road?

I knew there was a road because I'd seen it from the train, a slender ribbon that paralleled the tracks for miles on end. Parts of it may have been paved, judging from the speed of the few cars I'd seen, but then we'd hit long stretches where the dust clouds trailing behind the cars and horse-drawn wagons told another story. Depending upon the state of the road from this point west, it was barely possible that help might arrive in as few as three hours.

In just under an hour, the boss returned, the men cussed and switched out the trucks, and he took off with the third load.

'Miss Eleanor, do you think you and Miss Pamela could move quickly? I've been thinking. Those two thieves are hardly watching us. If we could scoot away into the darkness, they wouldn't follow. They couldn't take the time to search for us. They need to get that whiskey loaded and get out of here.'

Eleanor peered into the darkness. 'How would we see?' she whispered.

'Our eyes will adjust. There's almost a full moon. We wouldn't have to go far. Just until we find some rocks to hide behind. What do you think, Miss Pamela?'

'I don't know . . .'

'If your sister and I both support you, one on each side, could you move quickly?'

I could read the doubt in her eyes, but she understood the stakes. None of us voiced our fears, but it had crossed my mind and probably theirs that the thieves might find it safer to shoot all witnesses and dump our bodies in the desert along with Bowl Haircut. They'd already killed once, and I knew from experience that people who killed once found it easy to kill again.

'I can try. And Sister, if I fall, you and Miss Beckett go on without me. Promise!'

'I promise,' Eleanor said. I knew she was lying.

'All right. Now, here comes our chance. See how they're loading? One of the crooks is in the office car. He hands the case down to the man on the ground, and look how his back is to us, and that one hands off to Suddeth who puts it in the truck. Suddeth won't call out if he notices us moving, and the other two won't notice right away.' I hoped. 'Ready?'

Pamela pressed her lips together and nodded. She may have been weak in the heart but she wasn't weak in spirit. We stood and edged closer to the corner of the depot. The loading continued its monotonous rhythm. The thief on the ground never looked in our direction. The one in the office car – Jack Stubbs – was my main worry, but he remained intent on the case he was carrying, taking a half a minute to reappear each time with another.

'Now!' I whispered.

We moved, Eleanor and I supporting Pamela, who made every effort to stay on her feet. We rounded the corner and plunged into the desert, making our way gingerly across the rocky ground creased with gullies until our eyes could adjust. 'Good girl. Keep it up.' And she did, for several dozen steps, until suddenly Eleanor tripped and fell, pulling her sister down on top of her.

'Go on! Go on without us!' she hissed at me.

'Get up! You can do it. Get up!' They struggled to their feet, but we'd lost precious seconds. My ears strained to hear any sound that would suggest the men had noticed our flight. 'Keep going!'

A harsh voice cut through the cool air. 'Listen here, ladies,' said Jack Stubbs, sounding closer than I thought possible. 'I don't have time to come get you, so you better get your bustles back here pronto or the next sound you hear is gonna be a bullet through the head of this nigger.'

Eleanor gasped. 'We can't let him . . .'

'Come on,' I said, as we maneuvered Pamela around and headed back to the depot. I called out to Stubbs in a strong stage voice that carried through the night. 'Shame on you, Mr Stubbs, making such threats. We were right here behind the depot all along, just helping Miss Vandergrift answer nature's call. I told you she was ill. She can't manage on her own. No need to frighten us all to death.'

We rounded the corner. Stubbs was waiting, holding a handful of Suddeth's white coat with one hand and his pistol with the other. No Neck was beside him, brandishing his own weapon. We hobbled slowly back to our previous position against the wall. Pamela slumped to the ground and put her face in her hands. Stubbs played with his pistol, considering, no doubt, whether or not he believed my excuse. His one belligerent eye stared at me. I held my breath until he let go of Suddeth and holstered the gun under his jacket.

Noise from the approaching truck turned all heads. It was early for the boss to return. They had worked fast.

The truck jerked to a halt in the shadows of the depot, short of where it had stopped last time. My foggy brain noticed that the truck looked larger than before, but it wasn't until Stubbs and No Neck started shooting at it that I caught on. This wasn't the boss. It was our rescue!

Three of the men in the truck tumbled out the passenger side where they could use the truck as a buffer. Two others returned fire from inside the truck. In a burst of self-preservation, Stubbs hunched over to make himself a smaller target and darted to my side. He grabbed me for a shield and kept firing into the truck, as if he could kill the metal beast. No Neck followed suit, seizing Eleanor by the throat.

'Hold your fire!' called someone from the truck.

'Come on,' Stubbs said to No Neck, and they backed toward the dining car, keeping carefully behind us and firing the occasional shot just to keep the men from getting out of the truck. 'You, nigger, you get the other one and get into the car or I whack you both.'

Suddeth stooped, picked Pamela up with some effort, and staggered clumsily up the dining car steps.

Once inside, Stubbs turned me loose and gave me a shove. 'Pull all the shades,' he ordered. I complied, hoping the 'Hold Fire' command was still in effect outside. Suddeth reached the back of the car and deposited Pamela none too gently on the floor. Eleanor and I crawled under a table where, to my surprise, I found my handbag. It must have fallen there in the confusion. Having it back felt oddly reassuring.

'Now that the sheriff is here, we'll be saved soon,' Eleanor reassured her sister. I didn't contradict her. I hoped she was correct, that the men outside were lawmen, but if that were the case, why hadn't they identified themselves and called for the thieves to throw down their weapons and surrender? Or was I not thinking straight on account of the Veronal?

Stubbs broke a window with the butt of his gun, scattering splinters of glass on to the table and floor. 'You watch the other side,' he said to No Neck, 'in case they come at us that way.'

Hearing nothing from my cave under the table, I imagined the men in the truck were getting out now and positioning themselves around the dining car. Moments later, a thin voice called out. 'You men in there! Listen up! We found your dead friend, and we know there's just two of you left. You're outnumbered by a mile. We can shoot it out and kill you both, or we can play it smart and nobody gets hurt. What do you say?'

'I'm listening,' shouted Stubbs as he reloaded his gun. I wondered how much ammunition he had left.

'We just want the whiskey. We'll carry it off peaceable-like and go. You can wait where you are until the railroad gets here and tell 'em how brave you were, protecting the women and fighting us off.'

From her spot under the table, Eleanor looked at me, her forehead creased with confusion. 'They're not lawmen,' I told her, too exhausted to be scared. 'They're just more thieves.'

FORTY

'Look, Stubbs, I didn't count on getting killed,' said No Neck, wiping his forehead with his sleeve. 'Let's do what they say. We shoulda stuck with the original plan anyway, where we only got tied up. The pay was good for doing that much. We shouldn't a gotten greedy.'

'Shut up. We're sittin' pretty right here. Didn't you hear what they said? They think there's just the two of us. When Joe gets back, we'll have 'em from both sides with nowhere to hide. I say we stall.' And without waiting for No Neck to cast his vote, he leaned toward the broken window. 'You got yourself a deal, mister. Help yourself to the whiskey and never mind us. But come any closer to this here car and all bets are off.'

The sound of cases of whiskey being dragged and stacked drew me out from under the table. I peered over the windowsill. Four or five shadows were taking the whiskey off the small truck and loading it into their large one. They were the smart thieves, I thought. They'd brought a single, covered truck large enough to take the whole shipment and anybody they ran into would be none the wiser.

I dragged myself up to a bench seat and lay down. My limbs felt like lead. The night air made me shiver. Coffee, said my foggy brain. Coffee would help fight off that damned Veronal and warm me up besides.

And that's when the idea came to me. I swear it would have come sooner if my head hadn't been clogged with cotton stuffing, but at least it had come.

'Mr Stubbs? Excuse me, sir, but a nice cup of coffee would sure go down good right about now. Could I tell the waiter here to make us some? You might want some too. It would help keep you awake and alert while you wait to spring your trap.'

As Stubbs examined my proposal for tricks, No Neck spoke up. 'That'd be good, Jack. I could use some coffee.'

Stubbs gave a wordless nod. As Suddeth moved into the galley, Stubbs planted himself in the passageway by the galley door, gun firmly in hand. 'Just so you don't get any ideas. You so much as look at one of them knives and I shoot the ladies.' I heard the waiter opening and closing cabinet doors, clattering about in utensil drawers, and pouring water. No one was watching me as I took every packet of Veronal out of my handbag and stuffed them in my skirt pocket.

'I'll bet you could use some help, Suddeth,' I said as I slid past No Neck toward the galley. 'How do you like your coffee, mister? Cream or sugar?'

'Lotsa both,' he said.

'And you, Mr Stubbs?' He had the decency to look embarrassed.

'Uh, black.'

'Where is a tray, Suddeth?' I needed to put something between me and Stubbs so he wouldn't see me tear open the packets and stir in the powder. Suddeth reached above the stove and handed me a large silver tray. His dark eyes said he was puzzled, but I couldn't explain. I arranged several cups on the tray as Suddeth poured the coffee into a silver coffeepot.

'Mr Stubbs, sir, would you please ask the Misses Vandergrift how they take their coffee?'

I half expected him to snarl and cuss at me, but he meekly turned his attention away from me and relayed my question to the sisters. While his head was turned, I lifted the coffeepot lid and frantically began emptying the packets of Veronal. Suddeth caught on at once and positioned himself between me and Stubbs, blocking any glimpse of my actions.

I had no idea what sort of dose I was delivering, but this was no time to get stingy. As fast as I could, I dumped every packet I had into the coffee and then asked, 'Could I have a spoon, please?' He obliged and I stirred until the powder was dissolved. 'There. I think we're ready now. You carry the tray, Suddeth, it's too heavy for me. I'll serve.'

Together we walked back into the dining car and, starting with No Neck, handed out the coffee in china cups and saucers. I played it like a tea party in the Rockefeller parlor. 'One lump or two?' I asked him, and, 'Tell me when,' as I poured the cream. I stirred again, praying the taste would not be noticeable. Veronal is bitter when taken as one packet dissolved into water; what several packets in coffee tasted like, I could only guess.

No Neck took his cup and a big swallow. When he didn't blanch, I breathed more easily.

'Here, Miss Vandergrift,' I said, handing an empty cup to Eleanor. With my back to the thieves, I whispered, 'Just pretend!' Her eyes widened, but she took the cup and touched the rim to her lips.

'Perfect,' she said in a voice that carried to the men. 'I don't think Pamela will have any. She isn't a coffee drinker, are you, dear?'

Pamela, looking worse for wear, didn't respond.

'And I'll have cream in mine,' I said cheerily, bringing my own empty cup to my lips before turning to Stubbs. 'Here, Mr Stubbs. Are you sure you won't have any fresh cream or sugar? It's really too hot to drink right now.' I was desperately

worried about the taste. Without any cream and sugar to camou-
flage the bitterness, would he realize what was happening?

For an answer, he scowled, brought the cup to his lips and
took a swig. And a second one. I nearly fainted with relief.

Until without warning, he hurled the cup across the car. It
shattered into a dozen pieces. 'What is this pig swill?' he
shouted.

'Excuse me?' I stalled for time.

'Mine is delicious,' said Eleanor heroically. 'May I have
more?'

'Mine's good,' said No Neck, emptying his cup with a slurp.

Suddeth, ever the perfectly trained waiter, could not refrain
from kneeling to pick up the shards of china.

'Let me get you a refill, sir,' I said, picking up the tray and
pouring No Neck another cup, all the while frantically
searching for a way to get some more of the stuff into Stubbs.
'Mr Stubbs,' I said, moving toward the galley, 'how about a
fresh cup and see if you like that better?' I fetched a clean
cup and saucer from the cabinet, poured the last drop of coffee
in it, and set it on the tray. If he threw this one, we were
sunk.

'Here you go, Mr Stubbs. Perhaps sugar or cream would
help?' With a scowl for an answer, he took a swig, grimaced,
and set the cup on the table. My heart sank. Then, pulling his
bottle from his coat pocket, he poured a dollop of whisky into
the coffee and took several more gulps. Eleanor and I continued
to pretend to drink ours as I watched closely for some reaction
from the two thieves. I prayed Stubbs would finish the last
drop quickly, and he might have done so if No Neck hadn't
chosen that precise moment to slump unconscious to the floor.
Jack Stubbs watched him with an open mouth that clamped
shut as he realized he'd been had.

'What the hell's in this? What did you do, you liddle—'

Pulling out his revolver, Stubbs pointed it at Suddeth, still
mopping the floor at the other end of the dining car, and
prepared to fire. With not a spare second to consider the
options, I raised high the silver tray and brought it down on
the back of his head with every ounce of strength I possessed.
And then some.

I wasn't quick enough. Stubbs fired the gun, but my blow had knocked off his aim. He crumpled at my feet.

'Suddeth? Suddeth, are you all right?'

'Yes, Missy. He missed me, praise the Lord.'

'Quick! We need to find something to tie him up. That's— Oh, no. Oh, no!' As I looked toward the Misses Vandergrift, I saw Pamela, who had been sitting on the floor, slump over. The bullet meant for Suddeth had found her instead.

FORTY-ONE

I nearly tripped over Stubbs's body trying to get to Pamela at the other end of the car, but Eleanor was, of course, beside her tending to her. At that moment, a nervous voice from the platform stopped me cold.

'What's going on in there?'

No response would bring someone to investigate. A woman's voice, likewise. What could I say to reassure the outside thieves that the inside thieves were still in charge? The seconds ticked by as my drugged brain struggled to cope, and in the silence, I heard Eleanor whisper, 'Never you mind, Miss Beckett. Pamela has only fainted.' I nearly fainted myself as she fished in her enormous carpetbag for smelling salts to bring her sister around.

And then, Suddeth cupped his hands around his mouth to aim his voice toward the broken window and said, in an accent as white as any white man who ever spoke, 'Nothing to worry about, boys. Just shot an uppity nigger.'

Our eyes met. I couldn't speak. Suddeth grinned. 'Heck, Missy,' he whispered, 'I been fifteen years serving white folks. I 'spect I know how they talk.'

Knowing how someone talks and being able to imitate it are two very different skills, as anyone in vaudeville can tell you. True mimics are a rare breed. I didn't know what to say, so I said, 'Get his gun,' pointing to No Neck while I pried Stubbs's weapon out of his hand.

The nervous voice from outside said, 'Don't shoot the women, got that? You might need them later. Or we might.'

Suddeth cupped his hands around his mouth again. 'We don't need you to tell us that, mister.'

I gave the thumbs up signal to Suddeth, then gestured toward both ends of the dining car. 'You watch that door, I'll watch this one. Shoot anyone who tries to come in. No, wait. First we need to tie up these two in case they come to.'

'I know where there's twine,' he said, disappearing into the galley. He reappeared seconds later. Taking great care, he pulled Stubbs's arms behind his back and bound them tightly, then moved to No Neck and did the same.

'What was that you put in the coffee?' he asked.

'Just some sleeping powder I brought to help me sleep on the train. It's called Veronal. I took one a couple hours ago, and I'm about to fall over. Lord knows how much I stirred into the coffee. Everything I had.'

'Well, it worked,' said Eleanor. 'It was inspired!' The green bottle of smelling salts had brought Pamela around, although frankly, I thought it might have been better to let her stay unconscious and avoid all the fright. But I wasn't her sister.

'It was nothing,' I said modestly, although I thought it was pretty inspired myself.

'Honestly, I'm amazed I can even think straight, I'm so tired.' To prove it, I gave a great yawn.

'Things are quiet now,' said Eleanor, 'so you can nod off. We'll wake you if need be.'

But from the platform, where the five thieves were transferring the hooch from the boss's truck to the larger one, a man's voice said, 'Hey, where's the rest of the whiskey? This ain't all of it.' One of them had, I knew, climbed into the office car, discovered it was not full, and asked the obvious question. I braced myself.

The answer was an explosion of gunfire.

No one could see us inside the dining car with the shades drawn. Nonetheless, I felt safer crouching as I darted to the edge of one windowsill and lifted the shade to peer out. In the feeble light of the depot's single bulb, I saw the crooks who had been transferring the whiskey dive for cover even as they drew their own weapons. A new act had joined the line-up, and I knew who it was. The boss and Pockmark had returned, right on schedule.

Judging from the direction of the gunfire, they had situated themselves on opposite sides of the platform, one on the rocks and another behind the depot, where they could shoot at the upstarts from shelter. I put myself in their shoes. They would not have been entirely surprised at the appearance of the interlopers, but one thing was clear. They would expect friendly fire from inside the dining car to help them out.

'Suddeth,' I called softly. 'Shoot a few times out the window into the air.' I didn't need to explain the reason to him. This was one smart waiter. He nodded and let loose a shot or two.

So did I. The recoil knocked me off my heels. Sure, I'd fired guns before, but they'd all been loaded with blanks for the stage. It seemed real bullets packed a wallop. I gripped the gun with both hands this time and braced myself before firing again. Suddeth was smiling at my predicament.

This went on for maybe half an hour. I never knew exactly what happened outside, but someone must've circled around behind the boss and Pockmark and let them have it, because finally, the shooting stopped. The night grew quiet. The silence lengthened. I could hear my heart beat in my ears. As I tried to adjust to this new reality, the dining car door nearest me burst open.

I whirled around, pointing Stubbs's gun toward the door and prepared to blast the intruder to kingdom come.

'Jeez, kid, don't shoot. It's me.'

I blinked twice in disbelief. My mouth dropped open with shock. It was David Carr.

FORTY-TWO

This was a David Carr I did not know. Looking tense and as ruthless as any hired killer, he took two cautious steps into the dining car, gun at the ready. His ice-blue eyes scanned the room for a reason to pull the trigger. When he saw the two thieves out cold on the floor with their arms firmly tied behind their backs, his features relaxed and the David I knew reappeared.

Pushing the brim of his hat back a bit from his forehead, he drawled, 'Nice work, kid. I shoulda known you wouldn't need rescuing. You mind putting that gun down, pal?' He turned to Suddeth, who was still crouched in the rear of the car, perplexed but ready to shoot. 'She'll vouch for me. The excitement's over for now.' He prodded Stubbs with the toe of his boot and when he had no response, sent me a question with his eyes.

'We put sleeping powder in their coffee. That one didn't finish his so I had to brain him with the tray.' The dented silver tray lay on the floor where I'd dropped it.

David leaned toward the broken window and called to his men, 'No trouble in here. Two men tied up good. Get back to work.' Then he turned to the Vandergrift sisters and took off his hat. 'Everything's all right now, ladies. My name's David Carr, and I'm a friend of Miss Beckett here. And you might be . . .?'

'I'm Eleanor Vandergrift and this is my sister Pamela. We are very pleased to meet you, Mr Carr.'

'Miss Pamela, pardon me, ma'am, but you are looking poorly. Is there anything I can get you? Some water? Some whiskey?'

David's aw-shucks manner charmed the Misses Vandergrift and soon both women were simpering like girls.

'I'll be fine, Mr Carr.'

'My sister is ill, Mr Carr, and her medicine is on the train that left us here.'

'Well, I'm sure the porter will hold your belongings at your stop, and it won't be long before an engine gets here to take you on your way.'

All this front-parlor politeness was more than I could handle. I struggled up off the floor on to one of the benches and laid Stubbs's gun on the tablecloth. It looked odd beside the neatly folded linen napkin and perfectly positioned silverware. Making sense of what was going on was giving me a throbbing head,

but there was one thing I latched on to pretty quick. 'So now
it's you stealing the whiskey?'

'Me?' David blessed us with his most wounded expression.
'Hell, no! Oh, excuse me, ladies. Heck, no, Jessie. This shipment belongs to me. Bought and paid for. Lock, stock and
legal, and I've got the federal withdrawal permits to prove it.'
He patted his breast pocket. 'Me and my men are just rescuing
it from these thieves who were trying to steal it.'

Out the window, David's men holstered their weapons and
were preparing to resume the transfer of the whiskey from
office car to truck.

'Why . . . why are you loading the truck, then?'

'The truck'll be quicker. And safer.'

I yawned as I struggled to follow that logic. Before I could
reply, one of the men climbed into the dining car, looking for
David.

'Some of the whiskey is missing. What's on the truck and
what's in the private car doesn't add up to the whole load.'

'I'm coming,' said David.

The two men exited the dining car just as three gunshots
rang out and a voice from the darkness called, 'Everyone
freeze, and get your hands where we can see them.'

All I could think was, *Not again.*

FORTY-THREE

No need to caution the sisters to stay down – they were
pros at dodging bullets by now. Without a word, I
snatched up my gun and scrambled out of the dining
car and on to the platform behind David.

'This is Sheriff Barnes,' the voice continued. 'I got lots of
deputies here – let's hear it, deputies.' A chorus of voices
testified to their presence. 'And some Federals too, so you're
outnumbered by a country mile. No need for anybody to get
hurt long as you get your hands in the air.'

Without turning his head, David whispered, 'Hang on to

your gun.' Then he called out, 'Fair enough,' as he set his gun
on the ground. 'If you're the sheriff, step up and show us your
badge.'

He did. Out of the shadows he came, looking not a bit like
one of those sheriffs from the westerns who wear ten-gallon
hats, spurs and fringed vests. This man had on a rumpled suit
and a fedora like any small-town businessman. He had a scar
on his forehead and a badge on his lapel.

When David was satisfied, he broke into a wide smile. 'Well,
Sheriff, I am sure glad to see you! Wish you'd been here an
hour ago, we coulda used the help. But now, everything's
under control and there's nothing for your men to do. The
thieves outside are dead, but there are two more inside the
dining car all trussed up that you can have with our blessing.
This here's Miss Beckett, one of the passengers who got caught
up in the fracas. There are two more ladies on board and one
waiter. I'm David Carr, the owner of this shipment of medicinal
alcohol that they were trying to steal in that big truck. We
were just loading the cartons back on to the train when you
fellas surprised us.'

With that bit of effrontery, he pulled the ownership papers
from inside his breast pocket and surrendered them to the
sheriff who took them over to the depot light where he and
one of the federal agents began passing them back and forth.

I looked around uneasily. Something was wrong. 'Where is
the stationmaster? And the cook?' I asked David.

'Who?'

I spoke up louder so everybody could hear. 'I don't see the
stationmaster or the cook. Are they around anywhere?' When
there was no response, I continued. 'Two of the thieves took
them along on the truck to hide a load of whiskey. They came
back for another load and went off again. Aren't they in the
truck? The stationmaster is a little man, bald. The cook is
colored and wears a white jacket.'

One of the deputies took off down the road to check the
small truck that had been abandoned by the boss and Pockmark.
He trotted back after a few minutes. 'Truck's empty.'

'I have a bad feeling about this,' I said to David. 'Those
two little trucks weren't enough to hold all the cartons, so the

boss decided to hide them someplace until he could return
with a bigger truck. He took three trips, alternating trucks,
and took the stationmaster and the cook with him to help
unload. He made the stationmaster show him someplace to
hide the whiskey.' I looked over at the one small truck abandoned beside the tracks. 'I think two more truckloads would
have done it. Which means he'd have the four of them on the
last run in two trucks, and wouldn't need the cook and the
stationmaster . . . and they knew about the hiding place.'

David wasn't one to mince words. 'Then they're dead.'

Sheriff Barnes and the Federal returned to David and handed
back his papers. 'Looks like everything's in order, Mr Carr.
You can continue loading your whiskey back on to the train.
The railroad is sending an engine quick, so the incoming train
won't find the tracks blocked. Now, you, Miss Beckett, is it?'
I nodded. 'Let's see about these other thieves.'

David and the sheriff followed me into the dining car where
the Vandergrifts and Suddeth were waiting anxiously. I thought
it best to give them the bad news straight up.

'We can't find the cook and the stationmaster. It isn't
certain, but it looks like . . . well, it looks like they may be
dead. The boss thief probably shot them when he didn't
need them any longer. And to get rid of witnesses.' Suddeth
and the Vandergrift sisters took the news in silence, so I
cleared my throat and introduced the sheriff. 'This is Sheriff
Barnes and his deputy . . . uhhh . . .'

'Rankin.'

'Deputy Rankin. And these are the Misses Vandergrift and
Suddeth, the waiter.'

The sheriff tipped his hat, but his interest focused on the
trussed-up crooks on the floor. 'What happened?' he asked.

'Well,' I began, trying to marshal my thought so that I
explained in a coherent manner. 'They drank some coffee with
a sleeping powder and—'

The deputy crouched down beside No Neck and put his
fingers on his throat. Then he pulled a small mirror out of his
pocket and held it to the man's nose. 'This man's dead as a
mummy, sheriff.'

'What!' I nearly choked.

Sheriff Barnes knelt beside Jack Stubbs. 'So's this one. Just how much sleeping powder was in that coffee, Miss Beckett?'

'I . . . I don't know.'

'Are you responsible for this?'

'I, um, y-yes. I dumped everything I had into the coffee pot.'

'So you killed them?'

'I didn't mean to . . .'

'She didn't do it alone,' said Suddeth in a firm voice. 'I gave them the coffee.'

'And I helped,' said Eleanor.

'And I wanted to help,' said Pamela. 'We did it together. It was self-defense.'

'They killed the stationmaster and the cook,' said Eleanor. 'That one tried to shoot our waiter. They would have shot us next if it hadn't been for Jessie.'

The sheriff didn't need to give this much thought. 'Under the circumstances, I don't think there will be any charges. But what kind of sleeping powder kills people?'

'Veronal. I took a packet myself a couple of hours ago. I had no idea it was so powerful. The empty papers are in the galley.'

The deputy ducked into the kitchen to count. 'Nine papers. For two men? That's a helluva Mickey Finn.'

'You know who these men are?' asked the sheriff.

'Well,' I said, 'that one's name is Jack Stubbs, but I don't think it's his real name.'

'Why not?'

'Intuition.'

'And this one?'

I could only shake my head. It seemed sad to bury a man with no name for the tombstone. A lost soul in every sense. 'I don't know the names of any of them, except the boss, the one with the moustache and the slicked back hair. They called him Joe.'

'Grab his legs, Rankin. We'll get these two in the truck with the others and take 'em back to Holbrook as soon as the engine gets here. You folks will be on your way soon.' The unspoken implication was not lost on us: they would stick around to make sure the whiskey went safely on its way too.

As soon as the bodies made their exit, David drew me aside. 'I'm proud of you, kid, don't get me wrong. Still, I'm sorry they're both dead. I was counting on them to tell me where they stashed the rest of the whiskey. Unless I can find the stationmaster or the cook . . .'

I was sorry too. I'd never killed anyone before. Even by accident. Knowing they were going to kill us took the edge off my regret but didn't quite settle my stomach. And I was so very, very sleepy.

'Will you come back with us on the train?'

'Can't. I gotta start searching for that whiskey. More than half of it's gone missing. And no one alive knows where they stashed it.'

'I know.' His astonished expression made me laugh out loud. 'I heard them talking.'

'Then you're coming with me.'

Someone called out, 'Here comes the train,' and every face turned west. A pinhead light hung in the distance like a star low on the horizon, gradually getting brighter as it drew closer. The engine chugged into the station a short time later. Two men jumped off to hook up the cars.

Saying goodbye to Suddeth and the Vandergrift sisters proved surprisingly awkward. In the space of a few harrowing hours, we had whiplashed from knowing one another not at all, to a degree of intimacy shared only by people who had faced death together. It seemed impossible that we would never meet again.

David kept his arm tight around my shoulders as we sat in the front of the truck. One of his men drove while another rode in the back. He'd sent the other two to ride with the whisky as guards. I guided them seven miles west, then began squinting into the distance as I searched for sheds on my left. I don't think I'd have found it but for the nearly full moon that washed the desert with its pale light.

'There,' I said at last. The driver pulled off the road, making his own way across the desert toward the boxy silhouette.

'Stay here,' said David, and I was only too glad to comply. If the stationmaster and the cook were lying dead inside, I didn't want to see it.

As David and his two men headed toward the ramshackle building, I couldn't stop myself from thinking that something wasn't right with the entire evening's script. Like adding two plus two and coming up with three, some part of the equation had gone missing. How had David known . . .? Why was he . . .? Where did the . . .? I wanted badly to sort it all out, but I couldn't complete a single sentence. My thoughts felt thick as syrup.

The Veronal never gave up. I put my head down on the truck's seat and gave in.

FORTY-FOUR

C risp sheets and the drone of an electric fan told me I was in a fine place even before I opened my eyes to bright daylight. Someone had painted the ceiling and walls of this hotel room a cheerful, sky-blue color and furnished it with an iron bed and an oak chair and table. I was alone, but the dent in the pillow beside my head suggested that hadn't always been the case. The oscillating fan sent waves of cool wind across my bare skin. I was wearing nothing but my pink cotton step-in. I had no idea where I was or what time it was, but I was not confused or worried about it.

The hotel room was blessed with a private bathroom, and I wasted no time drawing a tub full of cool water. My stomach growled at the delay, but after three days on the train and a heart-stopping scare, I needed a bath more than I needed food. Besides, my clothes and shoes had vanished, so I could hardly leave the room in search of something to eat. Stepping out of my step-in, I soaked in the tub, immersing my head and scrubbing myself from hair to toe with a bar of lavender soap. After I had toweled off, I washed the step-in in the tub water and hung it across a ladder-back chair by the window to dry. With nothing of my own to wear, I fished through David's valise until I found a clean shirt. It was almost as long as my day frock.

Clutching David's comb, I sat between the window and the
fan to dry my hair. I didn't have a lovely, sleek bob like Louise
Brooks or a well-behaved, wavy bob like Gloria Swanson –
every strand of my hair had a different opinion on how my head
should look, and it took considerable effort to coax them into
some measure of agreement. The window opened on to a quiet
side street where only the occasional pedestrian passed by. As
I combed the tangles out of my hair, I thought about what I
was going to do when David returned. Seeing him yesterday
had been better medicine than any restorative on the market. I
was through trying to convince myself that I wasn't crazy about
him. I wanted him and I knew he wanted me. It was time.

The warm, desert air dried my hair in no time, but I was
still sitting beside the window when the door cracked open
and David peered into the room.

'Ah, you're awake.'

He came in with his arms full of parcels wrapped in brown
paper, saw what I was wearing, blinked twice and gulped.
'Holy Moses! My shirt's never looked that good in its life.'

'You didn't leave me anything else to wear.'

'I . . . well, that is . . . I needed to take your clothes with
me to show the, uh, the, uh, store clerks so I could, uh, buy
you some clean things . . . the right size.'

I met his eyes with an unmistakable invitation. 'I saw a
drug store out the window on the corner, if you don't have—'

'I do. Right here.'

'Well, then,' I said, standing up and starting with the top
button, 'let me give you back your shirt.'

Motionless, he watched as I took my time working down
the row until I reached the last button, then, like the performer
I had always been and would always be, teased his shirt off
my shoulders and let it fall to the floor, then sat naked on the
bed. 'I'm afraid I'm a little out of practice.'

'I don't mind.'

Dropping his parcels along with the last shred of his compo-
sure, he fumbled with the buttons on his own shirt and trousers,
nearly tearing them off, so impatient was he to take me in his
arms. He was beside me in the bed, wearing nothing but
his personality, before his clothes had hit the floor.

We came together so eagerly and explosively that the fun was over all too soon. Laughing at our haste, we curled up together to rest before helping ourselves to seconds.

'If that was you out of practice, I'm keen to see what's in store when you get a few rehearsals behind you.'

A few quiet minutes passed as we lay still, savoring the rhythmic sweep of the fan and the breeze that wafted across our damp skin. Finally I broke the silence.

'So, where are we?'

'Heaven.'

'And after that?'

'Holbrook. We got here last night just before dawn. You were completely out.'

That I could believe, although I felt no lasting effects from the Veronal. 'Where's your whiskey?'

'Probably in Los Angeles by now,' he said, turning on to his side and drawing circles on my shoulder with one finger.

'Was it all there in the shed?'

'Yep. I had the boys drop us here and sent them ahead in the truck. We'll go home by train later today.'

'What about the whiskey in the office car?'

'That's in Los Angeles by now too. Someone will meet the train and take care of it.'

His fingers moved to my breasts. His mouth followed.

'Someone you trust?'

'Mmm-hm.'

'You trusted the three guards and they double-crossed you.'

'Mmm-hm.'

That they'd ended up dead would not be lost on the current crop of employees.

'Were you expecting the double-cross?'

He looked up in surprise. 'What? Why would you think that?'

Why *would* I think that? I was having trouble marshalling my thoughts. 'Because . . . because you were there with a truck when they tried to steal your whiskey.'

'We were planning to unload the shipment here in Holbrook and take it the rest of the way by truck.'

'Why?'

'Safer.'

He kissed me until I couldn't think straight and didn't want to. There would be time for talk later. Now it was time for another rehearsal, one that was slower and more intense and infinitely more satisfying than any I'd ever known. All I could think – when I could think – was how good we were together and how crazy I was about this man.

FORTY-FIVE

'Y ou must be starving,' David said later. 'The hotel has a decent restaurant downstairs. Let's get something to eat.'

Clothes dry in a jiffy in the arid desert air, so my underwear was ready to put on again. I tore open the parcels to see what David had bought.

'The shop girls took your size from your old clothes and shoes. This is what they recommended. The store is only a block away – I can run these back for something else if you don't like them . . .'

No need for that. The railroad brought up-to-date merchandise to every town with a depot, linking women all over the country to as much big-city fashion as they wanted. Inside the box was a fetching pale blue and white frock in the popular straight profile with cap sleeves, a scooped neckline, and delicate cutwork piercing the bodice and hem – a dress that could have come out of any Hollywood shop. Those shop girls had David's number, all right. Taking their helpless customer in hand, they included such necessities as sheer white stockings, a cunning pair of thin-strapped shoes, matching gloves, and a white straw cloche with a dainty forget-me-not flourish. I hadn't been so fashionably attired since I'd impersonated the heiress.

The town was small, the hotel was small and the dining room was small, but the kitchen was open and the food tasted like big-city cooking to me. David watched with a satisfied grin as I polished off a lettuce salad, fruit cocktail, fried chicken, potatoes, snap beans, buttered cornbread, cherry pie, and vanilla ice cream and asked for a second scoop of the ice cream. When we finished, he pulled out his pocket watch.

'You feeling better now?'

I sighed happily. 'Much better, thank you.'

'Glad to oblige, madam. The next train's due in thirty minutes. You want to catch that one or wait for the one after? It comes in about four hours.'

'I'm ready now. I've nothing to pack.'

It took five minutes to gather up our things in the blue room and check out.

'You look so pretty, I think I'll buy all your clothes from now on.' It was the 'from now on' part that made me feel I was floating out the door.

We strolled hand-in-hand to the station, keeping to the shady side of the street where the breeze robbed the heat of its power. When forced to cross to the depot, we sizzled in the sun like fish in a frying pan.

The westbound train pulled into the station two minutes ahead of schedule. After we'd found our seats and had spoken to the porter, we went directly to the dining car to order iced drinks. I almost expected to see Suddeth there.

'That table in the back, please,' David said to the waiter, pointing to the far end of the car where there were several empty tables. As soon as we'd given the waiter our beverage order, David lowered his voice and leaned toward me. 'There's no one near enough to hear us. So tell me, what did you learn?'

Neither the incident at Navajo Springs nor even the goings-on in the blue room had knocked Ruby Glynn out of my thoughts. I had so much to report, I hardly knew where to start. So I started at the end.

'Ricardo Delacruz is not Cuban. He's a Negro passing as white.'

David's eyes grew wide. He gave a low whistle as the implications sank in. 'Geez Louise. Jumping the color line? If that gets out, getting strung up will be the least of his problems.'

'Back when he was a boy and his name was Sam Jeter, he

toured with Jessup and Shadney, an acrobat act listed on that
1910 program I found in Lila Walker's address book. Somehow,
Lila found out.' As David listened, I filled him in on my last
few weeks in vaudeville. 'I went to Hattiesburg to look up
Jessup. Before I could meet him, he was killed in a logging
accident – only it wasn't an accident. His widow didn't know
anything about the vaudeville years, but a nephew who used
to perform with the act was there. He showed me an old picture
of the act and right there, front and center, is young Ricardo
Delacruz. His real name's Sam Jeter, and he's from Florida.
Seems he grew up with some Cubans – must've gotten the
idea of passing as a Cuban from them.'

'So you think Delacruz was behind Jessup's death?'

'He must have been. It's my fault Jessup got killed. Delacruz
wouldn't have known I was in the area if it wasn't for my
telegrams. There I was, like an idiot, letting him know exactly
what I was doing and what I was thinking and how close I
was getting to the truth.' As I talked, I was seized with the
urgent desire to race home and get the police to arrest this
man who had caused so much pain. But arrest him for what?

David shook his head. 'How could you have known?'

'I should have been more suspicious. Why would the man
be sending me money and not paying for a real private
investigator?'

'Because you probably do a better job than a dozen so-called
real investigators, that's why. They didn't turn up anything
when he did hire them, before the trial.' He drummed his
fingers on the table and looked thoughtful. 'So you think
Delacruz killed Lila Walker? And left Ruby Glynn to take the
rap?'

'Maybe. I don't know.'

'Then how did he do it? How did he get into her rooms
and out again?'

'I'm still working on that. But I'm sure he was there, in the
closet. When Lila seemed to point to Ruby, she was really
pointing to the closet.'

'D'you think Ruby has been covering for him?'

'I don't know.'

'So what's next? You can ruin him with this and likely get

him killed, but you have no real evidence against him for Lila's death, so you can't clear Ruby Glynn.'

'I need him to confess.'

David snorted at the likelihood of that.

'I know he's not going to do it voluntarily, or he would have by now, so I need to trick him into confessing. I've got a plan.'

'Shoot.'

'When we get back to Hollywood, I'll telephone him and tell him I have some important news. I'll ask him to meet me at your house where we can be alone. When he arrives, I'll get him talking – I haven't scripted this part yet – but somehow, I'll tell him what I've learned and get him to admit his part in the killings. So we don't have to take my word for it, I'll have people hiding in the kitchen and in that coat closet by your front door who will overhear his confession. The police can arrest him after he leaves, and the eavesdroppers can testify against him in court.'

He stared silently out the window, deep in thought, his iced tea forgotten.

'We'll need a couple of important people to listen in,' I continued. 'People whose words are respected and who'll be believed in court. I was thinking of Douglas, for one.'

David shook his head. 'That could be seen as Doug getting rid of a younger rival. There's jealousy there, and it's widely known he doesn't like Delacruz.'

'Mary Pickford, then?'

'Doug will never allow it. Too much of the wrong kind of publicity. Not to mention dangerous. What if Delacruz checks the closet? If you're correct about him hiding in the closet in Lila's room, he'll be primed for that trick. And what if he brings a weapon and goes on a rampage? Besides, Doug and Mary haven't returned from their ocean voyage.'

'A cop, then. I have a cop friend who might do it.'

'The one who's always sniffing around you?'

I should have realized that David had noticed Carl Delaney's attentions. 'Him, yes, his partner, or another cop. Someone who could arrest Delacruz on the spot.'

He continued to stare out the window.

'Look, David, I know the plan isn't perfect yet, but it could work. And I don't have anything else. When there's no proof, our only chance to save Ruby Glynn is a confession. And we have only a little more than a week.'

'Lemme think about it.'

I sighed and played with my ice. We sat in silence for a while, our eyes fixed on the landscape as it moved past the window like a film on a theater screen. Speaking of traps, I'd been caught in one myself. If I did nothing, Ruby Glynn would die. If I exposed Ricardo Delacruz, he would die. There had been a lot of death clinging to me lately, and I was heartily sick of it. One man in Hattiesburg, seven men in Navajo Springs. Not all of them were my fault, but I'd played a part in each, and I despised my role.

'I feel pretty bad about killing those two men. I wish they'd gone to prison instead. I swear I'll never look at a packet of Veronal again if I live to be a hundred!'

'You can't think like that, Jessie. You didn't mean to kill them. And they weren't innocent bystanders like the cook and stationmaster.'

I summoned up enough courage to ask the question, even though I knew the answer. 'Did you find them in that shed?'

'Yep. The way I figure it, they planned to get rid of the bodies when they returned with the last two trucks full. Dumped in the desert somewhere, their corpses would be picked clean by vultures in a day. They'd've killed you too – you and those two old biddies and that waiter. You knew where they took the whiskey.'

'They didn't know I knew. I overheard them talking.'

'But you could identify them. All of you. And you can only hang once.'

I gave him a puzzled look.

'Once you've killed two people, you've nothing to lose by killing four more. Frankly, I wouldn't be surprised if Joe hadn't planned to kill off Stubbs and the others once he'd moved the whiskey to a safer place – you said he killed one man before we even got there. Fewer to share.'

I wondered if David had killed any of the men in the gunfight at Navajo Springs. Probably. I didn't want to know. But there was something I did want to know, something I didn't understand.

'Why did you pretend you'd been putting the whiskey back on to the train? You were taking it off the train and loading your truck, and when the federal agents showed up, you pretended you'd been putting it back.'

He gave a sigh of resignation. 'You remember I told you how I bought that carload of whiskey, fair and square? Government bonded, nothing illegal about it, right?'

'That's true, isn't it?'

'Utterly true. Remember that.'

I nodded warily, certain that I was not going to like what was coming.

'Well, you see, I had a plan . . .' He began a bit sheepishly, but as his story unfolded, his pace picked up and his voice tightened with excitement. 'A foolproof plan to double my money and then some. Naturally, I'd insured the whiskey, and that got me thinking that if the whiskey got stolen on its way to Los Angeles, I'd be reimbursed its full value. So I set it up so a few of my men would meet the train in Holbrook, uncouple the last two cars, and take it to Los Angeles by truck. You can't steal from yourself, so I wasn't doing anything illegal. That way, I would have the whiskey to sell in the drug store with prescriptions, like always, and the insurance money, plus I'd save tens of thousands of dollars by not paying the government tax that comes due when you take possession of bonded liquor. Because they'd think it had been stolen, see?' He couldn't stifle his boyish delight in the scheme.

I searched his guileless eyes for a glimmer of remorse and came away with nothing but clear blue sincerity. Either I was looking at the world's most accomplished actor or a con man who had capped his career by conning himself.

'Go on,' I said.

'The three guards were in on it, of course. We arranged that my men would tie them up so it would look like a real robbery and not a put-up job. I paid those three very handsomely, I might add. They knew what was coming and knew not to put up a fight. This very simple plan got messed up when those thieving bastards put everything into one car instead of two.

Then they betrayed my trust and recruited a couple of their friends to steal my whiskey in Navajo Springs, one stop before it was supposed to get stolen in Holbrook, where my boys were waiting with the truck. And they never let their friends know that they only needed to uncouple one car.' He shook his head at the stupidity of the crooks. 'I hadn't intended to be in Holbrook at all for such a simple job, but when I got your telegram, I realized you were going to be on the same train. I tried to wire back to tell you to take a later train, but you'd left the telegraph office. I don't mind telling you, kid, that started me worrying, just in case anything was to go wrong.'

We paused as the waiter came by to refill our iced tea. When he'd retreated a good distance, David resumed his tale.

'So I jumped the train to Holbrook where I could oversee the whole operation myself, and it's a damn good thing I did. When I learned that a dining car had gone missing along with my private car, and the porter said you'd been in the dining car, my heart almost stopped beating.' He reached over and took my hand in his, and placed it over his heart so I could feel it throb. 'Thank God you're safe. You know, Jessie, the whiskey, the money, the taxes, none of it matters to me like you do.' And he leaned across the table and gave me a brief kiss that failed to wash away my vexation.

Part of me wanted to throttle him for deceiving me yet again and for putting himself and others in such danger; another part wanted to throw my arms around him for caring enough about me to come out and handle the heist personally. And all of me wanted to drag him to the nearest bed and ignore everything except the pleasure of his body beneath, beside, on top and inside mine.

I disguised the war going on in my head by staring intently out the window, as if there was something fascinating about the endless scrub landscape flying by.

David and I stayed in the dining car sipping drinks and sucking ice cubes until the sun set and the outside temperature had dropped before we moved back to our seats in first class. We didn't say much. He knew I was upset; I knew he was thinking about my plan. After a while, he broke the silence.

'It will be late when we arrive at the station. And then we need to track down your luggage. I could drive you to your place, but you'd wake up your friends. How about staying with me tonight?'

I wanted nothing more than an entire night in bed with David, but I hesitated before answering, letting him stew a bit to keep his self-confidence in check. When he bit his lower lip, I gave in.

'That's good of you to be so concerned about my friends.'

'Well . . .'

'I'll stay.'

He took my hand and dropped a kiss on my knuckles. 'That's swell. Now, listen to this. I've been thinking about your plan, and I have an idea.'

Which made me wonder. Would he have told me his idea if I hadn't agreed to stay the night?

FORTY-SIX

'Here he comes. Places, everyone.'

Like a seasoned film director, David issued orders in a calm voice, setting off a flurry of motion as the actors and technicians in our drama took their positions, barely breathing, moving into position on sock feet as quiet as cats' paws. David left his post by the front window and prepared to follow Rob Handler and his assistant up the stairs. First, though, he locked eyes with mine.

'You ready, kid?'

Taking a deep breath, I nodded. Outside, a car door slammed. David gave me a thumbs-up and disappeared. The house grew so still, it was hard to believe I was not alone. The living room looked much the same as it had when David moved in a few weeks ago, save for the addition of a dried flower arrangement on the coffee table and a metallic chandelier too large for the ceiling. All of the wires had been painted white to blend with the ceiling or tan to match the wooden floor where scatter rugs didn't cover them. Rip dozed in his usual spot on the hearth rug by the fireplace. Untroubled by curiosity, he'd ignored the strangers traipsing in and out of the doors since morning, nor had he shown any interest in the equipment they carried. Now he watched with one eye as his master crept up the stairs, then he shut it and heaved a sleepy sigh.

The stage was set. The afternoon sun shone through the picture window that overlooked the backyard. A cross breeze swept in through the open sidelights and out through the windows that opened on to the front porch, windows that allowed me to hear every one of Ricardo Delacruz's footsteps as he came up the stone walk and, even louder, when he reached the steps and crossed the porch.

He paused so long I almost panicked, thinking he had noticed something odd or had sensed something amiss. At last he cleared his throat and rang the bell, and I let my breath out. In my head, I could hear the director say, 'Camera.'

I walked toward the door. I was just an actress playing a role, I reminded myself. I knew my lines and my vaudeville experience would stand me in good stead if forced to ad-lib. I was perfectly safe. David was upstairs, Carl Delaney was guarding the kitchen door, his partner, Officer Brickles, was stationed at the back, and two more cops were hiding in the bushes beside the street near Delacruz's car in case he made a run for it. What could go wrong? I opened the door.

Ricardo Delacruz had come alone, as I knew he would. He was splendidly dressed in a striped, double-breasted sack suit with a silk shirt and full trousers. Removing his Panama hat, he gave a courtly nod of his head. 'Señorita Beckett. Good afternoon.' He gave me a tight smile. I did not return it.

'Won't you come in, Mr Delacruz?'

The next few moments would establish our positions, and it was critical that I steer him to the middle of the living room. So as he stepped into the entrance hall, I closed the door behind him and, without offering to take his hat, walked into the living room. 'This way, please.'

Manners required I offer him something to drink, but I did not. I couldn't risk going into the kitchen myself or letting him wander in there. I made my way directly to the sofa where

I sat, putting the coffee table between us. A sweep of my arm invited him to take the chair opposite me. 'Please, make yourself comfortable.'

He did not follow. Pausing at the edge of the living room, he looked around cautiously, without haste, as if seized by a sudden passion for interior decorating.

'Are we alone?'

Had he heard something? Sensed something? It was clear he no longer trusted me. I did not let the tension show in my voice.

'As you can see . . . except for the dog.'

Still, Delacruz did not move. After some long seconds, he walked to the closet by the front door and flung it open. With no ceremony, he pushed aside the coats to make sure there was no one hiding behind them. I sighed with relief, thinking of my original idea to hide a listener in there. I should have known the closet would be the first place this man would look. I should have expected him to be suspicious. In my telephone call that morning, I told him I'd returned home early and had something important to report. He wanted to know at once. I said I couldn't talk over the telephone for fear someone might be listening in at the switchboard. He wanted to meet me at Musso & Frank's restaurant, but I stressed the need for privacy and insisted he come to David's address. I should have sent a telegram; all this back-and-forth had put him on his guard.

Without glancing at me, he walked into the kitchen, turning his head from right to left. Seeing no one, he jerked open a broom closet and jumped back as a mop fell forward. Grabbing it self-consciously, he shoved it inside and slammed the door.

At last he came into the living room.

I pointed to the chair that had been positioned close to the coffee table. 'Have a seat.'

With a phony smile, he sat, leaning back and crossing his legs, making a show of looking relaxed. 'I was glad to learn you had returned home. But I received your message with a heavy heart, because I fear your investigation is at an end and you had no success. Is it not so?'

'Yes, my investigation is finished. But I did learn something.'

His eyebrows arched in surprise. 'You can prove my Ruby is innocent?'

I shook my head. 'No, I'm afraid I can't.'

I am sure I saw a flicker of relief in his sad eyes. He leaned forward. 'Then I must thank you from the bottom of my heart for your efforts and offer—'

'But *you* can.'

'I?'

'You've always had the ability to prove her innocence. All you had to do was confess that it was you who stabbed Lila Walker moments before Ruby arrived.'

'I?' Now his acting experience paid off. His fingers touched his chest and his expression showed wonderment. 'How could I have done such a crime? I was far away.'

'I will tell you how. Please correct me if I make any mistakes. You came to DeWitt's that Saturday and hid in the bushes on the side of the house until the coast was clear. You're strong and used to doing your own stunts, so it was possible, if difficult, for you to jump up to the fire escape and pull yourself up the way a gymnast would. Then you climbed in the third-floor water-closet window, which was always left ajar and slipped into Lila's room when the hall was clear. You'd done it once or twice before, when you and Lila were having an affair. She had to have been the one to suggest it the first time, because you had no way of knowing where the fire escape led until you'd been inside. How am I doing so far?'

'Go on, please. This is most amusing.'

'Lila had developed a lucrative blackmail business. She was good at learning people's secrets and getting paid to keep them quiet. She learned something about you. When you couldn't come to an agreement on price, you stabbed her moments before Ruby knocked. In a panic, you dropped the knife and ducked into the only place large enough to hide you: the closet. From there, you heard everything. You heard Ruby scream when she saw Lila. You heard the girls rush in and soon after, the police. You heard their questions. Lila was trying to tell the police that her killer was still there, in the closet. She kept pointing to the closet and Ruby had the misfortune to be sitting on the floor in front of the closet, so it looked like Lila was accusing her.'

At this point, he squirmed a little in the chair and bit his lower lip.

'You stayed in the closet, not daring to move, until the rooms were empty. Then you left the way you came. As certain as I am of this, I have no proof, no evidence. So you got away with murder, as the saying goes. And I have nothing to use to free Ruby. You do, but you won't.'

'This story is so much fantasy, señorita. Why would I do such a crime? I did not love Lila, this is true. She was very cruel to my Ruby. But that is no reason to kill her.'

'You had the best reason of all. She'd learned your secret and threatened to expose you.'

'I have no—'

'Your real name is Sam Jeter. You're from Florida, by way of Mississippi, and you've been passing as Cuban for the last five years.'

'Madre de Dios!'

'Oh, cut the Spanish, Sam! You're no more Cuban than I am. Is that what made Lila suspicious in the first place – the language? You can usually fake it with a few phrases and the phony accent, but she must have known a little more than most.'

'You are very confused—'

'I certainly was, until I reached Hattiesburg, where I learned the truth about your background.'

'Impossible,' he said, his eyes shifting from side to side as if to reassure himself we were alone. 'You did not arrive until after Hal Jessup was killed. You told me so in your telegram.'

'Very true,' I said, watching him bite the inside of his cheek with mounting nervousness. 'But at the funeral, his widow showed me a photograph of her husband's old vaudeville act, Jessup and Shadney. You haven't changed that much in fifteen years. And your old friend, Ray Pigram, came home for his uncle's funeral. Were you planning to kill Ray and Frank too, in case they recognized you on the screen?'

'I killed no one,' he said angrily, his voice growing louder with every word. 'Dozens of people will tell you I was here in California!' He slammed his hand on the table for emphasis, shaking the flower arrangement. I noticed with horror that the microphone was slumping to its side. I spoke quickly to distract Delacruz from the microphone's movement.

'You arranged to have Hal Jessup meet with an accident.'

'As you say, you have no evidence for this either.'

'I have no evidence for the two murders, but I have evidence for your real identity.'

He shrugged in an effort to appear nonchalant. It didn't work. 'An old photograph that looks a little like me? I am not concerned.' A sly smile crept across his face. 'But I thank you for mentioning it. I predict the photograph will disappear within the next couple hours.'

With effort, I masked my dismay. I should have told him I'd taken the photograph with me. Now I'd carelessly given away my only bit of hard evidence, for he could send a telegram instructing whoever had killed Jessup to break into the Jessup home and destroy it. I could sense him getting ready to leave, and thus far, he'd confessed to nothing.

I played my last card. 'Before you go, if you would permit me one question? What had poor Ruby done to make you pin the blame on her? She loves you so much.'

Delacruz gave an angry cry and leaped to his feet. 'No! You are wrong! Never say that! I love Ruby! You know nothing! Nothing!' Suddenly wild-eyed and agitated, he sat down and stood up again, running his fingers through his hair and pulling at it in anguish. I don't think it was my imagination that his Cuban accent seemed diminished. 'I didn't intend to harm Lila. She would not listen to reason. She mocked me.'

'You knew Ruby was going to visit Lila.'

'Of course. Lila said as much. But I didn't know she would come at that moment and never did I think she would be blamed for Lila's death! I never thought it possible. I could not know Lila would point to the closet. Even then, I didn't think anyone would believe that Ruby, my sweet jewel, could have killed anyone. I was sure they would release her the next day. When they did not, I was sure the trial would result in an acquittal. After all, she is innocent! When that failed, I hired the best lawyer to appeal. I have left no stone unturned to save my beloved!'

All stones but one.

The outburst blew over; he calmed down a bit. I pressed him. 'Was it your poor Spanish that made Lila suspicious in the first place?'

He pinched his lips with his fingers, trying, I supposed, to decide whether to enlighten me any further. After a moment he continued, 'I had a letter last fall from Hal Jessup. He'd seen *Coronado's Gold* and recognized me. He wrote me, in care of Warner Brothers, that he was worried about me, that he would say nothing but others might. He put an old program of our act in with his letter. Back then, Lila was opening mail at the studio and she read his letter. She wasn't sure exactly what it meant. Hal had been careful with his words, but she took the program and passed the letter on to me. I didn't know until she told me in February that she had the program, and by then, she'd figured out why Jessup was worried about me. She claimed the program was proof of my identity.'

'You must have been surprised when I showed it to you.'

He shrugged. 'Not really. It proves nothing by itself. It is just a list of acts that no longer exist.'

'Then what good was it to Lila?'

'No good by itself. She didn't really need it. Her accusations alone would ruin me. People would look at me and see what they had not seen before.'

'So why didn't you just pay her off? Why kill her? Did she want too much?'

'You are not as smart as you think. I did not kill Lila because she was blackmailing me. I killed her because she *refused* to blackmail me. I begged her to name her price, I offered her thousands of dollars, but she preferred revenge to money. Lila was a passionate woman, in love and in hate. She hated me so much that she wanted to see Ruby cringe in horror when she learned who she was engaged to. That was her revenge, to deny me the love of the one person in the world I cared for.'

His eyes traveled absently around the room before coming to rest on my face. 'So, now you know the truth. You deserve to know. You have been helpful to Mr Kaminsky, and for that I am grateful. Because of the information you brought him, he is hopeful of a last-minute pardon from the governor. But your information against me cannot be proven, and you have no evidence that I killed Lila.' He started toward the door. 'Now I will leave you and continue my fight to free Ruby.'

I stood too. 'I can free her now. You've given me the evidence I need, right there.' I pointed to the dried flowers on the coffee table.

His eyes narrowed dangerously.

'There is a microphone there and another one above you,' I said, looking up at the chandelier. He caught sight of the wires running across the ceiling toward the stairwell and the others along the floor. 'Our conversation has been recorded with studio equipment. Your confession can be played in court when you are tried for the murder of Lila Walker and again in Mississippi, if the authorities want to try you there for hiring the killer of Hal Jessup. David!' I shouted. 'We're finished.'

Ricardo Delacruz watched in wonder as David appeared on the stairs, followed by Rob Handler. 'Stay where you are, Delacruz,' David warned.

Delacruz did not obey. Like a panther springing from a still position into a great leap at his prey, he grabbed me around the throat with one arm. The other hand clutched a blade that had appeared out of thin air. He held it to my neck.

'Stay where *you* are, my friend, or I will separate the young lady's head from her body.'

David paused half way down the staircase. This was not a part of any scenario we had planned for. I gasped for air, choking beneath Delacruz's vice-like grip, clawing ineffectually at his powerful arm, trying to scream but unable to make a sound. The knife gleamed inches from my face.

'Do not doubt me,' he said. 'I have nothing to lose by killing again.'

David held up his hands like they do in the westerns. When he spoke, his voice was matter-of-fact, like he was giving directions to a lost tourist. 'OK, Delacruz, take it easy. Just head out the door and—'

'No! You listen and obey. First you will bring me this recording. Then Miss Beckett and I will leave together—'

From behind us came a noise I can only describe as the

roar of an onrushing train. One heartbeat later, the train crashed into us with full force, knocking us both to the floor in a violent, snarling tangle of limbs, fur and fury that nearly scared the life out of me.

It was Rip. Sluggish, deaf, ancient Rip, whose bum leg prevented him from hobbling more than a few feet at a time and who raised his head from his paws barely long enough to eat, had turned into a weapon of war. The sight of the knife in Delacruz's hand must have alerted him to the danger I was in, or maybe he smelled my fear in some way known only to animals. He attacked as he had been trained to do by the Germans those many years ago, going for the arm that held the knife, gripping it in his still-powerful jaws, growling like a fiend from Hell. I twisted out of Delacruz's grasp and rolled out of his reach as Rip let go of the man's arm and went for his throat. Delacruz screamed, 'Get him off! Get him off!' and fought hard, but Rip was stronger.

David clambered down the stairs and pulled me into his arms, calling out in German, 'Halt! Halt!' Between Rip's deafness and the racket he and Delacruz were making, the dog didn't hear the command – or didn't choose to – for he never let up his attack. Then there was blood, a lot of it, all over Delacruz's clothes and Rip's fur, spilling on to the wooden floor.

The uproar reached Carl Delaney hovering at the back door, whose shouts brought his partner up from the basement. It took the three of them, David, Carl, and Brickles, to pull Delacruz out from under Rip who had collapsed as suddenly as he had attacked, his chest heaving from the exertion. Brickles pulled out handcuffs as Carl examined the man's wounds with the brisk efficiency of a medic on a battlefield.

'Cuff him,' Carl said. 'He's not bleeding much.'

But Rip was. The knife had gone deep into the dog's chest and his blood was draining fast, spurting on to Delacruz. With an anguished cry, David shoved me toward Rob Handler and scrambled across the bloody floor to where Rip lay panting. Dropping to his knees, he pulled the dog into his lap and cradled his head, heedless of the blood and oblivious to what was going on around him as the cops dragged Delacruz out the front door.

'There, boy. Good dog, good dog,' David crooned, the tears streaming down his face. 'What a prince! What a fighter! Rin Tin Tin's got nothing on you, boy, never did.' He put his face against Rip's and the dog licked his wet cheek. 'You saved her, Rip. You saved her, old boy, just like you did with me back in the day, remember? Sure you do. I remember. I'll always remember. You and me, Rip. You and me.'

Rip whimpered like a child wanting comfort. Then his head dropped and he went limp.

David buried his face in the soft fur at Rip's neck and sobbed.

EPILOGUE

I've never had stage fright, but I'll bet it feels like the sick knot I had in my stomach and the pounding in my ears that grew louder the closer I came to the police station. Lawyer Kaminsky was by my side, unruffled as a seasoned actor, but heck, he went to jail every day. The cop on duty took our names and pointed to the bench where we could wait. No one else was in the room, but we spoke softly anyway.

'So tell me how you got this confession on a phonograph record,' Mr Kaminsky said. 'I'm thinking there's some good possibilities here, assuming the courts will take recordings for evidence. I never heard of anything like it.'

'Well, you know how some studios are experimenting with sound for pictures? One way uses wax discs; it's called Vitaphone. Warner Brothers is working on that. Fox is experimenting with another method called Movietone, where they record the sound right on the strip of film. Douglas Fairbanks is interested in Vitaphone and he's got recording equipment at the studio. We borrowed some and set it up in the living room, with microphones connected by wires to the equipment that we stashed upstairs.'

'I thought nobody could get sound to work?'

'The recording part isn't the problem. That's been going on for years. It's the synchronization of sound with film that's so tricky. Getting the dialog to match with the lips.'

'Gotcha. So you got a good recording?'

'We hope so. They still have to transfer the wax copy to shellac and then it can be played.'

'So if it's messed up, Ruby's back in the clink?'

'We've still got my word, for what it's worth. But Carl Delaney, my cop friend, says Delacruz figured the game was up and confessed at the station.'

Word came that we could see Ruby. She was sitting in the same room, in the same chair, wearing the same clothes as she was when I'd seen her a month and a half ago. Her clenched hands rested on the table, her knuckles white. Before Mr Kaminsky and I could take the chairs across from her, she spoke.

'I heard someone confessed.'

'Nowhere does news travel faster than it does behind bars,' Kaminsky said. 'Yes. Someone has confessed. You should be released in a day or two, maybe sooner.'

She did not relax. I realized she had guessed the truth.

'Who killed Lila?' she asked.

'Ricardo Delacruz,' said Mr Kaminsky.

She stared at a spot on the wall behind us for what seemed like hours before saying, 'Tell me.'

Mr Kaminsky turned to me to explain. In as few sentences as possible, I relayed to Ruby what had transpired. She listened with a vacant stare. 'When the room was empty,' I concluded, 'he went out the way he came, never thinking you'd be charged, let alone tried and found guilty.'

'And now that I'm out of options, he's come forward to confess and give his life for mine.'

I didn't dare look at Mr Kaminsky. I did not correct her and prayed he wouldn't either. There was no harm in letting her think Delacruz was nobler than he really was. I thought back to that day last May when Mary Pickford called on me to stand in for her in the scene where Little Annie Rooney goes to give blood – all her blood – to save the man she loves. As young as she was, Annie understood true love. Ricardo Delacruz never would. He'd have felt terrible when his fiancée hanged, but he would not have saved her at the price of his own life.

'Why did he kill Lila?' said Ruby at last. 'I don't understand.'

'I don't think he planned to kill her. She had learned a terrible secret of his and he was trying to offer her money not to tell you. She refused the money. She was going to tell you that very day. That was to be her revenge. You would walk out on him as he had walked out on her, and his career would be ruined.'

She returned her gaze to the wall for several minutes. We

waited. Finally, she stood up and motioned to the guard watching through the glass in the door that she was ready to return to her cell.

I was baffled. 'But . . . don't you want to know . . .'

A tragic smile played about her lips. 'Secrets. They destroy us in ways we can't always foresee. I know about Ricardo. I've always known. I didn't care. I love him. I would have thrown Lila's cruel words back in her face if I'd had the chance. She couldn't have destroyed us. Ricardo and I could have escaped from all this hatred and run away to Mexico or some country where they don't kill you for loving someone who's different. I wish he hadn't confessed. I'd have happily died for him.'

HISTORICAL NOTE

So which parts of *Renting Silence* are fiction and which are fact? Jessie, David and most of the characters are my own inventions, but Mary Pickford and her husband Douglas Fairbanks, Les Hope and his partner George Byrne, Rudolph Valentino and his wife Natacha Rambova, Jack Warner, Myrna Loy, Gus Sun, and Rin Tin Tin are historical persons (or dogs), all famous in their day. Les Hope (he wouldn't be called Bob for two more years) may have been touring in Gus Sun's circuit with partner Lefty Durbin in the spring of 1925 (I can't be sure) but Lefty died some time in 1925. Since I couldn't learn what month that was, I decided to use Hope's next partner, George Byrne, in my story. They were a dance act at this juncture; the patter came a year or two later, but it isn't too far-fetched to think that they might have experimented with a few corny jokes during their early months together. Mary Pickford was working on *Little Annie Rooney* in 1925; copies exist if you want to watch this fine story and see the two important scenes I described. Douglas Fairbanks was preparing *The Black Pirate* in 1925, an exciting adventure with stunts that flabbergasted the audiences of his day.

Many people are surprised to learn that the KKK was an influential, popular organization in northern states, not just in the South. Indiana was one of the states where the Klan was hugely powerful (Oregon, the setting for *The Impersonator*, was another). In many places, virtually all white men were members because it was considered a patriotic, law-abiding organization. A horrific incident occurred in Indiana in 1925: a young teacher named Madge Oberholtzer was kidnapped, tortured, raped by the head of Indiana's powerful Klan. She got hold of some mercury bichloride and, to end her misery, swallowed the poison. The Klan boss then dumped her body at her parents' door, figuring her for dead. She survived for a couple of weeks, courageously summoning enough strength to accuse the Grand Dragon in signed testimony. Her written words were instrumental in convicting the man, and the resulting publicity destroyed the KKK in Indiana. I dedicate this book to Madge.

AUTHOR'S NOTE

I hope you enjoyed reading *Renting Silence* as much as I enjoyed writing it. If you'd like to see what Jessie's world of silent movies and Hollywood looks like, visit her Pinterest page at http://www.pinterest.com/mmtheobald/jessies-world-renting-silence/. If you have any questions or comments on *Renting Silence* or any thoughts for future books, you can contact me through my website: www.marymileytheobald.com, my Facebook page: https://www.facebook.com/pages/Mary-Miley/303906933020831, or my Roaring Twenties blog: www.marymiley.wordpress.com. I'll be glad to let you know when the next in the series comes out.

Lightning Source UK Ltd.
Milton Keynes UK
UKOW05f1101200617
303713UK00002B/57/P